The Boys Club

Angie Martin

This edition published by Angie Martin for CreateSpace
Text © Angie Martin 2014
ISBN: 978-1505678253

This book is a work of fiction. Any references to historical events, real people, or real places are used fictitiously. Other names, characters, places, and events are products of the author's imagination, and any resemblance to actual events or places or person, living or dead, is entirely coincidental.

All rights reserved. In accordance with U.S. Copyright Act of 1976, the scanning, uploading, and electronic sharing of any part of this book without the permission of the publisher constitute unlawful piracy and theft of the author's intellectual property. If you would like to use material from this book (other than for review purposes), prior written permission must be obtained by contacting the publisher. Thank you for your support of the author's rights.

Cover Art by: Novak Illustration

To learn more about author Angie Martin,
please visit her website at www.angiemartinbooks.com

This work of fiction contains adult situations that may not be suitable for children under eighteen years of age. Recommended for mature audiences only.

Novels by Angie Martin

False Security

Conduit

Poetry collections

the three o'clock in the morning sessions

Dedication

For Johnny, my forever. You are my strength, my courage, and my everything.

Prologue

"Logan comma Gabriel!"

Gabe peeked around the man who had him pushed against the wall and watched as a police officer scanned the mass of men in the overcrowded jail cell.

The man in front of him tightened his hold on his shirt and slapped his sweaty hand over Gabe's mouth. "Don't you say anything." His alcohol-infused breath seethed through rotting teeth and Gabe held his own breath to avoid the stench. "I'll kill you before you get two words out."

Gabe had started out the night in an empty, large cell after he broke into a home to steal a few small items to sell in the hopes of quieting his growling stomach. The owners came home early, retrieved the shotgun from their front closet, and held him at gunpoint until the cops arrived to take him away.

Not his first time in the back of a police car, he assumed he would spend another night in a cozy juvenile hall before being sent off to yet another foster family. Instead, the cops hauled him to the county jail. The empty cell lulled him into thinking the night wouldn't be so bad, but when large men of varying criminal backgrounds filled up the cell, all sorts of colorful threats floated toward the youngest, skinniest inmate.

"Logan comma Gabriel!" the officer called out again.

"Where the hell are you, kid?"

"Do you think these drunks are going to let him go?" another male voice asked. "Get some backup and go in there to get him."

The second man's angry, low tone scared Gabe a little more than the men in the cell, but smashed between the wall and a beer gut, he didn't want to stay in the cell a minute longer.

"Don't tell me how to do my job," the officer said.

"Then do your job. You shouldn't have put him in the drunk tank to begin with, let alone a jail cell."

"He's robbed four houses in the last month. Where do you suggest we put him?"

"He's a 15-year old kid. Get him out of there. Now."

Gabe decided to hell with the consequences. If he didn't speak up, they might never come in, leaving him at the mercy of the brutes around him. "I'm here!"

The man who held him smashed his fist into Gabe's lip and punched his stomach, while the guard called for backup. Gabe fell over and his forehead met the man's knee. The skin above his eye split open and Gabe cried out. Gabe's head flew back with the impact, but the man let go of him. Though half-blinded by the blood in his eyes, Gabe dropped to the ground and crawled around the man.

Officers grabbed the man and threw him to the ground. An unfamiliar face pulled Gabe to his feet and hurried him out of the cell, through the stale odors of alcohol and urine. When they left the cell, the man told Gabe to keep walking.

The main officer yelled at them to stop. The man next to Gabe whirled around with his index finger extended. "I'm taking him now. You're lucky I don't file a complaint about this matter." He pointed to the cell. "I want that man brought up on additional charges along with anyone else that even breathed in this kid's direction, and I will follow up on that, Officer."

Though his head pounded with pain, the adrenaline of getting out rushed through Gabe's body. He pointed at the cop and leered. "That's right, Officer!"

"You either shut the hell up," the man said through clenched teeth, "or you can spend the night in that cell with your buddies and I'll come back for you in the morning."

Gabe's hands flew up, above his shoulders. "I'm good, I'm

good."

As they moved out of the cell block and down the hall, toward the main lobby of the police station, Gabe got his first good look at the man. Gray strands peppered the sides of his short, brown hair. Wrinkles pointed toward hard, blue eyes, while more lines encompassed his downturned mouth. Gabe had not seen him before, but he already knew it would be suicidal to ever cross him.

"Who are you?" Gabe asked.

"Your guardian angel." He pinched Gabe's arm. "You sure are scrawny, but you'll do, I suppose."

Gabe scowled at the word 'scrawny.' Taller than most 15-year olds, he knew how to take care of himself without being bulked up with muscle. "Do for what?" he asked the man. "Are you like some pervert social worker? I don't know what they told you, but I don't do that for food like some of the other kids on the streets."

The man's hearty laugh answered Gabe's question.

"So if you're not a social worker or a pervert, who are you?"

The man pushed open the doors of the police station and stopped at the top of the steps. He pulled a handkerchief out of his jeans pocket and handed it to Gabe. "You're bleeding all over the place. You really know how to find trouble, don't you?"

Gabe took the linen and pressed it to the open wound over his left eye. "Who are you?"

The man held out his hand. "Jim Schaffer, but everyone calls me Schaffer."

Gabe accepted his hand in a firm shake. "Gabe Logan."

"Nice to officially meet you, Logan."

"*Gabe* Logan."

"If you don't mind, I'll call you Logan. Gabe is a scrawny burglar who gets caught a little too easily."

"Look, thanks for getting me outta there and all, but I got it from here." He started down the steps, but halted when he caught a glimpse of a car parked on the side of the street. His eyes widened and he lowered the handkerchief away from his face. "Whoa."

Schaffer smirked and walked over to the vehicle. He leaned against it and folded his arms. "You like it?"

"Are you serious?" He moved closer to the car and restrained himself from running his fingers over the freshly waxed burgundy exterior. "A 1965 Mustang Fastback, original paint, and what, a V-8?"

"You know your cars."

"Is it yours?"

"It is," Schaffer said. "But the real question is, have you ever stolen one of these?"

"I haven't stolen any cars."

"Wanna learn?"

Gabe narrowed his eyes and stared down Schaffer. "Okay, who *are* you?

"Former Special Agent Jim Schaffer with the FBI."

"Former?" Gabe laughed. "Did they kick you out 'cause you stole this car?"

"Not exactly. I decided to branch out on my own. I'm getting together a group of boys like you who have special… talents, if you will."

"To steal cars?"

"And save the world. To put things right that the feds and cops can't. There are a lot of people who pay a lot of money to make things right."

"And you think I can help?" Gabe turned to walk away. "You have the wrong man, Schaffer."

"I have the right boy for the job and I plan on turning you into the right man." Schaffer placed his hand on Gabe's shoulder. "When's the last time you had three meals a day? When you had a bed to sleep in at night? When you didn't have to fight for everything you have, only to find out you still have nothing?"

Staring at the front passenger tire, Gabe's vision glazed over. He had never been in that kind of position. Even in one of his many foster homes he had to sacrifice other things to get those meals, if three meals a day were even offered. On the streets he never knew when he would eat next, if he did at all, and he slept in a different alley almost every night. The idea of not being on the streets and not having to steal and fight to survive sounded better and better with each passing second.

"So what do you say, Logan? Wanna come save the world with me?"

Gabe took a long look at the Mustang, then glanced in Schaffer's direction and grinned. "I'm in."

Chapter One

Sixteen years later…

I 've been in far worse spots than this.

Though Gabriel Logan had repeated the same mantra for the past ten minutes, he failed to remember a single time he'd been worse off than now. After taking him hostage at gunpoint, a drug dealer who smelled like he climbed out of a sewer struggled with a frayed rope to tie Logan to a pole covered in red, peeling paint. Half of Logan's team had already left and the other half was probably trying to figure out where he had gone. Being stranded in the middle of the decrepit barn with no weapon had to be the worst of all of his messes to date, and Logan had no idea how he was getting out of it alive.

Several feet in front of Logan, a second man paced back and forth, his heavily tattooed hand gripping a nine millimeter. "Make it tight so he don't get out," he told the first man, "but not so tight that he gets hurt. They don't want him hurt."

Logan frowned. He didn't know who wanted him in one piece or what they were going to do with him when they had him, but if they didn't want him hurt then his best chance to escape was hurting himself.

The second man walked over to them. He tilted his head, his

greasy, slicked-back hair falling out of place. "Don't you know how to tie a knot?" He set his gun down on a haystack near Logan and walked around the back.

Logan almost laughed at the amateur move, but he was still halfway tied up so he couldn't celebrate quite yet. The tight constraints didn't allow Logan to reach the gun, but that wouldn't stop him from getting it.

As the two men argued over how to properly tie a knot in his peripheral vision, neither one of them paying attention to him, Logan clenched his jaw and squeezed his eyes shut. He counted to three and braced himself. Slacking on his left side, he grabbed onto a piece of rope, and pulled up and out as hard as he could.

He screamed and cursed as his left shoulder dislocated. He had pulled it out of the socket so many times over the years on accident that it now popped out with ease. Even though he prepared himself for the pain, it didn't lessen it in the slightest.

The two men stopped what they were doing and ran around to his front side.

"What the hell did you do to me?" he yelled at them.

The second man looked at the first man. "What did you do? You hurt him! They're gonna kill you for sure."

The first man appeared dumbfounded, his gaze shifting back and forth between Logan and the second man, apparently having a hard time determining how he hurt Logan by trying to tie him up. "I didn't do nothin' to him, I swear!"

Though he had adjusted to the pain, Logan moaned, exaggerating to make it sound as if he were dying.

"Get him out of there!" the second man ordered.

The first man ran around to the back of the pole and untied Logan. As soon as the rope fell away from his body, Logan launched himself at the second man. He punched the man's jaw, followed by an elbow to the side of his head. Logan raced toward the gun, while the second man staggered backward and the first man remained frozen with a confused expression.

Logan squeezed the trigger, firing two shots into the second man's head before he could attack. He whirled around to the first man and trained the gun on his head. Smiling, he shrugged. The man raised his hand for protection. The first round tore through his hand and cheek. When he screamed and lowered his hand, Logan fired a second bullet into his forehead.

Logan turned to regroup with his team, but a large body rammed into his, propelling him forward until he collided with the pole. The gun flew from his hand. He moved his head to the side so his nose didn't break, but the rest of his body seemed to instantly shatter, especially his left shoulder. A fist repeatedly crushed his side. The assault paused just enough so Logan could duck and scurry to the side. The large man's fist hit the pole, stunning him.

Staying low to the ground, Logan rushed the man and they tumbled over the haystack and to the floor. The man's weight pulled him down first, and Logan landed on top. He managed a couple of punches before jumping to his feet and running away. The man caught his ankle and Logan tripped. Only his right hand managed to cushion his fall, while his left arm twisted painfully between his torso and the floor.

Ignoring the flare of pain in his arm and shoulder, Logan used his right arm to drag himself away from the man. A strong hand landed on his left ankle and tugged. Logan pushed up with his right hand and flipped onto his back. He smashed the sole of his boot into the man's face three times until the man let go of his leg. When he pulled his foot away, the man reached for his flattened nose.

Logan got to his feet, but only took two steps before a bullet whizzed past his feet. He turned around with controlled, deep breaths. "You got me," he said. "I give up."

The man stood, blood flowing through the fingers covering his nose. He raised his gun toward Logan and laughed.

Logan took careful steps backward. "Your friends over there said your boss doesn't want me hurt."

"You think I care what he says?" the man asked, his voice nasal and strangled. "Self-defense."

The gun lifted, the barrel pointing at his head, and Logan closed his eyes. The shot sounded, but it did not penetrate his body. He opened his eyes just as the man fell to the ground.

"About time," he said, as he turned to the door.

"What the hell did you get yourself into?" Jack Sullivan asked. He pointed to the other two dead men. "Did we need three bodies on this one?"

"It's worth it," Logan said. "We need the gas can from the van."

"What for?"

"You mean besides getting rid of the bodies?" Logan walked over to the stacks of boxes on the back wall, one of which he had opened prior to the two men catching him. He picked up a DVD from the open box and tossed it to Jack.

"Kiddy porn," Jack said. He swore under his breath. "And here I thought these guys were run-of-the-mill, lowlife drug dealers."

"Looks like our source didn't have the full story." He shook his head as he stared at row after row of boxes stacked at least a foot higher than his six-foot three-inch frame. "Burn it all."

When they had taken care of the cocaine lab in the other barn earlier and were ready to leave, Logan had spotted the second barn, hidden behind some tree cover. Though the first half of his team had already left, he told the rest of them to stay put, positive he wouldn't find anything. What he saw in the box twisted his stomach and he knew they could not leave without doing something about it. Then the two men found him.

He followed Jack out to the van, holding his shoulder. Now that the adrenaline had worn off, fierce pain radiated from the injury. He thanked God they were less than an hour from the Church, where he could get it put back into its rightful place.

Jack passed by with the gas to burn down the second barn. Logan climbed in the back of the van and collapsed in the back bench seat. Lester Davis turned around from the driver's seat. "Kid porn, huh? Sick bastards."

"Jack's taking care of it," Logan said, as he lay down across the bench.

Lester's shiny, bald head jetted out over the top of the seat in front of Logan. "You okay, man? Jack said you had to take out a couple guys back there."

"They deserved it." Though he believed his words, he hated it when he had to kill someone. He wanted to hurry back before anyone else showed up that they would also have to kill, but knew they couldn't leave until the job was done.

"We'll get you home and fixed up soon enough." He looked up and out the back window. "In fact, I think I see smoke now."

Logan used his right arm to pull himself up in the seat. Through the dusky evening, small tendrils of smoke curled from the top of the barn into the sky. He smiled despite the pain. One cocaine lab and a barn filled with child pornography, both destroyed. All in all, a good day.

Chapter Two

"Damn!"

"Just hold still." Doctor Allison Connors removed her hands from Logan's arm. Shifting her eyes to his face, she said, "You've done this dozens of times in the past. Just a quick snap and it's back in."

Logan hated hearing about how quick of a procedure it was. Allie said the same thing the past two times she had put his shoulder back in place and every time it still hurt like hell. "You saying that doesn't make it hurt any less, *Doctor*."

She chuckled. "Then quit dislocating your shoulder and I won't have a reason to pop it back in the socket. From what I understand, you were already a pro at this when I came to work here."

Logan repositioned himself on the gurney. He gripped the side of the padding with his right hand, ground his molars against each other, and waited for the pain.

In his peripheral vision, Allie took her stance next to the table. She laced her fingers around his wrist and extended his arm. Before he could say anything else to stop her, she pulled on his arm, slow and steady to put tension on the muscles.

Logan groaned at the familiar pop of his joint going back into place. He blew out his breath and rotated his shoulder to make sure it still worked. "That doesn't get any easier. I swear you make it more painful each time on purpose."

She stood over him and glared. "You know what will make it easier? Surgery. You won't be down for very long and I can bring in a surgical team to do it here."

"Oh no," he said. He eased up into a sitting position and swung his legs over the edge of the bed. "I don't want something to go wrong and put me out of commission."

"I know a great surgeon who can—"

"I'm sure he or she is a miracle worker like you, but I'm not doing it."

"Then I'll see you back here the next time you decide to dislocate it. Probably in another week at your pace."

He grabbed her hands and pulled her body in between his legs. When Allie started working at the Church three months earlier, Logan first resisted the idea of getting involved with her, but his body wanted something different than his heart and mind. He made it clear to her that there would be no relationship and though she understood that, she fell in love with him. She didn't bother keeping it a secret, but he also didn't keep it a secret that he would never feel the same way. He cared about her as a friend and colleague, nothing more.

Sliding his hands over her hips, he said, "Quit worrying about me."

She shook her head and brushed his ash brown hair off his damp forehead. "Quit giving me reasons to worry."

Logan smiled in response.

She took his hands off her body and backed away. "I need to get you some ice for that shoulder and then we can work on the rest of your wounds."

Logan stared at the floor while she obtained supplies from the adjacent room. He lifted his hand to his shoulder and rubbed at the soreness. He knew he needed surgery, but he didn't want to chance a complication.

Yet it wasn't his shoulder or surgery, or even the rest of his minor wounds that weighed on his mind. While on the surface the job appeared successful, so many things had gone wrong. The cocaine lab was empty of personnel, just as they were told it would be, but how did the men find him in the second barn and where did they come from? If they had been there the entire time, why didn't they just come after them when his team was destroying the lab?

Their words about someone wanting him alive made Logan think that they knew he would be there. That raised a whole other set of questions, primarily, did they have a leak somewhere in The Boys Club?

As the first recruit into the program, Logan watched the organization grow from the beginning. The Boys Club started the day Jim Schaffer terminated his twenty-year career with the FBI. Schaffer had made a lot of friends during his tenure with the government, people who wanted to see injustices made right, but couldn't always do it the legal way.

Before he recruited Logan, Schaffer purchased a rundown, massive Catholic church and renovated it to suit the organization's needs. One of the earlier kids who came through the program coined the name "The Boys Club." Some of the boys left after a few years to pursue their own law-abiding lives. Others, like Logan, were lifers, the ones that Schaffer intended to help run the place when he no longer could.

Logan spent the last of his teenage years growing up with some of the men who still worked for The Boys Club, most of which he considered brothers rather than friends. The idea that one of the men could betray Schaffer and their group was too much for Logan to consider.

Allie came back into the room, wheeling a stainless steel tray filled with medical supplies. They went through the same routine every time he returned from a job in less than pristine condition. Logan pressed a cold pack to his shoulder while Allie gathered her long, golden blonde hair into a ponytail. As she tended to various wounds on his face and torso, Logan kept himself occupied thinking about the job and who could possibly want him alive. Only one name came to mind, but with that name came a rush of bad memories.

"Alright," Allie said. "Take off those jeans and let's have a look at the rest of you."

He slid off the gurney and to his feet. "I think you're just saying that to get me naked."

"Don't flatter yourself."

He laughed and worked on getting his jeans off. Whenever his hand touched his hip, he groaned with pain.

"What is it now?" Allie asked, as she put on a fresh pair of latex gloves.

"My hip's just a little sore," he said, stepping out of his jeans. "No big deal."

"Whenever you have a physical reaction to pain, it is a big deal. Which hip is it?"

"The left one, but like I said it's... ouch!" He jumped back when she tugged down the side of his boxers and touched his hip.

"That 'no big deal' needs stitches."

"You've got to be kidding."

"Hop back up on the table."

"I'm never getting out of here tonight," he said. He lay down again, with his left side toward the outside of the table. "Next time I'm not saying anything about any pain. I think you were just looking for a way to operate on me. If you can't get to my shoulder, you'll settle for stitches."

Allie rolled her eyes and moved her tray closer to his hip. "Or maybe it's your track record with stitches that made me grab the necessary supplies just in case." She laid two syringes down on the table next to him.

"Whoa, wait a minute. What are those for?"

"Antibiotics and lidocaine."

"I just had a shot with antibiotics last month."

"And yet here you are, getting cut up in a rusty old barn again. Every time you do that, you get another good dose of antibiotics. You're just lucky you're up-to-date on your tetanus booster or there would be three syringes here." She pouted at him. "Did you want me to hold your hand? I can always give you a lollipop when we're done."

"Funny," he said.

"Never did get that. Big, strong guy like you scared of a little needle."

"Just hurry it up."

She wiped the skin on his upper arm with an alcohol swab and took the cap off the first needle. It punctured his skin and he grimaced as the medication burned through his arm. The next one didn't hurt quite as bad, but he groaned anyway to try and make her feel bad for sticking him.

She set the used syringes back on the tray and prepared a third syringe.

"What's that one for?" Logan asked. "And why did you put the lidocaine in my arm when you're stitching up my hip?"

"Oh, I was mistaken." She held up the new syringe. "This one is lidocaine. The other must have been morphine." She shrugged with a playful grin. "Sorry!"

"You're the worst doctor ever. I told you no pain meds."

She patted his arm. "You'll thank me later."

After she administered the lidocaine and started stitching him up, the morphine kicked in and gave him a bit of reprieve from all his aches and pains. He always gave Allie such a hard time as a patient, even though she had his best intentions in mind.

Once she finished stitching, she covered up the wound with a bandage. Taking off her gloves, she said, "All done. The bandage is waterproof. I'll want to see you back here tomorrow to check on the stitches and re-bandage you." She handed him a navy blue sling. "Put this on in the morning and wear it until I tell you otherwise."

"Yes, doctor," he said, sliding off the gurney once more. "Am I your last patient tonight?"

"You are. Are you staying here overnight?"

"Sure am." Whenever any of the men returned from a job, they stayed at least one night at the Church, mainly for debriefing and any medical attention. After they were released, they went to their own homes until the next job came in. Allie, however, always went home after her workday ended.

"I was hoping you could come over to my place tonight," she said.

He moved closer to her and slipped his hands around her waist. "Why don't you stay here with me instead?"

She laughed and shook her head. "Schaffer would never go for that one."

"He'd never find out." Logan touched his lips to hers. "He's long gone and won't be back until the morning. We'll sneak you out before then."

She smiled and gave him another kiss.

As he gathered up his clothes and followed her down the hall to his room for the night, the guilt over sleeping with Allie once again gnawed at him. He knew it made him quite the jerk to take advantage of her feelings for him, but she also knew what she was getting into from the start. One more night together wouldn't hurt anyone.

Chapter Three

The numbers on the computer screen blurred until they doubled and ran together in an indecipherable mess. Sara Langston lowered her head into her hands and rubbed her temples. She had been working on the account for hours and had found nothing to help solve her ongoing mystery. At well past 3 a.m., answers were not coming anytime soon.

A noise from behind her snagged her attention and she whirled around in her office chair. Stephen Mathers stumbled into the room, yawning and wearing only black boxer shorts. "When are you coming to bed, babe?"

"In just a few minutes."

"That's what you said two hours ago." He wandered over to her, leaned over, and gave her a quick kiss. "We have too much happening in the next few days for you to keep late nights."

Sara looked him over, but kept her thoughts about the big events to herself. In less than two days, they would take their vows and pronounce their love in front of almost 800 people, a love she had yet to experience. She was still unsure if Stephen loved her. He acted like he did, but she figured he could fake those emotions, the same as she.

Neither of them chose their relationship. Her father pushed it on them so that one day they would marry and she would give birth to a boy who would eventually take over his empire, after Stephen had his turn at the reins. Stephen, as most men, would definitely marry someone he didn't love for that opportunity, but it didn't stop him from pretending.

She rotated her chair to face the computer again. "I wanted to finish up some work before we leave on our honeymoon, that's all."

His hands landed on her shoulders and kneaded her muscles through her cotton top. "There's nothing that can't wait until we get back," he said. "Isn't Mary picking you up in a few hours to finalize arrangements for the wedding?"

Sara's eyelids fell, part at his slow massage and part at the anxiety growing in the pit of her stomach. "Mary will be here at ten."

He leaned over her shoulder and stared at the computer monitor. "What are you working on that can't wait?"

"Just this mystery account. I can't figure it out. There are all of these crisscrosses of deposits and withdrawals between every account, and yet they're all tied to this account in some way or another. Then there are the discrepancies I found between the statements and the books. I've asked Dad for the information several times, but he always tells me to talk to Daryl, who sends me to someone else, and down the line. No one seems to know what I'm talking about." She turned back around to face Stephen. "How am I supposed to do accounting for Dad's company if I keep getting the runaround?"

Stephen knelt down in front of her. "I'm sure you're not getting the runaround. You're only doing the books for one of his companies and you know he moves things around from business to business all the time, even though you tell him not to. It's got to be a misunderstanding, that's all." He tucked some stray curls behind her ear. "Why don't you come to bed? It's so late that you're not thinking clearly."

"I would love to, but I feel like I'm on the verge of figuring this out. If I can just work on it for another hour, I'm sure that—"

"You're tired, Sara. Come to bed."

She smiled, despite her desire to keep working on the accounts. "You're right," she said. "I'm too tired to finish this tonight."

He slid his hands up the outsides of her thighs, making his

way up to her hips. "If you want to stay up and work, I'm sure we can find something much better for us to work on together."

Though not in the mood for a late night encounter, she wrapped her hands around his neck and leaned over for a kiss.

"That's better," he said, accepting her kiss.

She ran her hands through his disheveled, dark hair, enjoying his kiss far more than she wanted. Though she hated the idea of spending her life with someone just to appease her father, he could have picked out someone worse for her than Stephen. She may not love him yet, but she was learning.

He broke away from her and grinned. Taking her hand, he pulled her out of the chair and led her out of her office, toward the stairs. "Listen, Sara, I know it's not the time to talk about it, but when we come back from our honeymoon, I want you to reconsider teaching at West Hills Academy. You have a job there whenever you want it and then you won't have to pull late nights or worry about your father's accounts. I think it would be a much better job for you, especially when we start a family."

Sara's mood soured again. Everyone seemed to know what was best for her, and between her father and Stephen, her whole life was planned. Even if she didn't want to teach at the academy, she had a feeling that within a few months of returning from their honeymoon, she would end up working there. She wanted to tell Stephen the career change was out of the question, but telling him that was the same thing as telling her father, who had also been on her about taking the teaching position.

Stephen stopped walking at the bottom of the stairs and turned to face her. "Besides, when your father retires, you don't want to work for me, do you? I wouldn't want our marriage to fall victim to us working together." He fingered a chunk of hair in front of her ear. "You know you could always stop working altogether. We don't need the money and I'm sure you can find lots of other things to keep you busy."

The newest push, Sara thought. He had only brought up the idea of her staying home once before and she had hoped he wouldn't remember. Now that he had said it again, she wondered if it his new goal was to have her as a stay-at-home wife and mom where he could better keep her under his thumb.

Too tired to disagree at the moment, she gave him a strained smile and nodded. "We'll talk about it when we come back from the honeymoon."

His palm cupped her cheek. "I'm so glad to hear that." His mouth claimed hers again.

Sara fell into his kiss and tried to ignore all the same old concerns about marrying Stephen flooding her mind.

Chapter Four

"Doctor Connors!"

Jim Schaffer's voice thundered through the room, making Logan jump straight up in bed.

"I won't embarrass either of you by turning on the light," Schaffer continued, "but I want you both fully dressed and in the hallway in the next two minutes."

After the door shut, Allie sat up, the blanket covering her bare chest. "I suppose I've just lost my job."

Logan lifted his hand to her cheek. "No, you haven't. I'll make sure of it." He kissed her gently and said, "We better not push it, though. Time to pay the piper."

They rushed through getting dressed and moved to the door. Before she could open it, he scooped her close and kissed her again. "Whatever he says, don't worry. You'll still have a job in the morning. I promise."

Her eyebrows shot up and she glared at him with a flash of despair in her eyes. "I better."

"You will. It's my fault you stayed here."

"Damn right it is."

He stared into her eyes, his own narrowed with concern. "I'm sorry, Allie."

"I know you are." She lifted herself onto her tiptoes and

gave him one last passionate kiss.

Logan reached around her and opened the door. They walked outside, an angry Schaffer leaning against the wall across from the door. Logan turned to Allie, who kept her eyes down to the tiles.

Schaffer crossed his arms and stared Allie down. "Doctor Connors, did your house get foreclosed on yesterday?"

Allie hung her head low. "No, sir."

"Gas leak? A fire?"

She squirmed and clasped her hands in front her waist. "No, sir." Her quiet voice wavered, as if on the verge of tears.

"Anything else that prevented you from returning home after your shift last night?"

"Schaffer, don't," Logan said.

Schaffer turned to Logan and held up his hand. "I'll deal with you in a moment." Looking back at Allie, he asked, "Well?"

"No, sir."

"Then I suppose since you have no reason to be here, you should be home right now." He took a few steps toward her and lowered his voice. "What the hell are you thinking sleeping with Logan? You have to know he's 15 ways messed up."

Logan glared at him, but couldn't find a good argument against what he said.

"You may be a damn good doctor," Schaffer continued, "but you'd make a horrible psychiatrist. Go on home."

"Yes, sir." She started down the hall, but stopped when Schaffer spoke again.

"Doctor Connors, I'll expect to see you in my office at 9 a.m. sharp. We still need to discuss the repercussions from this violation of your contract."

"Yes, sir," she said without turning around, and then continued down the hall.

Once she turned the corner, Logan looked at Schaffer. "You don't have to talk to her like a criminal. She didn't do anything wrong."

"What was the one rule I had when I brought her on? The only rule that I made more than clear to all of you before I hired a female to work here?"

His turn to be punished, Logan lowered his eyes and his voice, like a child in trouble with his father. "No fraternization."

"There are reasons for that," Schaffer said. "I don't need any of you distracted while you're here. You were the last person I expected to break that rule."

"I'm sorry. I don't know what I was thinking."

"Don't act like this was a one-time deal. I've held my tongue for over two weeks now and I'm sure you've been with her longer than that. Since you two were keeping it quiet, I didn't say anything, but when you bring it here…" He sighed. "Come on, Logan. I have to draw the line somewhere, even with you."

Logan folded his arms and locked eyes with his longtime friend, mentor, and boss. "Yeah, I suppose you do and I'm sorry."

"It's not me you should apologize to. What the hell are you doing to that poor girl? You must know she's in love with you."

He did know. There was no misunderstanding that point. She had even told him again tonight, as if expecting his feelings to have changed.

"I know she is," he said. Saying it aloud to someone else brought on a wave of self-loathing and disgust over his actions.

"Ah hell, Logan. That makes it even worse."

"It won't happen again."

"You're damn right it won't. If it does, I'm putting her on a two-month suspension."

"You can't—"

"She's getting off easy. You'll have a six-month suspension with mandatory psych visits."

"That's not right."

"Yes, it is. It's the only thing I'll have done right since I let you come back so soon after Karen died. Either get yourself together or I'll force you to."

Logan balled his fists at his sides and suppressed his anger. Nothing Schaffer said was wrong and Logan knew he deserved every ounce of that punishment now, despite only getting a warning.

Schaffer leaned against the wall again. "You know I started this organization to help you boys, not to screw your lives up completely. Most days I wonder if I've failed in that mission, especially where you're concerned."

Logan raised his eyes to Schaffer's worn face. The mass of wrinkles around his tired blue eyes told the tale of his life. Every single strand in the mess of gray hair came from either Logan or one of the other boys Schaffer brought onto the program. Though most of them were men now, all of them ranging in age from 24 to 35, save one new 17-year old recruit, Schaffer would always view them as his boys. The thought of disappointing him weighed heavily on Logan.

"You haven't failed us," Logan told Schaffer. "You brought all of us out of the life of failure we were already living. If anything, I've failed you."

Schaffer stared at him, but Logan could not read his expression. "From here on out your relationship with Doctor Connors is strictly patient-doctor. Unless you love her. Since that's not the case, we won't need to have that discussion anytime soon." He pushed off from the wall. "Get some sleep. In the morning, you'll be debriefed and go home. Take a couple weeks off to get your head together. I won't put you on a job before then."

Logan nodded. "Thank you." He went back to his room, exhausted and embarrassed. He had failed not only Schaffer, but Allie. Somehow, he'd have to find a way to make it right.

Chapter Five

Logan woke in a mess of tangled sheets and damp pillowcases. He wiped the cold sweat from the back of his neck and the fatigue from his eyes. Making his way to the bathroom to clean up, he yawned and rubbed his chin, the growth a few days past a reasonable stubble length and a cruel reminder of how little he cared anymore.

After returning to bed earlier in the morning and smelling Allie on the sheets, he tossed and turned over his bad decisions and the effect they had on others. He didn't know what possessed him to sleep with Allie at the Church after months of being careful and meeting at her house. He assumed on some level he had a desperate need to get caught. If he couldn't stop sleeping with her on his own, Schaffer would force cessation on them both.

Sleep finally greeted him with another nightmare about Karen. The dreams had grown infrequent over time, but every so often one found him and choked out his desire to keep going in life. This one had been no different, as he watched her death unfold before him with her in his ear, telling him all the reasons why it was his fault.

When he met Karen six years ago, life took on new meaning for him. He proposed marriage a year later, married her a year after that, and left The Boys Club for a life of happiness. Schaffer found him a legitimate job on a road construction crew and everyone expected him to be gone forever.

At the time, he did not know that Hugh Langston, a man he had undermined and crossed many times over the years, had uncovered his identity. Langston took out a contract on Logan, resulting in a car bomb gone wrong.

Almost two years into their marriage and six months pregnant, Karen postponed a trip to visit her parents due to a nasty bout of nausea. She spent the morning throwing up, and Logan convinced her to go see the doctor.

Logan walked her to the car, which sat in the middle of their driveway, since boxes from their recent move filled the garage. He ran back into the house to get his wallet while she started the engine. He went back outside to a smoke-filled car and his wife screaming in pain. Then he saw the flames. A second later, the car exploded, throwing Logan back into the house through the open door.

A bomb intended to explode upon turning the ignition key and instantly kill Logan did not perform its designed function. Investigators believed the smoke started first, confusing Karen so she couldn't find the seatbelt latch or the door handle. The fire started soon after that, searing her skin for a full minute before Logan came back outside.

Since that day, Logan had often tortured himself by watching the clock as a grueling minute ticked by, wondering what she thought about while her skin bubbled and boiled under the intense flames. He questioned if she blamed him, if she thought he abandoned her while she died, if she worried for the baby, or if the pain denied her any coherent thoughts. Had he been in the car with her, he could have found the door handle for her and pushed her to safety, giving her time to escape before the bomb finally did its job.

But he had been in the house, performing the mundane and meaningless task of retrieving his forgotten wallet from the kitchen counter.

Logan rushed through a shower and shave, after which he threw on an old pair of jeans, black T-shirt, and his sneakers. He secured the sling Allie gave him over his bad shoulder. He would take it off when he got home, but did not want to get called out on his way out of the building. With his duffel bag slung over his good shoulder, he took one last look around the room to make sure he had not forgotten anything. Pain stabbed his heart when he caught sight of the bed and he hoped Allie was okay.

Heading down the hall to the elevator so he could get to his debrief and hurry home to his small apartment, Logan heard a commotion overhead. When he reached the first floor, almost everyone who worked at The Boys Club was gathered in the main lobby.

"Where do you think you're going?" Jack asked, as he walked up to Logan.

"To my debrief and then home for a couple weeks, which is exactly where you should be going." Logan gestured to the sling on his arm. "I have a few injuries to take care of."

"Funny how you were the only one on the whole team who was injured," Jack said with a laugh. "But we're not going home anytime soon. Schaffer called everyone in for this job. I'm surprised you didn't get the memo."

Logan glanced around the room and saw the other members from last night's team with their own bags in their hands. It appeared as if they also thought they were going home for some time off between jobs, but got stuck here like he had.

"What are we waiting for?" Logan asked Jack.

A loud click sounded through the lobby and men started moving toward the main doors.

"That," Jack said. He turned to file in after the others.

Logan followed suit, walking with the last of the group down the long hallway that led to the main chapel. Though the pews had been replaced by chairs and the Catholic artifacts donated back to the diocese, the stained glass windows remained. Sunlight filtered through the colorful scenes of Jesus, Mary, angels, and saints. Logan wondered if Schaffer left them in place to give the boys a sense of calm when entering the chapel, like the one that came over Logan now.

He found a chair toward the center of the chapel next to Jack and set his bag down on his lap. His eyes landed on the empty podium at the front of the room where Schaffer usually stood to brief them on a new job. A large white screen filled the majority of the back wall, where pictures related to the job would be displayed. After Schaffer announced the job, the assigned leader picked his team and planning began. Yet in all his years working for The Boys

Club, Logan had never seen the chapel so full, which made him all the more curious about the job.

Schaffer came through a side door with a file in his hand, followed by his assistant, Kyle, and Allie. Logan watched him step up to the podium. Kyle went to the projector and plugged in a laptop, while Allie settled into a chair to the left of the podium. Logan made eye contact with her for a brief moment before Schaffer called for everyone to settle down.

"I know you are curious why so many of you are here this morning," Schaffer said into a microphone. "Right now we have three teams in the field, but everyone who isn't active on a job is here in this room. A new job came across my desk an hour ago, one that will require three teams. Even though it's the biggest job we've ever done, we have only 24 hours to plan it."

Murmurs came from the all over the room and Logan frowned. How did Schaffer expect them to plan such a large job in such a short time? He was grateful that he had just returned from a job. The chances of getting stuck on another job so soon after finishing his last one were slim, especially since he had been injured.

Schaffer's voice boomed across the room again, silencing the whispers. "I know it seems impossible, but we have to get it done. A life is at stake, so we don't have a choice." His eyes roamed around the room until they landed on Logan. "I'm putting Logan in charge of this one."

Logan's lips parted in surprise as the others turned their heads until their eyes fell on him. A few strong whispers came from around him, expressing outrage over Schaffer's decision.

"With all due respect," Logan said, "I'm not ready for another job. I just returned last night and with my shoulder and the stitches, I don't know if I'm able to take on such a huge job so soon."

His words shut up the rest of the group, who turned to Schaffer for his response.

"I wondered that myself, but I reviewed Doctor Connors's report and she's cleared you for duty." Schaffer held his hands up at the start of the protests from the others. "I would much rather have someone who is rested, but I think when you hear about the job you will all agree with me that this one needs to go to Logan."

Anxiety knotted in Logan's stomach. "What's the job?" he

asked.

"Hugh Langston."

Gasps came up from around the room and some men turned to look at Logan, who had tightened his jaw at the sound of that name. He was certain the other men no longer objected to his taking charge of the job, not when it involved the man who had killed his wife and unborn child.

"Are we taking him down?" Logan asked.

"Not exactly. He's taken out a hit on someone and we need to stop it before it happens next week. She'll be the one to take him down."

"Who's the target?" Jack called out from beside Logan.

Schaffer locked eyes with Logan. "His daughter, Sara."

Chapter Six

Sara rolled over in bed and reached for Stephen. They had decided to sleep in, and she sent Mary a text earlier in the morning to delay their plans. With the wedding racing toward her at light-speed, she welcomed the opportunity to be lazy for a change.

Watching Stephen sleep, listening to his soft snores, she wondered once again what marriage would change between them. They had lived together for three months, ever since her father insisted on buying them an early wedding present in the form of the immodestly large house, staffed with maids, a personal chef, and gardening crew. She hated the obnoxious display of money, but he claimed he wanted to spoil his only child, especially since they had lost so much time together.

He had missed out on the first twelve years of her life, mainly because her mother had been his mistress and not his wife. When her mother passed away from cancer, he took Sara into the fold as if she had always been a welcome child. Sara, however, knew that if her mother had not died, she would still not know her father.

After Stephen had become her father's right-hand man, her father encouraged them to date. Even when she told her father that she didn't think things were going anywhere with Stephen, he pushed their relationship, convincing her time and again to give him one more chance.

She continued dating him to keep her father happy, but it didn't take long for her to figure out his motivations. Her father wanted them to marry so Stephen would become his legitimate heir. Then they would have a child, a boy if her father got his way, and another heir would be in place. The arrangement had nothing to do with her happiness. She would be taken care of for the rest of her life, as long as she gave her father what he wanted.

When they moved in together, she fell into a comfortable routine with Stephen. Sometimes she believed she loved him, but other times she regarded her feelings for him as forced. Stephen always told her that he loved her, and for the most part he acted like he did, but she never knew whether it was a ploy to stay in her good graces. Yet, he had a tendency to push her like her father did, to talk her into things she didn't necessarily want. They were so much alike that it was hard to believe Stephen wasn't on board with all of her father's ideas. The rush to get married after dating for less than a year, the constant mention of starting a family, the push for her to take the teaching position. They played the same record to her all the time and just as she had given into their wishes for the wedding, she would do so with everything else.

Sara closed her eyes to try to catch some more sleep rather than think about how out of control her life had become, when Stephen stirred beside her. He rolled over to face her and she greeted him with a good morning kiss.

Running his fingers through her hair, he asked, "What are your plans today?"

"Just boring old wedding stuff that wouldn't interest you."

"Of course our wedding interests me. It's interested me since our first date."

She grinned and her eyebrows shot up. "Really?"

"Yes, really." He slid his hand under her and flipped her onto her back. After her giggle died down, he became serious and ran his thumb over her lips. "I really do love you, Sara." He lowered his mouth to hers.

The little statements and gestures always made her think he did love her, and not just her father and his money. As he pulled the covers down from their bodies and lifted her top over her head, Sara told herself that it wouldn't be so bad to live the rest of her life with him. She could learn to like it, maybe even love it.

Chapter Seven

"His daughter?"

Logan's question echoed through the suddenly quiet chapel.

"Sara Langston," Schaffer said. He used a small remote to bring the projector to life. A photograph of an attractive girl flashed on the screen behind him. "Langston had many mistresses over the years, but only one resulted in a pregnancy. Sara's mother, Ruth Bennett, passed on his last name to Sara on the birth certificate. Of course, Langston refused to have anything to do with his daughter, or even the mistress once she announced her pregnancy."

Logan looked back to the woman on the screen, her windblown, shoulder-length russet curls captured by an unseen cameraman at the end of a zoom lens. With his connections to Hugh Langston, he had heard mentions of his daughter in the past, but had never seen her picture before now. He recognized bits of Langston in her small, rounded nose and deep-set, brown eyes, but had he passed her on the street he wouldn't have guessed their relation.

"Sara's mom died from a brain tumor shortly after Sara turned twelve," Schaffer continued. "Apparently her mother had raised her with full knowledge of her father's identity because Sara wouldn't quit talking to social services about her famous father.

When the authorities checked her birth certificate, Langston's name was listed as the father.

"Some reporter picked up on the story and when the media looked deeper into the facts, they discovered that Sara most likely was his daughter. Langston claimed to have never known of her existence, but he went through the paternity tests. When those came back a match, he transplanted her from Indiana to California.

"Sara, however, didn't live under his roof for long. Langston shipped her off to boarding school, where she graduated at the top of her class. She went on to earn her Master's Degree, again with honors. She came back into the picture a couple years ago and he's been trying to corral her ever since."

"Why does Langston want her dead?" Jack asked.

"She's been heading up the accounting for one of his front companies for the past two years," Schaffer said. "She's discovered a few things she shouldn't have and she asked too many of the wrong questions."

"So Langston falls back on his old standby," Logan said. "Kill her to get her out of the way."

"Father of the year," Lester said from the other side of the room.

"Our job is to get her to safety and turn her over to the FBI," Schaffer said. "She'll go into the Witness Security Program and hopefully she knows enough to testify against him. The feds have tried to get to her and it's impossible with her security."

"She's not going to come with us if we ask her nicely," Logan said. "She also won't believe us when we say that Langston is trying to kill her."

"Which is why your team is going to kidnap her," Schaffer said. "Once she's safe, then you'll explain everything. She might not believe you, not until we get her in the hands of the FBI, and that's okay. Our main priority is her safety, but you're going to need to do your best to convince her to surrender willingly to the FBI."

"What's the plan to get her away from Langston?" Austin Moore asked from the front row.

"Sara is getting married on Saturday," Schaffer said. "It's about the closest thing to an arranged marriage one can get." He clicked a button on the remote and another picture filled the screen.

Logan scooted to the edge of his seat and squinted at the

32

new photograph. Sara stood next to a man who appeared to be almost a decade older than her. He immediately recognized the man and tension crawled into his shoulders. "Stephen Mathers," Logan said, contempt dripping from each syllable.

Schaffer pointed at Logan. "Second in command, set to take over Langston's empire once Langston retires. Since Langston has no male heirs, he's been grooming Mathers for the position for years. The best way for him to take over without question is for Langston to marry him off to his daughter. The hit is scheduled to take place on their honeymoon."

"That way Mathers is married into the family already when she dies," Logan said. "Does Mathers know about the hit?"

"That we don't know," Schaffer said. "Mathers is up to his neck in Langston's illegal dealings, but whether he has a part in the hit is still unclear. Langston did hire a professional to do the job so even if Mathers is in the know, he won't be suspected."

Logan's stomach churned. He knew long before Karen's death that Langston was a despicable man, evil in every possible way, but Logan never would have thought him capable of killing his own child. If Mathers knew about the hit, it made things so much worse.

"From what we understand," Schaffer continued, "Mathers is continually updated on her whereabouts and activities, another reason the FBI can't get to her. They can't take a chance of alerting either him or Langston."

"Nothing like marrying your stalker," Jack said.

"Tomorrow night, Sara is meeting with her wedding planner prior to the rehearsal dinner. All of Langston's cars will be busy picking up wedding guests from the airport, so he has hired a car service for his daughter." Schaffer turned to Logan. "You'll be driving."

Logan nodded. "Will anyone else be with her?"

"Her best friend and maid of honor, Mary Flynn, who has no allegiance to Langston. We'll take both of them and immediately separate them. We need two teams, one for Sara, one for Mary. Four men each. Then we need a four-man team to stay here and run point. I'll oversee that team." He motioned for Allie to come up to the podium.

Allie adjusted the microphone to her height. "I'm preparing several syringes of sedatives according to the heights and weights of both girls. Sara has two medical issues to note. She has a severe peanut allergy. You will have to be careful with any food preparations, but I'll send along some EpiPens to be safe. She also has asthma. Our reports do not indicate what inhalers she uses, so I'll have several different kinds and she'll have to tell you which ones she uses. I'll also send you with a nebulizer. Because she will be under duress, she may need breathing treatments. Before you leave, I'll teach the team that will be with her how to prepare and administer the treatments." Her eyes scanned the room. "Any questions?"

"Does Mary have any health issues we need to know about?" Lester asked.

"None," Allie said. She smiled at Schaffer and stepped away from the podium.

"Alright, boys," Schaffer said. "Next 24 hours is hardcore prep. We'll start sleep shifts now so that you can adjust for when you're in the field. I wish we had more time to prepare, but we absolutely have to save this girl's life. We can't fail. Logan, come pick your teams."

Logan rose from his seat and walked to the front of the room. He glanced in Allie's direction, making quick eye contact. Standing in front of the podium, he said, "Let's start with my team for Sara. Head to the back when I call your name."

He looked at his colleagues, mentally dividing them into categories by expertise, and he called their names one by one. There was no doubt he needed Jack, his closest friend and the jack of all trades in the group. Lester was an expert driver who would help with the initial getaway once they had Sara in the car. Finally, Charlie Cantor was a caring individual with a soft voice. He would be what Sara would need as she adjusted to her circumstances and was told the truth about her father. Charlie was also one of the rare cooks in the group and would best know how to handle her peanut allergy.

The three men moved to the back of the room to await further instructions. Logan looked at the remaining men and decided to mirror Mary's team from the one he constructed for Sara.

"The team for Mary," Logan said. "Bill, you'll head it up, followed by Tuck, Jonesy, and Stu." After the men joined the others in the back, Logan took note of who was left, thankful he had plenty of technical guys available. "For Schaffer's team here, we'll go with Phil, Austin, and Kyle."

"Very good," Schaffer said. "The rest of you will be on standby in case you're needed. We're not taking on any other jobs until our other three teams return. Sara is our primary focus until she's in the hands of the FBI." He clapped his hands together. "Let's get to work."

Chapter Eight

Sara took steady breaths as her feet rebounded against the pavement, the impact of every step jarring her legs. She had maintained the same brisk pace that she always did on her morning run, and so far her breathing had held up just fine. A familiar burn spread through her calves and thighs, and her hamstrings tightened up, reminding her she was nearing the end of her five-mile course.

Before she left the house, Stephen disagreed about her running with her asthma acting up. He did not want her to have breathing problems before the wedding, but unlike everything else in her life, she never compromised on running. It gave her a sense of freedom that she didn't have in the rest of her life. Out in the open morning air, she had control over everything. Where her feet landed, which path she turned down, how fast she moved. No one could guide her otherwise. Not even her security detail.

She had long ago grown accustomed to the men that followed her all over town. Their surveillance started when she met her father for the first time and subsequently moved three states away for boarding school. Having Hugh Langston as a father became a very public matter in those first few years after her mom's death, resulting in constant security. As a budding teenager, she found school difficult with the eyes of her security always on her, but she soon learned to live with it. She gravitated toward kids who had the same problem of intrusive bodyguards, if only because they understood her plight.

After heading off to college, she learned to ignore the men who watched her, but it didn't make it any easier. Whenever she made friends, her father knew about it and dictated whether she could keep them. If she tried to date, her father ran a background check and immediately deemed any potential suitors off-limits, an order her security detail enforced. Boyfriends ran for the hills and warned all the other men that she was more trouble than she was worth. Stephen was not only the first man she had ever been with intimately, but the first man she had ever dated, exactly as her father wanted it.

Returning home two years ago, she thought that life would be easier and give her more freedom, but the opposite was true. Working for her father made her feel inadequate all the way around, as he always had someone in the company watching her closely. The discrepancies in the accounts were only her latest set of problems, but no one dared help her resolve them. By the time she returned from her honeymoon with Stephen, they would have been swept under the rug and she would be on her way to a cushy teaching job at West Hills Academy or even staying at home full-time, another change in her life that her father, and Stephen, would force upon her.

Sara turned a corner to head in another direction. Glancing over her shoulder, she saw two men following at a safe distance. Ordinary jogging outfits concealed their weapons and their earpieces allowed them to keep in touch with their boss. Sara had watched them press the ear pieces into their ears many times, but had never met the person that spoke to them, at least not knowingly. She had never managed to engage the men in conversation, even though the same ones had followed her for the two years since she graduated from college.

A large group of firemen on their morning run approached her on the running path. She had seen the group from time to time, but today the sight sparked something in her. In all the years of having a security detail, she had never once tried to ditch them, not even as a precocious teenager. Now, she needed to give them the slip, as if she had to prove something to herself before marrying the man and living the life her father chose for her.

Sara picked up her pace. If she timed it right, she would top the hill just as she passed the firemen. She resisted the urge to peek over her shoulder again to look at her security guards so she wouldn't accidentally alert them to her plan. Her feet hit the smooth concrete faster and faster, and she focused all her thoughts on her breathing to keep it even and under control.

She smiled and waved at the passing firemen just as she started downhill. Off to her left, thick woods concealed a lesser-known running path. She had only taken it one time since she started running in the park. With the firemen covering her movements, she zipped off to the left and raced as fast as possible around the first several turns.

After running a couple of minutes, she slowed down to a brisk walk. She lifted two fingers to her neck and counted out her pulse rate. Though much higher than normal, she attributed it to the adrenaline coursing through her body. She carefully controlled her breathing so she wouldn't have an asthma attack, but heard the slight wheezing that told her she would need a treatment when she got home. Rotating her head, though, she forgot all about her asthma.

The men were nowhere to be seen.

A large victory grin overtook her mouth and the first real pangs of excitement in quite some time hit her chest. Though it seemed like an adolescent stunt, she had done it, that one thing she always wondered if she could do. She turned up the volume on her iPod and settled back into a comfortable jog through the thick trees.

Forty-five minutes later and still fueled by the high of her mini-adventure, Sara keyed in her passcode on the front gate to her house and ran up the steep driveway. She paused at the front door to stretch. She had barely pulled up her right leg up behind her when the door swung open and Stephen dragged her inside.

"Where the hell have you been?" he asked, the anger on his face mixed with concern.

"I went for my morning run," she said.

"That's not what I mean. Your security detail lost sight of you and couldn't find you."

"I'm fine, Stephen. I just went down a side path and I guess they couldn't keep up with—"

"So you *knew* that you lost them?" His eyes narrowed. "Did you do that on purpose?"

Sara stepped away from him. "I don't understand what the big deal is—"

"What the hell is wrong with you?" He moved toward her and grabbed her wrist. "You can't do something like that. I've been going crazy thinking something happened and Hugh is on his way over."

She twisted her arm under his grip. She almost cowered under the tone of his voice, but remained defiant. "He doesn't need to come over here," she said. "I'm not missing."

"We didn't know that. Any number of things could have happened to you." He loosened his grip and placed his hands on her upper arms. "You have security for a reason. You're Hugh Langston's daughter."

"What exactly does that mean anyway?" she asked with a raised voice. She shrugged his hands away and walked out of the foyer, toward the back staircase. Taking the stairs two at a time, she raced to the second floor and down the hall to their bedroom. Shoving open the door, she stormed onto the marble flooring of the master bathroom and ripped out the elastic band that held her hair in a short ponytail.

At any moment, she could break under the smothering weight of Stephen and her father. She had one little victory in the past 14 years of her own making and now they had taken it away. Stephen was upset, her father was on his way over, and she was destined for another lecture on how she should live her life.

Sara slid open the shower door and turned the water up as hot as she could get it. She stripped off her top and sat on the edge of the standalone bathtub to take off her socks and shoes. Mary would be here in a couple hours to go with her to take care of more wedding details, and Sara didn't have the time or the desire to deal with Stephen or her father a second longer.

The bathroom door opened, letting the built-up steam flow out along with some of her anger. She straightened up, as Stephen sat down beside her and took her hand.

Rubbing his fingers over hers, he smiled. "You know we only want to make sure you're safe. You're the most important girl in both of our lives."

She glanced sideways at his handsome face. The care and concern in his green eyes shone on her and provided some comfort. Some of the tension eased out of her shoulders, but she didn't respond.

"Are you okay?" he asked. "I've been a little worried about you lately. Is the wedding starting to be too much for you?"

Sara ran her tongue over her bottom lip. Maybe it was only the stress of the wedding that weighed on her, causing her to magnify things which never upset her in the past.

"Do you want to put the wedding on hold?"

Her lips parted and she gasped. Though she had never been sure about whether she loved him, his words pierced her heart. She didn't want to lose the only thing she'd ever known, the one constant in her life.

She grabbed his arm. "No, Stephen. I don't want to postpone the wedding. I'm sorry about this morning, I just…" She paused and looked past him, staring blankly at the wall, as she tried to untangle her emotions.

"It's okay," he said. "We all have moments where we don't feel like ourselves or we just want to do something out of the ordinary."

Her gaze fell to his hand clenching hers and guilt washed over her.

Stephen lifted her chin until his eyes locked onto hers. "Just promise me you won't do anything like that again. It's much too dangerous."

"Why?" she asked, eliciting a look of confusion from him. "Why is it dangerous? Why do I have security following me everywhere?" She had asked the question numerous times without ever receiving a true answer.

"Let's just say that Hugh has stepped on a number of toes over the years. It's the best way to make sure that you're safe."

"Do you step on toes?"

"When I have to." He pushed up from the bathtub and pulled her to her feet until her body rested against him. Wrapping his arm around her back, he asked, "Why don't you take a bath instead? The jets would be nice on your muscles after your run."

Though a great suggestion, that nagging feeling of being controlled latched onto Sara again. "I think I'll just stick to the shower today."

He tugged at the strap of her sports bra. "Too bad I'm already dressed or I would join you."

"I know you're busy and I wouldn't want to keep you. Isn't

Dad still coming over?"

"I called him and told him that you were found and everything is under control." He frowned at her. "You sound a little wheezy, though. You should do a treatment before you go with Mary."

A strong urge to disobey his command possessed her, but she didn't want to make a poor health care choice because she decided to act like a spoiled, rebellious teenager. "I'll do it after my shower."

"Good," he said and pressed his lips to her forehead.

Once he left the bathroom, her smile fell. She always assumed she had security assigned to her because her father was beyond rich and others might exploit that somehow, but she never dreamed that he was involved in something dangerous. He wasn't the greatest man in the world, but what toes had he stepped on that would require her to have constant security and why was her soon-to-be husband stepping on those same toes?

Sara went to the shower and regulated the temperature before stripping off the rest of her sticky clothes. As she climbed under the steady stream of lukewarm water, tension formed new knots in her shoulders and back. The bubble her father and Stephen had formed around her suddenly seemed a very unsafe place to live.

Chapter Nine

"What did he say?"

Allie kept her eyes glued to Logan's hip no matter how hard he had tried to get her attention while she examined his stitches. "This is looking a lot better even though it's only been half a day."

Logan groaned with frustration. Still tired from yesterday's job, he now had to rush off and save the daughter of the man who had killed his pregnant wife and he couldn't get Allie to talk to him about anything other than his injuries. He let her re-bandage his hip in silence, but wasn't about to give up trying.

"You're good to go."

He hopped off the gurney and slipped on his jeans while Allie cleaned up her supplies. "What did he say?" he asked again.

"I'll take another look at you tomorrow before you leave and send you off with some bandages to keep it clean. I'll also give you a pair of small scissors, in case you aren't back in time for me to remove the stitches."

Logan grabbed her arm and spun her to him. "What did Schaffer say in your meeting this morning?" he asked, stressing each word.

Allie briefly met his eyes. "He asked me why I would want to destroy my career over someone who was just using me."

Logan's mouth dropped and a sharp pain struck his heart.

"Allie, I wasn't using you."

"Weren't you?" She looked up at him. "I knew what the stakes were and I knew nothing would ever come out of what we were doing, but damn it, Logan. I can't help how I feel about you."

"Allie—"

"Maybe you're right, though, and you weren't using me. Maybe I was the one using you." Tears spilled from her eyes, dripping from her cheeks down to her white doctor's coat. "Maybe I kept thinking that one day you'd wake up and see me for who I am and that you would love me, too."

"Allie, stop." He brought her to him and circled his arms around her in a tight embrace, and she pressed her face into his chest. "I'm so sorry, Allie. I never should have done this with you. I should have ended it the minute you told me how you felt." He placed his hand on the back of her head. "I never meant to hurt you."

She pulled away from him and wiped her cheeks. "I know you didn't. It's entirely my fault for sticking it through when I knew better."

"I wish I could tell you that I love you, but I can't do that to you."

"Things with Karen are still too raw for you to love anyone right now."

Logan nodded and swallowed back his own tears. "It's more than that. Karen is dead because of my life here. I can't put anyone else in danger like that, especially not you. You deserve so much more than that."

Allie touched her fingers to his cheek and wiped away the dampness beneath his eyes. "Now I know you weren't using me, at least not on purpose. You're too big-hearted to intentionally hurt someone."

He didn't feel as if that mattered. He had hurt her, and badly. It also didn't matter if she knew what she was getting into. The blame rested with him.

She placed her palm over his heart. "You have so much pain in here. It started with Karen and the baby and you've just let it build up. I know you were only sleeping with me to try to expel some of that pain before your heart explodes."

Logan covered her hand and pressed it to him. "I'm sorry, Allie. I don't—"

"Let's just leave it at that. You're sorry and I'm sorry and we'll get over it eventually." She pulled her hand out of his, but kept her eyes on his face.

He wanted to say more, but the finality in her voice warned him against further discussion. "Are you coming into the meeting now?" he asked.

She shook her head. "I have to get some things together first and then I'll come in to demo the nebulizer for your team."

He brushed her cheek with the back of his knuckles. "Just for the record, I always saw you for who you are, but I couldn't act on it. I want you to find someone who is not only going to see you for who you are, but who will know what to do with it." He pecked her smiling cheek. "I'll see you in a bit."

Logan walked out the door, but only made it a few feet before her voice found him again.

"And wear your damn sling, Logan!"

He laughed, but to give her the win, he adjusted it from where it hung around his neck and secured his left arm in it.

In the planning room, his team waited for him. On the table, scattered folders waited for his review. At a glance, he saw over a dozen folders. While grateful for the amount of intel on Sara Langston, it also triggered concerns.

"What do we have so far?" he asked, as he chose the seat at the head of the table.

"Everything," Charlie said. "We have pictures, reports, more pictures, more reports."

"Basically Sara's life on a platter," Jack said.

Logan picked up one of the folders and opened it. Sara's smiling face stared back at him. Her beauty jumped out from the photo, with her wide smile that revealed the top row of perfect teeth, sparkling brown eyes, and dark, reddish-brown curls that framed her slender face. His forehead creased as he studied her and he reminded himself that she was the job, not someone for his imagination to enjoy.

He closed the folder without looking at the other pictures and grabbed another folder. Inside, a report gave a full account of her wedding plans for the next two days. He saw the meeting with the wedding planner listed, the one after which they would kidnap the women.

Looking at Lester, he asked, "Do we have a map of the

area?"

Lester retrieved a map from the folder in front of him and spread it across the table, close to Logan's end.

Logan stood up and planted his palms on the table. "Tell me what's what."

Pointing to a red circle on the map, Lester said, "This is where the wedding planner's office is." He picked up a pen, and dragged it along the road heading east. "We need to first follow the designated route to Langston's estate where the rehearsal will take place so the girls think nothing is wrong."

"Do we know what her security will be like?"

"Two men are assigned to her at all times," Jack said. "They've been with her for a couple years now, so they are pretty aware of her movements."

"Is there any way to derail that and have someone else as security?" Logan asked.

"Negative," Jack said.

He ran his finger north along the street, toward the green circle, which marked Langston's estate. "We need a distraction. Something that will put distance between us and her security."

"An accident is always a good way to go," Lester said.

"We have enough guys here that aren't assigned to the job that we could easily create an accident," Charlie said.

"Let's do it," Logan said. "Les, I want you to pick a few men and work with them on how to create the diversion. We only have one shot at this, so everything has to be timed perfectly." He pointed to a spot ten blocks away from the wedding planner's office. "I want the distraction here. Then we can drive another four blocks, to here." He moved his finger along the route, as Lester marked the indicated locations with a black marker.

"From there, we turn west, into this alleyway. We won't have long to do the exchange. I'll make sure Mary is on the passenger side and Sara on the driver's side. I'll stop at the intersection here," Logan motioned to a cross-shaped intersection in the alleys. "I want two cars to come up on either side. Les, you'll approach from the south and Austin will come in from the north. One person opens the doors on each side at the same time and administers the sedatives. Then we pull them out and move them into the main cars. I'll have a driver replace me in the car and we'll head out from there. We should be able to do it in less than two minutes in order to stay ahead of her security detail."

"Then we get to tell her that dear old dad is trying to kill her," Jack said. "That's not going to be easy."

"No, it won't. We'll lay low in the safe house 30 minutes outside of town, since we'll be eight hours away from here," Logan said. "As soon as Langston and Mathers realize she's gone, which won't be long, there will be an immediate call to action to find her. We'll keep her sedated until Saturday afternoon and then Charlie and I can deal with telling her. We'll redirect the team with Mary to a safe house on the other side of town. We need the girls as far away from each other as possible."

Logan fell back into his chair and looked around the table. "Any questions or thoughts?"

His team shook their heads.

"Les, get going on working with the diversion team." Logan glanced at his watch. "Charlie, it's about time you get started on your sleep shift. I'll wake you in four hours and we'll have Doctor Connors demo the nebulizer then."

Both Lester and Charlie left the room, leaving Logan alone with Jack. Logan picked up the folder with the pictures again and sorted through them. The first several photos were only of Sara, while the last half had her with Stephen in various locations.

Flipping through the pictures of Sara with Stephen, Logan picked up on a recurring theme. In every photo, Sara leaned away from her fiancé. In the one picture where Stephen kissed her cheek, she appeared disconnected, her face absent of a smile that most women in her position would have.

"There's something missing here," he said.

"What's that?" Jack asked.

Logan straightened out the pictures in a neat stack. "Love," he said, setting them down in the middle of the table.

"What are you, a premarital counselor or something?" Jack asked.

Logan ignored the joke. "It's evident from the pictures that she doesn't love him and we can use that to our advantage." He turned his head as Schaffer walked through the door, and rose from his chair. When he reached Schaffer, he asked, "Can we talk for a minute outside?"

Schaffer turned back around and Logan followed him into the hall. "What's going on?" Schaffer asked.

"We have too much intel."

Schaffer laughed. "Normally, you're complaining that we have too little intel. Now you're complaining because we have too much. Exactly how much intel will make you happy?"

"It's not that," Logan said. "The norm is that we have too little intel. So why, all of a sudden, do we have an overabundance of intel on this particular job?"

Schaffer studied him for a moment. "Are you worried about something?"

"We haven't had time to debrief from the last job, but something was off there, too. We were sent out to destroy a drug lab, and we did so, with no one in sight. Once we took care of it, over half my team left. I see the other barn, and it's only when I'm inside alone that I get ambushed. That barn was filled with child pornography. Not something we'd expect to see from drug dealers."

"Do you think it was a setup?"

Logan hesitated. He had yet to voice his suspicions and he worried about Schaffer thinking him to be a conspiracy theorist. "I don't know what it was, but something wasn't right. The men who caught me said something about their boss wanting me in one piece. Who else wants me outside of Hugh Langston? And now we're getting massive amounts of intel for a hit on his daughter?"

Schaffer took a deep breath. "If you're right about this, we could have a leak."

Logan nodded, grateful Schaffer brought it up first. "What if Sara is in on this? What if we're meant to bring her back here to infiltrate us? She could be wearing a wire or have a bug or transmitter when we pick her up."

"I trust your instincts. I always have. When you get her, sweep her for any bugs, however you feel necessary. Make sure she's clean. If this hit is legit and we do have a leak, you will need to limit access to Sara until we can get her to the FBI. Someone could be using us to get her into the Church, like you said, or even so that we get her out in the open so they can go through with the hit that way, while she's in our custody."

"Setting us up for the murder since we kidnapped her." Logan shook his head. He hated thinking anything like that could happen, but he had to remain on high alert. "I trust my team, but I'll limit access to her to be safe. If someone on my team is the mole and they are working with her or they want to kill her, they'll have to get through me."

"I'll work the leak from this end and see what I can find out. Be careful and get a backup plan ready that only you know about."

They moved back into the planning room. Schaffer's acceptance of his theories made Logan happy to have Schaffer on his side. The idea of a leak or a possible setup added a whole new layer to the job.

Logan sat down at the table and picked up a random picture of Sara. He didn't know what he would do if he found out she was involved, not after everything her father put him through. She didn't seem the type, but he wasn't about to rule anything out.

Chapter Ten

"I'm famished," Sara said. "Let's stop for a late lunch."

"You read my mind," Mary Flynn said. "I never thought I would tire of wedding preparations. I swear if you divorce this man, you better elope with the next one. I'm not going through this ever again. Well, maybe I will for my own wedding someday."

Sara laughed. "I don't think that will be an issue. If I divorced Stephen, Dad would have a massive heart attack, then survive just to tell me off."

"Where do you want to go to lunch? Our usual?"

A childlike smile filled Sara's face. "Where else would we go?"

Sara opened the tinted glass that divided them from her driver and gave him new directions. When the glass rolled up, she leaned back in the seat and turned to watch the shops pass by. The day had exhausted her and it was only midafternoon. From the excitement that morning of slipping her detail, to meeting with the wedding caterer, having their nails done, and checking the final alterations on her dress, Sara wanted nothing more than a strong drink and her comfortable bed.

The car pulled up to their destination. Sara hopped out of the car when the driver opened her door, already salivating. At the food truck, Sara placed their usual orders and handed over a twenty, telling the owner to keep the change. After a year of coming here, the owner of the truck always treated her right and she always doubled-down on the tip. She received far better service here than at any of the expensive restaurants Stephen or her father insisted on going.

With their food in hand, they walked across the street at the crosswalk and made their way onto the beach, toward their normal spot on a short wall in front of the bike path. When they sat down on the concrete wall, facing the water, Sara kicked off her sandals and curled her toes into the soft, warm California sand. She spread a napkin over her lap and prepared her tacos for consumption.

Taking her first bite of the overstuffed, corn tortilla, she took note of the activity all around her. She enjoyed the tranquility in her surroundings, watching the surfers lost in their own world of waves, the competitiveness of the volleyball game to her right, the healthy mix of tourists and locals on the pier, and the families enjoying the water.

"Where are Tweedledee and Tweedledum today?" Mary asked with a mouthful of burrito.

Sara's mouth turned downward, as she glanced at the two unfamiliar faces watching them from a distance. "Apparently I got them fired this morning."

Mary's mouth opened, giving Sara a glimpse of her half-chewed food. "What?"

Sara leaned in as her friend resumed chewing. With a mischievous tone, she said, "I slipped my security detail on my run."

Mary smiled, a combination of surprise and admiration. "How did you manage that?"

"Right time, right place, I suppose. I just wish Stephen hadn't fired them."

"What possessed you to do it?"

Sara shrugged and took another bite of her taco. She had been asking herself the same question since that morning. Sure, she had always wondered if she could do it, but she was 26-years old and preparing to marry the most powerful man in her father's empire, right under her father. With a wealth of money and all the best in life, expectations of her were high. She couldn't run around like a teenager rebelling against her overbearing parents.

Her teeth sunk into the thick taco and the juice from the

tender meat ran down her fingers, coating her engagement ring. She threw the taco into the tray and ripped off her ring. She dipped a napkin in her water and wiped off her hand first, then poured a little water over her fingers.

As she polished it off with a clean napkin, Mary asked, "Why are you marrying Stephen?"

Sara finished drying off her ring and secured it back on her finger. She twisted the gaudy thing around her finger and stared at the five karat square-cut diamond, flanked by half karat square diamonds. Everything about it screamed Stephen, with nothing in it reflecting her personality. Stephen insisted on yellow gold, but she preferred white. Stephen demanded a large ring while she wanted something inconspicuous. She didn't care if it was a single solitaire of only a tenth of a karat. If she loved him, it wouldn't matter if she had no engagement ring, as long as they were together.

"You don't love him," Mary said. "You never have."

Sara shot her a glance, wondering how Mary could know that. She had never expressed her concerns about getting married, never once disclosed her nonexistent feelings for Stephen.

Mary laid a hand on Sara's arm. "I've supported you through this wedding and I've held my peace. But you're also my best friend and have been since prep school. As such, I have the obligation to tell you how I feel. Tomorrow you're marrying someone who doesn't give you the happiness you deserve. And why? Because Daddy told you to."

"Mary—"

"Someone has to say it, no matter how much it hurts. Maybe I should have said it a long time ago." She gestured to the security men. "That's not your life. This is your life. Right here, with a greasy food truck taco and your feet half-buried in the sand."

Sara looked down at her feet, which were just as Mary said. She couldn't help that she loved the way the soft granules felt between her toes, just as she couldn't help it if she craved greasy food truck tacos.

"Can you imagine what Stephen would say if he saw us?" Sara asked.

Mary scrunched up her face. "Food truck tacos are not suitable for my future wife and mother of my children," she said, with an awkward impression of Stephen that sounded nothing like him.

"Stop it," Sara said, despite the laugh that left her lips. "This is your life, too. You're not cut out for any of that socialite stuff."

"That's because we were raised poor. We're not like all the other rich kids on the block. If my parents hadn't won the lottery and actually managed their money, then you and I never would have met at school."

Sara fingered the small heart locket around her neck, the one her mother gave her before she passed away. "The same goes for if my mother hadn't died."

Mary shifted to the side, threw her leg up on the wall, and grabbed Sara's arm with both hands. "Don't do it. Don't marry him."

"But everything's in place and ready. The dress is—"

"Screw the dress. You're not happy with him and you don't love him. Just walk out on this wedding like you slipped your security this morning. Your dad will forgive you eventually. Until then, you can hang out at my place. We can have a dress-burning party and pawn the ring."

Sara laughed. She didn't know why, but she couldn't stop herself. Mary joined in and they laughed until tears rolled down their faces.

Sara wiped the tears from her eyes and pulled her best friend to her in a tight embrace. "I love *you*," she said. "That's all I need."

Mary broke the hug. "No, that's not all you need, but I'll still support you if you go through with this. Just think about it, okay? It's not too late to call it off, not until you've taken your vows. In fact, until the priest says man and wife, you can still get out of it."

"I appreciate your concern," Sara said, "but I'm going through with it. Just because I don't love him now doesn't mean I won't someday."

"That's about the saddest thing I've ever heard," Mary said. She shifted until she faced forward again and resumed devouring her burrito.

Sara touched her fingers to the ring again. It may be the saddest thing Mary had ever heard, but it felt much worse saying it.

Chapter Eleven

"Good afternoon, boys."

"Good afternoon, Doctor Connors."

The playful, singsong response from his team put a smile on Logan's face for the first time that day. Allie grinned and shook her head, as she moved to the table at the front of the room with a machine in her hands. The members of his team shifted in their chairs, each with notepads and pens ready to take notes.

"Today we are going to learn about asthma," she said, her tone keeping up the classroom pretense. She set the machine down on the table along with an inhaler. "Sara Langston has your run-of-the-mill asthma. During an attack, her bronchial tubes become inflamed, partially closing off her access to air. Should she have an attack, she'll be short of breath, have some audible wheezing, and may cough. She'll feel tightness in her chest and may panic a bit due to not getting enough oxygen. Everyone's symptoms are different, however, so her symptoms may present slightly different."

Logan looked to his left, as Jack raised his hand. Allie laughed and called on him.

"Will she know she's having an attack?" Jack asked.

"Absolutely, although maybe not right away. Watch for things like her taking shallow breaths while talking and excessive yawning or sighing. You might also hear wheezing or her struggle to take breaths between words before she states she's having an attack."

"What do we do if she has an attack?" Charlie asked.

"The first thing you'll do is give her a rescue inhaler." Allie held up the inhaler. "This is your standard albuterol inhaler and should help open up her airways. If it doesn't, she'll need an immediate treatment. You'll also want to inquire if she does regular treatments to maintain her asthma in addition to using maintenance inhalers."

Logan's head spun with the whirlwind of information and he scratched down notes as fast as he could.

Allie picked up the nebulizer. "Time to prepare a treatment."

For the next several minutes, Logan and the rest of his team watched as Allie walked them through connecting tubes and adding medication to the machine in great detail. She flipped a switch on the machine and it roared to life. Within seconds, steam came from the mouthpiece.

"So the medication is in the steam?" Lester asked.

"Correct," Allie said. "She breathes it in through this mouthpiece. The average treatment takes 10 minutes, maybe a little more. After the treatment, she might feel jittery and shaky throughout her body, as well as have increased and rapid heart rate. These are all normal and, in fact, when she uses the rescue inhaler she may also have these symptoms, but to a lesser degree. The treatment may make her speed up her speech pattern because of the shakiness. Just make sure she has access to cold water and take it easy on her."

Charlie stuck his hand up and Allie called on him. "What if the breathing treatment doesn't work?"

"Take her to the nearest hospital. I know that's going to be tough given your job circumstances, but you cannot save her life just to risk it again with a bad attack."

Amidst the sudden rush of groans, Logan raised his voice. "We'll figure that out if we come to it. I'll work on a contingency with Schaffer. Les, time for your sleep shift. Charlie, Jack, stay here with Doctor Connors and practice preparing a treatment until you have it down."

"Where are you going?" Jack asked.

"I need to check in with the other team." He flicked his gaze in Allie's direction. "Doctor Connors, can I see you in the hallway for a moment?"

She gave a slight nod and led the way into the hall.

"Schaffer said you're going shopping later," Logan said once they were outside.

"I'll get both Sara and Mary enough clothes and things to last two weeks."

"The report said Sara runs every morning."

"I'll make sure to get her something to run in."

"Did he give you a budget?"

"Open."

Logan raised his eyebrows. "Open? Lucky you. I never get an open budget."

"They are used to the finer things in life." Her eyes combed over his face. "But you didn't bring me out here to talk about my budget."

"No, I didn't. These inhalers, the nebulizer, and EpiPens that you're giving us for Sara. I need an extra set of everything and I don't want you to tell anyone about it."

Her face scrunched up and eyes narrowed. "I have to clear all expenses with Schaffer."

"That's fine, just no one else. Can you do that for me?"

"Of course. I don't suppose you're going to tell me why."

Logan pressed his lips together and smiled.

"Can you at least tell me if everything is okay?"

He didn't respond. He couldn't without lying.

She touched his arm. "I'm worried about you. I know this has to be hard. Saving the daughter of Hugh Langston."

"She's not responsible for what her father did. She deserves to be saved just as much as the next person." *As long as Sara's not setting us up*, he thought.

"Be careful, Gabe. Please."

Her use of his first name struck him with how deep her concern was for him. He'd only ever heard her say it in bed. "I will be," he said. "I will be."

Chapter Twelve

Everything laid out across his bed, Logan packed his go-bag, mentally checking off items on his list. He had packed the same go-bag for every job since his first job with The Boys Club, when Schaffer instilled in him the importance of having one. Though the safe house had personal hygiene items and plenty of clothes for just about every size man, Logan still believed in his go-bag. He never knew what might happen.

A pair of jeans, a T-shirt, two pairs of boxers, and two pairs of socks went in first. A thin blanket and a roll of toilet paper followed. Flashlight with extra batteries. A lighter and a box of matches. A small first aid kit. Paracord and hunting knife. His trusty Smith & Wesson M&P nine millimeter and extra clips. Two bottles of water and a handful of granola bars. A small bag of cash. The list continued until his bag was almost full.

In the front zipper, he added the final two items on his list: the last picture of Karen he ever took and his wedding ring. He had stopped wearing it almost a year ago, but still carried it on his jobs as a good luck charm.

He ran his hand over his freshly shaven head several times and thought about his list to make sure he didn't miss anything. It had been a long night of planning with only four hours of sleep starting at 2 a.m. Now only an eight hour drive away from kidnapping Sara Langston, Logan's nerves were on high alert and his mind overanalyzed everything, right down to if he missed something in his go-bag.

He had balked at the suggestion of shaving his head down to a quarter inch of hair, but after they decided late last night that Carlos would take his place as the driver of the car service vehicle when Logan got into the other car with his team and Sara, he had little choice. Though half-Mexican, Carlos looked most similar to Logan out of all the men in The Boys Club. Unfortunately for Logan, Carlos also regularly shaved his head. Logan agreed to go down to a fourth of an inch to get a better match, but not completely bald. Anyone following the car service vehicle wouldn't be able to tell the difference under the hat they had to wear with the suit.

His bedroom door opened. He turned to greet Allie as she closed the door.

Allie shook her head. "Just when I thought you couldn't get any more handsome, you have to go and shave your head."

"That's not what we were going for, but thanks. Carlos is taking over for me in the car when we take Sara and Mary."

"You need a lot more of a tan to look like Carlos, but not a bad match. Where's your suit?"

"I'll change into it when we get there. Don't want to get all wrinkled on the drive."

Allie grinned. "You mean you don't want to be uncomfortable in a suit longer than you have to."

"That, too." He gestured to the nebulizer and a small bag in her hands. "Are those for me?"

"They are," she said, handing them over. "Duplicates of everything that I officially gave to Jack a few minutes ago. Schaffer is the only one who knows about this. The teams already have the suitcases for Sara and Mary as well."

He packed the items in his bag and zipped it up. "I appreciate it, Allie."

"That bag also has some bandages for your hip and some scissors if you can't make it back for me to take out the stitches. I know I won't be able to get you to wear your sling, so I'm not even going to try."

Logan heaved his go-bag over his right shoulder. "Can't let anyone know I have a weakness."

"No, you sure can't."

Considering the meaning of her words, he followed her out of the room to the elevators. The only two people he'd ever let in were Schaffer and Karen. Despite his close friendship with Jack, he couldn't open up in the way he should, no matter how much Jack opened up to him. However hard she tried to get in, Allie only saw his external wounds, though she knew of the internal ones.

They rode up the elevator in an uncomfortable silence. With the numerous things he wanted to tell her, he couldn't say anything. Allie wouldn't understand the incredible pain that Karen's death still caused him after two years. That pain swelled in his chest now, just from thinking her name. Allie knew nothing of his life as a juvenile, running away from foster parents that ranged from mediocre to horrific. How he tried to keep food in his stomach by starting with pickpocketing and working his way up to burglary. He could not carry his burdens on his own, but he wouldn't dare ask another to help him with the load.

The elevator doors slid open and he gestured for Allie to exit first. Stepping out of the elevator, barreling into a situation that held little possibility for a positive outcome, Logan turned his thoughts to the job ahead.

They walked into the chapel, where the rest of his team and the other teams waited. Allie moved up to the front of the room and Logan took a seat in the front row. Schaffer eyed them both, as if searching for signs they had broken his decree.

"Now that we're all here," Schaffer said, "let's make sure everything's in place. Logan, run down the job one last time for us."

Logan rose from his seat and stood next to Schaffer. "The teams assigned to Sara and Mary will both leave here and drive to our previously designated meeting place where the car service vehicle will be waiting. I'll drive that to the wedding planner's office, while the other teams get into position. I'll make sure Mary sits on the passenger side and Sara on the driver's side. Those who are assigned to creating the diversion will make sure there is an accident involving her security detail."

Jack's hand shot up. "We got some good news in that regard. Sara slipped her detail yesterday on her morning run and Mathers fired them both. She now has two new security men who are unfamiliar with her."

Logan tilted his head. Why would she pull a stunt like that? The actions made no sense for a privileged girl. Maybe she wasn't as tied to her father or money as he originally thought. Maybe she was more... normal.

"That is surprisingly good news," he said to the group. "It could also be bad news. Apparently she's resourceful and thinks fast on her feet. We'll have to watch her closely so she doesn't slip away from us.

"Once I pass the accident, I'll get to the exchange spot as quickly as possible. I'll pull up, Jack and Tuck will administer the sedatives, and we'll put them in their respective cars. Carlos will take over driving for me and we'll head out to the safe houses. The team here will maintain communications with both teams every hour as well as monitor and disseminate any new intel. Are there any questions?"

His eyes flitted about the room, from team member to team member, but saw no uncertainty in their faces. "What about medical? Any questions about that?"

Again, no one responded.

"Boys," Schaffer said, stepping up next to Logan, "I cannot stress how important this job is. We must execute it precisely and I trust you will. Thank you."

The teams filed into the center aisle and headed toward the front door. Logan gave a backward glance at Schaffer and Allie, who now stood next to him, and nodded at them as an affirmation that everything would go smoothly. He wished he believed it.

Chapter Thirteen

Sara and Mary couldn't stop laughing as they left the wedding planner's office. Everything still seemed like such a mess, but Sara had to trust it would all work out in the end. The wedding had put an incomparable amount of stress on her shoulders. There was nothing to do but laugh it all away.

"I still can't believe she booked an accordion player for the wedding instead of a harpist," Mary said.

"I don't even want a harpist," Sara said.

"But Stephen thinks it's 'proper' for the occasion," Mary finished for her.

"Whatever that means."

"You're the one running around getting everything in order and Stephen is just telling you what to do. Again. Is there anything in this wedding that belongs to you? Something you picked out that you would like?"

As they walked down the two flights of stairs in front of the building, Sara thought about every aspect of the wedding, from the harpist to the cake to the location, even the date. "I picked out nothing. He shot down my suggestions in the beginning, so I stopped making them."

"What would you change if you could?"

The corners of Sara's mouth turned up and she stared into

the dusk of the evening sky. "We'd elope," she said. "No fancy wedding, no show of money and prestige. Just me and him and a couple close friends to sign as witnesses."

"And of course I'd be one of those close friends."

"Well, I was thinking about asking Heather, but now that you mention it, you might be better suited for the job."

Mary smacked her arm and they laughed again. As a black car pulled up to the curb in front of them, all humor left Sara's bones. Time for the rehearsal at her father's estate, followed by a boring rehearsal dinner that she wished she could get out of attending.

"Do you know this driver?" Mary asked.

"Not that I'm aware of." Her father had her normal driver drop her and Mary at the wedding planner's office before rushing off to the airport to pick up guests.

The new driver exited the car and Sara didn't have to look at Mary to know her eyes were wide with lust. Mary's hand poking Sara's leg told her that.

"Do you see that?" Mary asked in between clenched teeth. "You need to hire him full time."

Sara had to admit the new driver was quite attractive. Her teeth raked over her bottom lip as he approached. He greeted them in a professional manner and ushered Mary into the car. Shutting the door, he coaxed Sara to the driver's side and opened the door for her there. Though her other drivers always let them get in through the same door, Sara didn't complain. She was too busy stifling her rampant thoughts.

When he shut the door, Sara turned to Mary, whose large eyes and smile said she had the same thoughts running through her mind. Words failed them both as the driver climbed into the driver's seat. Looking at Sara in the rearview mirror, he confirmed her father's address as their destination. Sara then rolled up the window between them and the driver.

"What are you doing?" Mary asked. "I can't see him anymore."

"We look like giddy schoolgirls that just found their first crush."

"He's my first, second, and third crush."

Sara laughed. "He is a bit on the side of good-looking."

"Just roll down the damn window so I can look at the eye candy while we have him captive."

Sara swatted Mary's arm. "You're so bad. Just don't be obvious, okay?"

"I can't guarantee anything."

Sara rolled down the window between them and the driver. She kept her eyes focused on her hands in her lap. Out of the corner of her eye, Mary molested the driver with her gaze.

"Ma'am?" the driver asked, making eye contact with Sara in the rearview mirror.

Sara realized he thought she rolled down the window because she needed something. "We're fine," she said. "Just wanted some fresh air."

Mary giggled at her words. "I need a little more of that fresh air, please."

Sara pressed her lips together to stop even more laughter. After a few minutes passed, she lifted her eyes to the rearview mirror to get another look at him. Focused on the traffic in front of him, the driver didn't notice her scrutiny. He appeared to be in his mid-thirties, but had small lines jutting out from his ice blue eyes, which mesmerized her with the stories they told. Hard and weary with lots of pain, and something else she couldn't quite grasp. Regret, maybe. She couldn't explain why they drew her in, but it was the first time she had looked into someone's eyes and caught a glimpse of their soul.

His gaze rose to the mirror and he caught her staring. She tore her eyes away and crimson filled her cheeks. She focused instead on the view outside the tinted window and rested the side of her head against the glass.

A loud crash came from behind the car, just after they flew through an intersection. Sara jumped and looked out the slanted, rear window.

"What was that?" Mary asked, also turned around.

"Looks like an accident," the driver replied.

Though they were moving farther away, Sara recognized one of the cars in the accident. "Oh, no! That's my security detail." She whipped around in the seat. "Sir, I'm so sorry, but can we go back? I need to make sure they are okay."

The driver nodded. "I'll turn around up here."

"Thank you so much," Sara said. "I just can't leave them there."

She turned back to look at the accident, but enough distance had passed that she couldn't see it. She bounced up and down in her seat, anxiety flowing through her veins. The driver turned right into an alley and slowed the speed of the car.

"I hope they're okay," Mary said.

"I hope so, too. It's my fault those two guys were there."

"How do you figure?"

"I got the other two fired, remember?"

Mary touched her arm. "If it hadn't been these two guys, it would have been the other two. It's not your fault."

"How much farther?" Sara asked the driver.

"We're here," he replied. The car stopped.

Every instinct in Sara's body sounded an alarm. "What are you doing?" she asked, looking at the driver in the rearview mirror. "Why did we stop?"

The blue eyes she had admired for most of the drive gave away nothing. The silent stare of the driver raised her heart rate and level of fear. Sara jumped as her door opened up at the same time as Mary's. A man reached in and grabbed her. She screamed, competing with Mary for volume.

She turned her head back to the driver. "Help us!"

The man slapped a hand down over her mouth and told her to be quiet. The driver continued watching her without moving to save them.

Something pierced her neck and her vision dimmed, not once taking her eyes off the driver's, pleading with him for help that never came.

Chapter Fourteen

Guilt consumed Logan while he watched Sara struggle with Jack. Her eyes begged him to help her, but he remained still while the needle slipped into her neck and she faded away. He fought his instinct to help her and reminded himself that it had to be done to save her life.

As soon as both women were asleep, he jumped out of the car and Carlos got in. Jack and Tuck dragged Sara and Mary out of the car and into the cars that contained the teams assigned to them. Logan shut the doors to the car, and Carlos climbed into the driver's seat. Logan raced back to the car that had Sara in the back and hopped in the front seat next to Lester. Right on schedule, all three cars took off in their assigned directions.

Logan buckled his seatbelt and turned around to look at Sara seated between Jack and Charlie. With her head leaning on Jack's shoulder, a peaceful sleep claimed her face. The easy part of the job was done. Now they had to convince her that her father had taken a hit out on her and she needed to cooperate with the FBI. Her whole world was about to be turned upside-down.

"Did you have to stick her in the neck?" Logan asked Jack.

"She was struggling and I couldn't get to her arm. The needle would've snapped in two had I tried."

Logan frowned and kept his eyes on her, hoping Jack didn't

hurt her too much.

"You okay?" Jack asked.

Logan nodded and shifted in his seat until he faced the front again. According to Allie's instructions, they would give her another sedative as soon as she started waking from the first one, in order to keep her out for almost a full day. If they could keep her asleep until after the scheduled time of her wedding, she would have one less reason to fight to get away. The wedding was scheduled for 1 p.m. tomorrow, which meant keeping her asleep for just under 19 hours.

Everything had gone perfectly so far, but when she woke up tomorrow afternoon, anything could happen.

He wished there was a way to have taken Sara without the trauma of being kidnapped. During all the time they planned, he hadn't thought about how a kidnapping could affect both of the girls. Yet, walking up to Sara and telling her that her father was trying to kill her would never have worked. Her security wouldn't have given him the chance. He kept telling himself he was saving her life, but he couldn't help but wonder if there had been another way.

The panic in her eyes during her struggle with Jack did that to him. Made him question everything they did and everything they were about to do. They had never kidnapped anyone before, let alone two people. The complexities of the job were difficult enough without having to see Sara's amber eyes in the back of his mind.

From the moment he saw her waiting on the sidewalk, he knew she wasn't caught up in her father's business. She had no idea what he did or how he got his money. She didn't have it in her to set up Logan and his team, nor did she have anything to do with Karen's death. Yet he still had to treat her as if she did until he confirmed otherwise.

"I talked to Schaffer before we left," Charlie said, interrupting Logan's thoughts. "The safe houses are both well-stocked with food and everything else. We could live there for a few weeks if we need to."

"Thanks, Charlie," Logan said without looking at him. He didn't want to see Sara's sleeping face again. He shifted his attention to the passing scenery.

An hour later, Lester pulled the car into the safe house

driveway. Though they had safe houses all over the country, they were all in different settings. Some were apartments in the middle of a busy city block while others had more rural locations. The safe house they picked out for Sara fell into the latter category. Sitting on five acres, it allowed plenty of privacy. With four bedrooms on the main level, a fully furnished basement, and a large, second-story loft, the house satisfied every need for their job.

Sara would stay in a secret room at the back of the house. After Schaffer had acquired the home, he blocked off part of the master bedroom along with an entrance hidden in the back corner of the walk-in closet. Most of their safe homes had similar rooms or hiding places for emergencies. Sara's room allotted her a separate bathroom and plenty of space, but before she could sleep there, they had to proof the room.

Logan instructed Jack and Charlie to put Sara in a smaller bedroom until they could finish preparing her room. He had Charlie stay with her while he, Jack, and Lester went to work. They first removed all furniture except the bed, relocating the furniture to another room. They then went to work on the bathroom, removing the shower curtain and rod, the towel racks, all items from the drawers, and the lid of the toilet tank.

After they cleared the bathroom, they took the mattress and box springs off the frame and hauled the frame into the other room. Logan did one last check throughout the room to make sure they had everything. There was only one window in the bedroom, which Lester boarded up. Jack installed a new lock on the door, one that could be locked or unlocked from either side using a key.

Looking at the bare room, Logan felt disgust. They were treating her like a prisoner, but they had little choice until she accepted the circumstances of her kidnapping. As he gave Jack the okay to bring Sara in, he hoped she would soon understand that the situation necessitated their actions.

Chapter Fifteen

"Schaffer said to turn on the news."

Logan lifted his head off the back of the couch at Charlie's voice behind him. He had almost fallen asleep, having sat in the same position for several hours. Lester had taken his shift to watch over Sara in her room, while Logan and Jack passed time in the living room.

Charlie set a plate of sandwiches for dinner on the coffee table. Logan picked up the remote next to him and turned on the television. He flipped the channels until he came across a news broadcast.

The words "Breaking News" filled the bottom of the screen and Logan's heart seized. He'd assumed that once Langston and Mathers knew of Sara's disappearance, they would work quickly to find her, but seeing a press conference already made him worry about their chances of success.

On either side of a man in front of the podium stood Hugh Langston and Stephen Mathers. Logan caught his breath and pushed his anger aside. He'd only seen Langston a handful of times since Karen's death. A tall, gangly man with wire-rimmed glasses, at first glance Langston didn't appear capable of causing anyone's nightmares. Logan knew much better, as he once underestimated Langston's reach. Never again.

The bottom of the screen identified the man in the middle as FBI agent John Shelby, who spoke to the cameras. Logan turned up the volume with the remote and leaned back against the couch.

"…kidnapper or kidnappers have not yet been identified. We are interested in speaking to the driver that picked up both Sara and Mary this evening so we could get more information on where he dropped them off."

"Could they be any more obvious?" Jack asked. "They want to find you because they think you took them."

"Good thing they have no witnesses to do a sketch," Charlie said. "Langston would recognize you in a heartbeat."

Logan knew that even if Langston knew it was him who took his daughter, the only way he would find Logan is if there were an informant on the inside. Though the FBI was already investigating, Schaffer had far more prominent contacts there than Langston could ever imagine. The agent with Langston and Mathers probably had no idea that a couple of his higher-ups were helping to cover Logan's tracks.

A reporter shouted off an indecipherable question. "We have not yet received a ransom demand," Agent Shelby said. "Sara's fiancé would like to say a few words to the kidnappers."

Mathers stepped up to the microphones. He looked far worse off than Logan had anticipated. Reddened, tired eyes combined with constricted facial muscles gave the impression of a man who experienced loss. Logan recognized himself in the face that filled the screen. For the first time, he wondered if Mathers knew about the hit on Sara.

"I would like to speak to the man or men who have Sara and Mary. Sara is my fiancée and we are to be married tomorrow. She's 26-years old and is very smart with a bright future. She has asthma and…" He looked down at the podium. "We just want her home safe, so she can be with those who love her. Sara is…" he broke off as tears streamed down his cheeks. "She's… I can't…" he shook his head and walked away from the podium, wiping his eyes. A nearby woman helped him away from the prying lens of the camera.

"As you can imagine," Agent Shelby said, "this is a very trying time for both Sara and Mary's families. We ask for any witnesses to please come forward and help find them. Thank you."

Reporters shouted out unanswered questions and Logan

muted the television.

"What do you think?" Charlie asked.

"Mathers is sincere," Jack said. "You can't fake that."

"You *can* fake it," Logan said. "I just didn't expect him to be so good at it, if that's what he's doing."

"Why didn't Langston speak?" Charlie asked. "And where is Mary's family?"

"They know Sara's the real target, so they had her family front and center," Logan said. He snatched a sandwich off the tray on the coffee table. "Langston didn't speak because he can't fake emotion, not like Mathers." He took a bite of his sandwich, happy to find it was turkey instead of ham, Charlie's favorite.

"Nah, man," Jack said. "Mathers convinced me. He doesn't know anything."

Charlie picked up the tray. "I think I'll get a couple sandwiches to Lester and see how he's doing."

Logan lifted his eyes to Charlie and watched him walk out of the room.

"What's going on with you lately?" Jack asked, sitting in the recliner next to the couch.

Logan took another bite of his sandwich instead of answering.

"You've been on edge, not acting like yourself. It's like this job is too much for you, not that anyone would blame you for—"

"I was sleeping with Allie." Logan hadn't intended to blurt out the confession, but out of everyone, he trusted Jack the most.

"Doctor Connors?" Jack laughed, a reaction Logan hadn't expected. "No way."

A corner of Logan's mouth turned up. "Yes, way."

"You lucky son of a—"

"Not that lucky," Logan said. "I mean, yeah, it was fun, but I never had any feelings for her and she did for me and it all became a mess. Then Schaffer found out—"

"Schaffer? Oh, man. That must have been hell."

"More for her than me, I suppose. He told her I was using her."

"Were you?"

"Yeah, I was," Logan said. "I told myself I wasn't and I told her I wasn't, but the more I think about it, I definitely used her. I sure didn't mean to."

"Well, if you meant to, it would tarnish your armor a bit." Jack shook his head. "Doctor Connors. Man, if the other guys knew that—"

"They don't know and they won't know. Ever."

Jack studied him for a moment. "Karen was a good woman. We all loved her. All of us lost something that day, and not just Karen. We lost you, too."

Logan blinked several times to stop the tears that welled in his eyes.

"I know you don't want to hear this, but there are other women out there. Karen wouldn't be mad at you for sleeping with Doctor Connors or even if you found someone else to spend your life with. But she'd be pissed as hell that you're living like a zombie. It's been two years, Logan, and you're acting like it happened yesterday."

"It doesn't matter if it's been ten years."

"Time does heal, man, but only if you let it. This job is opening up a lot of wounds. You have Langston's daughter in the next room and it's a very bad reminder of the past."

"I'm going to take some time off when we're done here."

"That's the smartest thing you've done in a long time. Besides baggin' Doctor Connors, that is." Jack let out a roar, and Logan couldn't help but laugh a bit himself.

"You know it's not just Karen," Logan said after the laughter died down. "Something about this job is…" he hesitated.

"What is it?"

Logan shook his head. "Never mind. I'm not thinking quite straight." He had almost told Jack about the suspected leak. He knew Jack was safe, but he didn't feel comfortable telling anyone. If only he and Schaffer knew, he could keep it contained.

Charlie came back in the room. "I'm going to relieve Les for a bit so he can get some rest. It's about time for his sleep shift."

"How is she?" Logan asked.

"Still snoozing," Charlie said. He set the tray with two remaining sandwiches on the coffee table. "How are the sandwiches?"

"Fine, but I want to know where our steak is," Jack said.

"I'm saving all the good stuff for Sara," Charlie said.

"I need some fresh air." Logan stood up and yawned. "I'm going to take a walk around the back, make sure everything's okay.

"Don't forget your gun," Jack said.

"I'll get it now. If Schaffer calls back, let him know that I need to talk to him." Logan made his way back to the bedroom where he stashed his go-bag. He retrieved his gun, then secured it in the harness he pulled over his shoulders.

When he stepped back through the door, he turned to the right and looked at the door to the master bedroom. He walked through the room and opened the door in the closet, where Lester greeted him.

"How's she doing?" Logan asked.

"She's good. Not a peep outta her."

Logan crept to the bed and stood over her sleeping figure. She seemed so peaceful, and he had to focus to see the rise and fall of her torso with each breath underneath the blanket. Lost in merciful dreams, she had no idea she was missing or that her father was trying to kill her. Logan wished he could keep her in that state forever, but eventually she would have to wake up and face the truth. No matter when it happened—tonight, tomorrow, in a year—it wouldn't be pleasant for her.

He moved back toward the door to leave, but paused next to Lester. If they had a potential leak, Logan couldn't leave Sara alone with anyone for long. He needed to limit access to her, just as he told Schaffer he would. There had been something on Langston's face during the press conference, something in his eyes. A nonchalance that almost translated into disconnecting himself from the situation. He didn't care that Sara was missing or if she ever returned. Why would he? He had already planned on having her killed. He was probably hoping some kidnappers had saved him the trouble and wouldn't demand a hefty ransom that he'd have to pay for show.

Logan's other thought troubled him much more. Langston might have been disinterested because he already knew Sara's location. He had a mole inside The Boys Club, someone who would reveal her location once they had a chance, giving him access to both Sara and Logan.

No matter what the case, Logan had to be the primary face Sara saw. The one she spoke with and confided in, once she believed them about the hit.

"Les," Logan said, "do me a favor. When Charlie relieves you for your sleep shift, bring a mattress from one of the other rooms and put it on the floor right here, next to the door."

"You sleeping in here?"

Logan twisted his head and glanced at the sleeping girl he had sworn to protect. "Yes, I am."

Chapter Sixteen

Logan tucked his hands behind his head and stared at the ceiling through the dark. He'd been awake most of the night, which allowed him to react when Sara stirred in the early hours. Before she regained consciousness, he administered the sedative in her arm, putting her right back into a deep sleep.

Despite staying the night in Sara's room and keeping the others away, Sara's safety still concerned him. Not knowing the identity of the mole rendered him incompetent to protect her. Once she woke, he might be able to learn more about the leak and find out if she was setting him up. Watching her throughout the night, he grew more convinced she knew nothing about her father's activities, but he wouldn't know for sure until they swept her for bugs.

The door opened and Logan sat up. It took a moment for his eyes to adjust, but he recognized Charlie's hushed voice. "You hungry?" he asked.

"Yeah," Logan said. "What time is it?"

"Just after five."

"Where are Jack and Les?"

"They went out for a morning run."

Logan rolled off the mattress and followed Charlie out of the room.

"Sara's going to be starving when she wakes up this afternoon," Charlie said, as they walked to the kitchen. "I'll make sure to have some food ready for her."

"Good idea." Logan looked at the spread of food Charlie prepared for breakfast. Scrambled eggs, bacon, sausage, toast, and pancakes were laid out across the breakfast bar like a buffet. He loaded up a plate, filled a mug with coffee, and went to the kitchen table.

Charlie sat in a chair across from him with his own plate of food. "You look exhausted. Did you sleep at all?"

"Not much."

"I'm not trying to question your judgment, but why are you staying in her room? I thought we were taking shifts watching her?"

Had the question come from anyone else, Logan would have thought it was a clue that the person was the leak. Charlie's soft demeanor, however, told Logan that his question was more curiosity than anything. He'd been up half the night bouncing around the idea of getting Charlie's help with the leak. Normally he would have gone with Jack, but his gut said that Charlie was the man for the job.

Instead of answering Charlie's question, he said, "I need your help later with Sara."

"I'm already talking to her about her father and the hit."

"No, not that." Logan took a small sip of coffee. "We need to check her for bugs or wires."

"Why do we have to do that?"

"Schaffer and I think there's a leak."

Charlie's eyes widened. "A leak? How is that possible?"

"I don't know, but we received too much intel on this job. My last job didn't go so well, either. I think that Sara is either here because Langston sent her to infiltrate us or someone wants her out in the open to kill her and get to me at the same time."

"I couldn't imagine anyone helping Langston. There's not one person working with us that would want to help him get to you. Everyone knows what happened with Karen. Who in the hell could be involved in that?"

"I don't want to think about it either, but it's a strong possibility. Don't say anything to the others. The only reason I told you is I know you're not him and you can help me calm Sara down enough to check her."

Charlie picked up a slice of toast and tore off the crust. "She's not going to be very cooperative if you're manually checking her for bugs."

Logan had thought about that most of the night, too. "I know, but we have to do it, as much as I don't want to. It's bad enough we kidnapped her."

"You're right, though. We can't take a chance in case she's wired. We should have searched her already."

"Not while she's sleeping," Logan said, "and not against her will, if we can help it. I don't want to upset her more than we already have."

"I am not looking forward to this afternoon," Charlie said, stuffing half the piece of toast in his mouth.

"You and me both."

Chapter Seventeen

Sara groaned as she woke, having been in the middle of a nightmare. She reached out to the other side of the bed, but didn't find Stephen next to her. Her stomach growled like a fierce lion, and she hoped Stephen had the cook prepare breakfast. She couldn't remember ever being so hungry. Wondering where Stephen had gone, she tentatively opened her eyes and looked around her bedroom.

Except it wasn't her bedroom.

She shot up in bed and clutched a blanket to her chest. After scanning the unfamiliar room, she lowered the blanket away from her body and saw she still had on the same dress she wore to the wedding planner's office, minus her high heels. Memories trickled in: being picked up by the attractive driver, joking around with Mary, an accident, a man with a blurry face drugging her while the driver watched.

"Where the hell am I?" she whispered into the empty room. Her chest heaved with frantic breaths and she coaxed herself to calm down. She had to think clearly if she hoped to get away.

Climbing out of bed, she first noticed the boarded up window. The only furniture in the room consisted of two mattresses and the box spring under her mattress. There seemed to be nothing she could use in the room as a weapon against whoever took her. She tried the doorknob on the only door in the room, but the lock held it shut.

In the bathroom, she realized that all potential weapons had been removed as well. She turned her attention to the mirror. She looked like hell, but she didn't care much about her appearance. On the sink counter, a bath towel and wash cloth called to her. She shut the bathroom door, careful not to make a sound. Picking up the bath towel, she arranged it so the material was doubled in half and held it over the mirror. She took a deep breath and smashed her fist into the mirror. The sound of a slight crack came from behind the towel. She turned her body and used her elbow to finish the job.

Once the mirror broke, she brought the towel down perpendicular to the mirror, curving it up to catch the broken glass. She sifted through the shards, careful not to cut herself, and found one that would work. With the washcloth, she lifted the jagged shard and enclosed her hand around it. Opening her hand, she was happy to see that the glass had not cut her through the thick cotton.

Sara left the bathroom, closing the door behind her. She didn't want her assailant to see the broken mirror and know she had a weapon before she had a chance to use it. She climbed back into bed and covered herself up with the blanket, concealing the glass.

Not a minute later, the door to her room creaked open. Sara lay very still in bed, keeping her breathing deep to feign sleep. Footsteps neared her bed and her heart raced out of control. Someone bent over her and she lashed out with the shard of glass. Her arm caught on the corner of the comforter, but she managed to cut into a forearm.

The man, who she recognized through the shadows as the driver, stepped back and she jumped out of bed, holding the glass with both hands like a sword. "Stay away from me," she said.

He held up both hands in a surrender stance, blood dripping down his arm and onto the floor. "Sara, put it down. I don't want you to get hurt."

She let out an exasperated laugh. "I am not putting it down. You're going to show me how to get out of here and let me go."

The man watched her for a moment and then turned his head toward the open door. "Charlie! Get in here!" Looking back at Sara, he said, "I'm sorry, but I can't let you leave. It's for your own safety that you stay here with us."

She flinched. What did that mean? He was the one holding her hostage, him and someone named Charlie. If anything, her safety depended on her escaping.

"I'm getting out of here right now!" She jabbed the glass toward him as a threat.

A smaller man, presumably Charlie, walked in and flipped on the overhead light. After assessing the situation, he said, "Oh, Sara, you have to put that down. This won't help you at all."

Her eyes darted back and forth between the two men. "I'm not putting anything down until I get out of here."

Charlie took several steps forward and she swung the shard at him. Before she could react, the driver raced to her and scooped her up from behind, lifting her inches off the ground. He applied pressure to her wrist and palm until it became too much. The piece of glass and washcloth tumbled out of her hand. Not knowing what else to do, she flailed in his arms, kicking her heels at his legs while she screamed for help.

"Get the syringes." The driver struggled to get the words out, as she continued fighting as hard as she could. "We have to put her out again."

"Not yet," Charlie said. "Sara, calm down. I don't want to drug you, but I will have to if you don't calm down."

Sara slowed her pointless resistance. The man who held her was much too large to defeat and fighting only left her exhausted.

"That's better," Charlie said. "Logan's going to set you down now. I want you to sit still on the bed while I explain some things to you."

The driver, Logan, lowered her to the floor, next to the bed. He removed his arms from around her and helped her sit down on the mattress.

"Thank you, Logan. Can you bring me a chair?"

Logan left the room and Charlie turned toward her. "Sara, there's a lot of things we need to talk about and most of it will be very difficult for you to hear. But you have to start out by trusting us."

Sara rubbed at her damp eyes, but couldn't stop the tears from tumbling down her cheeks. "You kidnapped me. Why would I trust you?"

"Because you don't want to die. You have a lot of fight in you, which tells me you want to live. We also don't want you to die, nor do we want to hurt you. We kidnapped you to save your life."

Logan came back into the room with a chair and set it down so it faced her. Charlie thanked him again and sat down.

"Can you tell him to go away?" Sara asked Charlie. Logan's ability to handle her so easily frightened her. She didn't want him to do that again if she did or said something wrong.

Charlie shook his head. "Logan is in charge and he's going to have to stay."

Sara glanced at Logan, who leaned against the wall behind Charlie with his arms crossed. The idea that he was in charge surprised her. She had thought of him as the muscle and Charlie the brain.

"Sara," Logan said, "no one here is going to hurt you, least of all me. But I need you to listen to what Charlie has to say."

She turned her eyes back to Charlie. Though Logan's calm voice assured her, he had still been the one to kidnap her and Mary. The thought of her friend made Sara worry for her safety. "Where's Mary?"

"Mary's fine," Charlie said with a warm smile. "She's with another team and she will be returned to her home in a couple days."

"Team? How many others are here besides you two?"

"There are four of us total and we're all dedicated to keeping you safe."

Sara's face scrunched up at his words and the tears came again. "I don't understand what you mean. You kidnapped me. How is that keeping me safe?" Another thought rushed into her head. "What day is it?"

"It's Saturday," Logan said.

"Saturday?" Sara drew in shallow breaths and her mind raced. "I'm supposed to get married today!"

"Your wedding was scheduled to start about a half hour ago," Charlie said. "It was put on hold due to your disappearance."

She couldn't control her rapid breathing, as she thought about the wedding being placed on hold, wondering what Stephen and her father must be going through with her kidnapping. Did they know she had been kidnapped or did they think she had run out on the wedding? She hoped these men had already made a ransom demand and the money would change hands soon. If not, surely Stephen and her father were searching for her and would find her very soon.

"It's a good thing that you missed your wedding," Logan said. "You don't want to marry Stephen Mathers. Trust me."

"What Logan is saying," Charlie said, "is that marrying Mathers isn't the right thing for you to do."

"I don't understand," she said between shallow breaths. "You kidnapped me to stop me from marrying Stephen?"

"No, Sara." Charlie placed his hand on her arm. "You need to slow down your breathing, please."

Sara's chest tightened and she tried to take more breaths to get oxygen into her lungs. She lifted her hand to her chest and closed her eyes, but only heard the familiar wheezing that came with an asthma attack.

"Logan," Charlie said.

Sara looked at Logan, who left the room without a word.

Charlie brought his chair closer to the bed and took her arms. "Slow your breathing, Sara. Try to calm down."

Sara watched his dark eyes and listened to his words, but couldn't stop gasping for air. She felt as if she were drowning as her airways constricted. "I need... I need..."

"I know," Charlie said. "Logan's getting it."

A moment later, Logan came back into the room with a nebulizer and a small bag. He handed the nebulizer to Charlie, who prepared a treatment. Logan dumped the bag next to her on the bed. Several inhalers fell onto the blanket and Sara quickly sorted through them until she found a rescue inhaler. She struggled with getting the cap off, and Logan took it from her hands to help. He handed it back to her and she took two puffs.

Her breathing calmed down just enough for a bit of air to flow through her lungs. Charlie turned on the nebulizer and handed her the mouthpiece. She wrapped her lips around it and breathed in as much of the medication as she could. She coughed several times with the first few inhales, but her breathing improved. After a minute, she was able to take deeper breaths, allowing the medication to open her airways.

Logan, whose eyes had never left her, turned to Charlie and lifted his arm. Blood had dried on his arm, dripping down from where she cut him. "I'm going to clean this up. I'll be right back."

Sara turned her head and watched him walk into her bathroom. He stood in front of the sink, and his blue eyes caught hers in the broken mirror. She spun back around to face Charlie, almost embarrassed that Logan caught her watching him, the same way she had in the car yesterday. As she stared into Charlie's caring eyes, considering their words that they were saving her life by taking her, she realized these were no ordinary kidnappers.

Chapter Eighteen

Logan stood over the sink, washing the dried blood from the still stinging wound. Sara was barely 5'2, but she had a hell of a swing and had cut him almost to the point that he needed stitches again. He hadn't prepared for her tenacity and needed to exercise more caution with her until she accepted the situation. She seemed to be coming to terms, he thought when he caught her watching him. Maybe she understood that they would not hurt her.

Her asthma attack had terrified him. Though Allie explained Sara's asthma to them, when the attack happened Logan had sudden flashes of her not being able to breathe and passing out, possibly dying. As she got her breathing under control, Logan realized he had been holding his own breath. She was the key to bringing Hugh Langston to his knees. Logan couldn't let anything happen to her.

Logan surveyed the damage to the mirror. He'd have to get it cleaned up before they left her alone again. With the nebulizer still running, he left the room and went into the bathroom next to the guest room. He took a first aid kit out from under the sink, applied an ointment to the wound, and wrapped his arm in gauze. He then headed into the kitchen for a broom and trash bag.

After he cleaned up the broken glass and removed the rest of the glass from the mirror, he threw away the bag and retrieved a cold bottled water from the refrigerator. When he returned to the room, Sara handed Charlie the mouthpiece and turned off the nebulizer. Logan offered her the water, and she thanked him. She took several small sips before replacing the cap.

Logan watched her for a few moments before saying, "Charlie, we need to…" He gestured with his eyes to Sara.

Charlie nodded and turned to her. Removing the pulse oximeter from her finger, he said, "Sara, before we explain why you're here, we need to take care of something. You're not going to like it, but it's for your own safety, I promise."

Fear flashed on her face and her chest heaved with deep breaths.

"Just stay calm, we're not going to hurt you," Charlie said. "But we do need to check you for wires. We'll also need you to change into another pair of clothes and we will have to burn what you're wearing now, just to be safe."

Sara looked back and forth between both men, as if not understanding what Charlie was saying.

"We can do this two ways," Logan said. "It's up to you as to what will be easiest for you. We can pat you down, but it would be much more invasive than you would get at the airport. Or you can remove your clothing here, keeping your undergarments on, and we can do a quick visual inspection. Then you can go in the bathroom and change."

Sara crossed her arms over her chest, as if covering herself even though still fully dressed. "No," she said.

"We don't want to do this either," Charlie said. "It's necessary for your safety and for ours. We have to make sure there are no wires."

"Why didn't you just check me while I slept?" she asked.

"I wouldn't do that to you," Logan said. "But you do have to make a choice."

"Why do you have to burn my clothes?"

"In case there's a bug or tracking device sewn into the material," Charlie said.

Sara looked away for a moment and shook her head. "I can't," she said. She tightened her mouth and tears rolled down her cheek.

"Either you can comply," Logan said, "or I have two more men out there that will come in and hold you down while we cut off your clothing and check. I don't want to do things that way and I'm sure you don't either." He wouldn't do it, especially since Charlie was the only one who knew about the possible leak, but he hoped the threat would spur her into action.

She climbed onto her knees and moved backward on the bed, her eyes darting between the two men.

"I'm really sorry, Sara," Logan said. "I have to be sure that we've not been set up."

Her forehead wrinkled and eyes narrowed. "I haven't set anyone up. I don't know what you're talking about." She got off the bed on the other side, her eyes making quick glances at the door. "I don't even know who you people are or why I'm here."

Logan took a deep breath, remaining patient only because he recognized her fear through her actions. She distanced herself by putting the bed between them and kept looking at the door, as if she had some sort of escape.

"I promise you," he said, "we are not going to hurt you. If we wanted to hurt you, we wouldn't have let you do a breathing treatment and we would have searched you while you slept. Go in the bathroom and strip off your dress. Then wrap a towel around you, come back out, and we'll make it very quick."

She stood still for a moment, and Logan braced himself in case she tried to run out of the room. To his surprise, she turned around and went into the bathroom.

As soon as the door shut, Charlie turned to him. "Do you really believe we have a leak?"

"This job came around way too quick after this last one, and it just happens to involve Langston's daughter. I don't know if that's just coincidence or if someone wants us to take her back to our camp. Either way, I'm not going to take a chance."

"She's scared, Logan. I don't think she knows anything."

Logan stared at the closed bathroom door. "I don't think so either, but to keep her safe, we have to be careful."

"Hello?" Sara called from behind the door.

"We're here," Logan said, as he walked toward the bathroom.

"I can't do this with both of you in here."

Logan looked at Charlie, who nodded. "I'll go get her suitcase."

"Give us five minutes, but knock before you come in." As

soon as Charlie left the room and shut the door, Logan said, "Sara, it's just you and me now. I sent Charlie out to get your clothes."

The doorknob rotated and the door creaked open. Sara poked her head out, as if making sure he had told the truth. She came out of the bathroom, gripping a towel around her body.

Seeing her frightened broke down Logan's defenses. More than ever, he abhorred the idea of searching her, but knew of no other way to make sure she wasn't wired.

"Sara," he said, "this is not something I want to do. We have no intentions at all, other than making sure you're not wearing a wire."

She fixed her gaze to the floor. "Let's just get it over with, please."

"Bring the opening of the towel to your front."

She turned the towel until the knot was centered on the front of her body.

"I just need to take a quick look and then you can cover back up," Logan said. "Then we'll do the same for the back."

She squeezed her eyes shut. Her fingers fumbled with the knot, but managed to loosen it. Her cheeks turned pink and she opened the towel.

Logan scanned his eyes over her exposed skin, skipping over her bra and panties. He saw no wires and turned his attention back to her undergarments. There were no unusual bumps that signaled a wire or bug underneath the black material. He instructed her to close up the towel.

Sara turned around and moved the knot to her back. She struggled with opening up the towel again and asked Logan to do it for her. Logan hesitated, not wanting to touch her at all. He had not prepared himself for a physical reaction to seeing her half-naked. While easy to admit that he found her attractive, as the others in the house did, he needed to suppress any thoughts about her outside of the job.

His fingers quickly opened up the towel on the back and his eyes ran over the soft curves of her tanned skin. Seeing no indication of a wire under her panties or bra strap, he covered her back up.

She latched onto the towel and opened her eyes. "I told you," she said. "I haven't set anyone up."

Her quiet voice wracked his heart, making him feel so much

worse for putting her through the inspection. "I have to check the bathroom to make sure there's nothing in there." He checked every area of the bathroom, including rifling through her black dress on the floor, but found no wire or tracking device.

He exited the bathroom and she looked at him for the first time. "Why would you think I had set you up to kidnap me?" she asked.

"It's complicated," Logan said. "In a minute, Charlie will come back in here, you'll get dressed, and then we're going to tell you some things that you won't want to hear. You probably won't even believe us, but I want you to listen with an open mind. Beyond that, and this is the most important thing that anyone will tell you today, I need you to trust me."

Sara searched his eyes. "You kidnapped me. Why would I trust you?"

"I get that I'm asking you to do something that is near impossible for someone in your position, but there are reasons we took you. I swear to you that it had to be done to save your life. The reason I tell you to trust me is that I don't know who else in this house you trust. I hand-picked this team to come here and protect you, but while I trust them, I don't want you to. If there's anything you need to tell us, you tell me and only me. If you have questions, only ask me. I'll be spending most of my time with you, but if I'm away and someone asks too many questions of you or you feel like they are probing too much, let me know right away. Believe me when I say that your life depends on it."

"I don't understand anything that's going on here and I don't know how you think you saved my life by kidnapping me the night before my wedding. For all I know, you're all crazy and this is some kind of trick."

"It's not a trick. My only concern while you're in my custody is keeping you safe, no matter what it takes to do that. Your life and safety mean more to me than you could possibly know." Logan closed his mouth before he kept talking and gave away that her importance had everything to do with getting back at Langston for killing Karen.

Sara held his eyes for a long moment without giving away her thoughts. "I will keep an open mind. If what you and Charlie say makes sense and I can believe that you did save my life, I promise I will trust only you."

Logan breathed a sigh of relief. "Thank you, Sara." A knock on the door interrupted. "Come in."

Charlie walked through the door rolling the suitcase Allie packed for Sara, with extra bath towels tucked under his arm. "I don't know what you women put in these things," he said with a grunt. "I can go away for two weeks with a small duffel bag."

Sara gave a small smile, making Logan believe that she was coming around. After what he just put her through and everything that they were about to tell her, the smile was a sweet reward for a grueling task.

Chapter Nineteen

Sara surprised herself by smiling at Charlie's joke. She didn't want to like anyone here, but if they were telling the truth that they saved her life, then Charlie was easy to like. His quiet voice and calm demeanor contrasted Logan's serious nature.

She wasn't sure what to think of Logan. She remembered back to when she and Mary first saw him and they joked about how attractive they found him. He still had those same physical qualities, but there was a much darker side to him that she didn't see before. She felt it when he had her in his grip and forced her to let go of the glass. She saw it in the intensity in his eyes when he pled with her to trust him. Something about him made her want to believe his words, yet she was more apt to trust Charlie than him based on instinct.

Gripping the towel tighter to her body, she turned her feet inward so her left foot overlapped the right. The idea that Logan had seen her almost naked embarrassed her and she wanted Charlie to see as little of her exposed skin as possible.

Charlie wheeled the suitcase into the bathroom. He came out with her dress in hand and placed it in a plastic bag. "I hate to ask you for this," he said, "but when you're done dressing, I need the rest of what you're wearing to go into the bag, too."

"We had another woman pick out your clothes and personal

effects for you," Logan said. "She assured us that you'll like everything and that it will all fit."

"I'm sure it's fine." She went into the bathroom and closed the door behind her. Opening the suitcase, she smiled at the sight of the clean clothes and personal items. She had never been so happy to see a toothbrush and deodorant in her life, but she desperately wanted a shower and a hot meal.

She settled on a pair of jeans and a simple black top. After doing her best to sponge bathe herself, she brushed her teeth. Once she had dressed, she closed the suitcase and balled up her underwear and bra in her hands. She didn't want them on display in front of the men while she put them in the bag.

Sara exited the bathroom and Charlie held out the plastic bag. She deposited her undergarments, and he closed the bag.

"You'll be able to keep your toothbrush and toothpaste, some shampoo and conditioner, and a few personal items in the room with you, but the rest of the things we'll take out of here," Logan said.

"Can I keep the inhalers?"

"Of course," Charlie said. "Just choose the ones you normally use and we'll leave those with you. One of us will bring you the nebulizer whenever you need a treatment."

"We need you to remove your jewelry," Logan said. "Earrings, necklace, and ring."

Sara touched the necklace around her neck. "I… I can't give these to you."

"It's not a request," Logan said.

Hoping to make a compromise, she removed the earrings first and handed them over to Charlie. "I can't give you my engagement ring or the necklace."

"You don't want that ring," Logan said.

Sara frowned and studied her engagement ring. Stephen had given it to her during a romantic night on the town a year ago. They had only dated for a few months, but he had told her he knew she was the girl for him the first time they met. The ambience of the night made her believe him then, although she had never truly been sure about him being the man for her. Now she didn't know if he ever meant those words.

"I know you don't love him," Logan said in a low tone.

Her eyes flew up to his face. How could a stranger possibly

know how she felt about Stephen? First Mary mentioned it, and now Logan. Was it that obvious?

Watching Logan's face, she twisted the ring and pulled it off her finger. She held it for a second before handing it to Charlie. As soon as he took it, a weight lifted off her shoulders, as if in that moment she made the decision not to marry a man she didn't love. When she returned to Stephen, things would be different and she would end up spending her life with him. For now, she was free from a life without love.

"The necklace, Sara," Logan said.

She held her hand over the small locket. "I can't," she said. "This necklace belonged to my mother. It's all I have left of her."

As he examined her, something shifted in Logan's eyes. After a tense moment, he said, "That's fine. Keep the necklace. Why don't you get comfortable?" Logan gestured to the bed. "Are you hungry?"

"Famished."

"Why don't you eat before we talk?" Logan asked. "We want you to be as comfortable as possible while you're with us, so if there's anything you need, just let us know."

"I have baked chicken breasts already prepared with broccoli and rice on the side," Charlie said. "Is that okay? If not, I can make something else."

"No, that's fine," Sara said.

After Charlie left the room, Sara lowered her eyes to the floor so she didn't have to look at Logan. The behavior of the men made no sense. They gave her a breathing treatment, apologized for having to search her, and now they asked her if chicken was okay for her meal. She supposed they might be keeping her in good condition for a ransom demand, but what did they mean that they saved her life? And why was Logan so interested in her trusting only him?

As much as she didn't love him, she missed Stephen. Living with him for the past three months helped her grow into their relationship, and she would give anything to hear his voice right now.

Sara's face scrunched up and she leaned over, elbows on her thighs, head resting in her hands to catch her tears. She didn't know Logan had left the room until the door shut. Her head shot up and the emptiness of the room made her cry harder. The unknown terrified her, not knowing yet what these men wanted with her. She only knew her life was in danger. Whether from these men or someone else, someone wanted her dead.

The door opened again and Logan came in with a box of Kleenex and a plate of food. She accepted both, and he moved back to the door.

"Where are you going?" she asked.

"Giving you some time to adjust," he said. "Are you okay with water or do you want something else to drink?"

She glanced at the bottled water next to her. "Water's fine."

"Feel free to eat, take a shower, whatever you need to do." He picked up the chair Charlie used and started toward the door.

"Thank you," she said, her voice timid and strained.

He nodded and left the room. The clicking of the lock shuddered through her body. She used the Kleenex to wipe her tears and picked up her plate. They had given her a plastic fork and the chicken breast was precut to small bites, eliminating the need for a knife. Despite the sinking feeling in her stomach, she stabbed a piece of chicken with the fork and set about eating.

Chapter Twenty

"How's she doing?" Jack asked when Logan walked back into the living room and sat on the couch.

"She's struggling, like we thought," he said.

Charlie came into the room. "Just heard from Kyle. They got a call from the other team and all is good there."

"How's Mary?" Logan asked.

"Surprisingly well," Charlie said. "Then again, she's been awake for about half a day longer than Sara. They explained everything to her and she seems to understand what's going on. She's worried about Sara, of course."

"Of course," Jack said. He turned to Logan. "How much more time do you think we should give her before we're ready to move her?"

"As much time as she needs," Logan said.

"Staying out in the open for too much longer isn't good for any of us," Jack said. "We should just go in there now and—"

"No," Logan said. "We're going to give her time to adapt before Charlie and I approach her again."

"Are you sure you don't need help?" Jack asked.

Logan glanced at his friend. He knew he was trying to help, much as Charlie had been earlier, but it still bothered him that Jack was so eager to talk to Sara. He was glad that he chose Charlie to speak with her. Jack was much too blunt to be in there with him. There was one thing, however, with which Jack could assist.

"I may need your help, actually," Logan said. "Sara likes to run, so if she's doing better tomorrow morning, maybe we can take her out around the property."

"I'm sure not going to volunteer for that," Charlie said. "Les might want to go, though."

Logan realized he hadn't seen Lester most of the afternoon. "Where is Les?"

"He slept for a few hours and then went outside to tinker around with the cars in the barn," Jack said. "You know he can't sit still for long."

Part of the appeal of the safe house for Logan had been the extra two cars in the barn. He had chosen the location partly because of the additional means to get away if needed and he was glad to hear Lester worked to keep them in good condition.

"Hungry?"

Logan turned around to see Charlie holding out a plate of food. "Not right now. Thanks, though." He pushed off from the couch and moved down the hallway back to Sara's door. He stared at the door for a moment, and then dug in his jeans pocket for the key to the room. Only he and Charlie possessed keys to her room and he intended to keep it that way.

He slid the key into the lock and rotated it until it clicked. Taking it out of the door, he put his hand on the doorknob, but hesitated before entering. He knew it was too soon to go back in and talk to her, but he also had a desperate need to put her at ease and not let her sit too long thinking they had kidnapped her for malicious reasons.

Instead of entering her room, he left the door unlocked. Leaning against the wall, he sat on the carpet next to the closet door. It wouldn't be long before she decided to come out and talk.

Chapter Twenty-one

Sara had consumed almost all of her plate of food when she heard the click of the lock. She watched the door for a moment, but no one came through.

She set her plate down on the floor and cautiously rose from the bed and crept over to the door. She stood still for a moment before putting her ear to the door. No noises penetrated the wood, piquing her curiosity.

She moved back to the bed and finished her meal, keeping her eyes on the door. No one entered, not while she ate and not while she sat still, waiting for someone to turn the knob. She wondered if Logan was testing her to see if she would try to escape.

Sara decided to take her mind off the unlocked door by taking a shower. Seeing the missing shower curtain and no lock on the bathroom door dismayed her, but she had to shower at some point. Logan seemed genuine about not wanting to search her and she had no reason to think he would embarrass her by barging through a closed bathroom door. With him in charge of the others, she figured he'd keep everyone else in line as well.

The only question she had, besides why they kidnapped her was why there was a mattress on the floor by the door. She imagined they took turns sitting there while she slept, but she felt a bit awkward about someone being in the room while she rested.

In the bathroom, Sara turned the showerhead toward the wall so the water wouldn't soak the floor too much. She stripped her clothes and laid them on top of the vanity countertop. After she climbed into the shower, she regretted breaking the mirror in the bathroom. She thought having a weapon would better her position, but she only ended up hurting Logan. She had never done anything like that to another person, and though remorse tugged at her heart over doing it, at least they knew she would fight back if pushed.

Sara finished her shower while wondering where Stephen was and if he was looking for her. Surely he knew she was missing, but did he miss her as much as she missed him? She wished she could see him now, but Logan's words about her not loving Stephen plagued her heart. Logan had also said that she didn't want to marry Stephen, as if he knew Stephen and didn't approve of him. Yet out of all of Stephen's friends, she had never met Logan before, or even Charlie. Maybe she would recognize one of the other two men in the house as an acquaintance of Stephen's.

Dressed in the clothing she had on before, she contemplated asking one of the men to bring the suitcase back so she could find something else to wear. It would be a good excuse for opening the door. They might even let her out a bit, giving her a glimpse of the rest of the house. If she could map out the rest of her location, she might be able to find a way out.

First things first, she thought. She walked over to the boarded up window and examined it. Screws held the board into the wall on all sides. Though she knew it wouldn't open, she pressed her fingers into the right side of the board and tugged. Nothing.

Sara leaned over and squinted as she studied one of the screws. They had used screws that required a funny shaped screwdriver, one that looked like a hexagon, she determined by counting the number of sides inside the little hole. She only knew about flatheads and Phillips screwdrivers from helping her mom fix things around the house as a kid. If they had used one of those types of screws, she could have figured out a way to open it by using a nail file, a pair of tweezers, or a knife, if she could get access to them.

She moved away from the window. Her escape would not be through there. She stared at the doorknob, inching closer to it. Just one little, quick turn of the knob and she could leave the room and find someone, hopefully Charlie.

She sealed her hand over the knob and opened the door before she lost her courage. She lifted a leg to walk out, but froze when she saw the wall in front of her. Turning left, she took careful steps down the small hallway. Only when she reached the light at the end of the hall and saw Logan sitting against the wall in another bedroom did she realize her room was hidden behind a closet. She sucked in her breath, worried he would get mad at her for leaving her room.

"Hi, Sara," he said, as he got to his feet. "How was your meal?"

She hesitated before answering, wondering if his warm tone and question were a trick. "Um, good."

"What can I help you with?"

She looked around the bedroom and every plan she had thought up for escape quickly left her mind. There was no getting through this maze and into the main house without someone noticing.

"Sara?"

She stumbled a bit on her words before asking, "Is Charlie here?"

"I can get him for you."

"I think I'm ready to listen to what you have to say." Though deceiving him with her words, she didn't know what else to tell him except what he wanted to hear.

"Why don't you take a seat in your room and I'll grab Charlie?"

Her nerves shot up with his words. She wanted to find a way to escape, instead of listening to some fanatical tale they probably made up to make her think they were good people, but she had no way out. If she tried to run, Logan would catch her before she got more than a couple feet away. Best to go back into the room and listen to them. If she could convince them that she trusted them, maybe that trust would go both ways. Once she earned their trust, they would afford her more leniency and allow her to freely move around the house. Then she'd escape.

Chapter Twenty-two

Logan shut the door behind Sara and locked it. She had lied to him when she said she was ready to talk. She only opened the door to push her boundaries, but had to come up with a viable excuse when she saw him sitting there. He wasn't about to take a chance that she would attempt an escape if he left the door unlocked with no guard.

He found Charlie in the living room with Lester watching a national news station that had on information about Sara's kidnapping.

"Any news of importance?" Logan asked.

"Nothin'," Lester said.

"They have no leads and no ransom demand has been made," Charlie said. "Which we already knew. Oh, they've issued a reward for her safe return."

"How much?" Logan asked.

"Two hundred grand," Charlie said. "Langston and Mathers each contributed to the pot."

Logan laughed and shook his head. "They're billionaires and that's the value they assigned her life?"

"Are you gonna tell her?" Lester asked.

"No," Logan said. "It's better not to say anything to her that she might construe as positive, even if we know it's a measly amount."

"Good point," Charlie said.

"Speaking of which," Logan said, "she's ready for us."

"Already?" Charlie asked, as he stood up.

"I tricked her into it. She's still looking for a way to escape, so we need to watch her closely. Just ease her into this. Let's not hit her with everything all at once."

"Got it," Charlie said.

After grabbing a chair from the kitchen, Logan followed Charlie into her room, where Sara sat cross-legged in the middle of her bed. She seemed to relax at the sight of Charlie, but tensed when she laid eyes on Logan. Her body language convinced Logan he needed to stay in the background of the conversation and contribute as little as possible to it.

He set the chair down for Charlie. Moving to the wall behind him, he stood off to the side so he could study Sara as she spoke. With Charlie guiding the conversation, it gave Logan a chance to watch Sara and determine where she was in terms of accepting the truth. He didn't expect it to happen today, but he hoped she was at least a little closer by the end of their conversation.

"Why did you kidnap me?" she asked Charlie.

"What do you know about your father?" he asked.

Her gaze wavered. "I don't know what you mean."

"How much do you know about what he does?"

"I don't understand. What does he have to do with kidnapping me?"

Logan picked up on the frustration in her voice. "You do accounting for him, right?" he asked.

"I try."

"Try?" Charlie asked.

"I mean... yes, I do. For one of his smaller companies."

"Have you ever noticed anything out of sorts?"

Logan almost stopped Charlie from asking the question. Sara's furrowed brow and constant fiddling with her necklace not only gave him the answer, but revealed her discomfort with the topic.

"I don't understand what this has to do with you kidnapping me."

Logan stepped up to the bed, unable to keep out of the

conversation like he wanted. He knelt at the side of the bed, diagonal to her, in order to keep her at ease and not feel threatened. Softening his voice, he said, "You've noticed some discrepancies, right? Things you can't figure out or explain?"

She turned to him, fear flooding her eyes alongside her tears. "Is that why you kidnapped me? Did I do something wrong? I won't ask about it anymore if that's what you want." Her chin quivered and she rubbed her forehead. "I just want to go home."

Logan wanted to put her at ease, but didn't know how. "Charlie, this isn't working. Can you give me a minute with her?"

Sara lifted her head and her chest heaved with deep, frantic breaths, as if he had asked Charlie to leave so he could kill her.

He placed his hand on her knee and caught her eyes. "Sara, I am not going to hurt you."

Charlie stood up. "Let me know when you need me."

Logan nodded at him and waited for him to leave. He took a seat in the chair and pulled it up so he sat inches in front of Sara. "I'm not going to hurt you. I meant what I said earlier. My job is to protect you. I need you unharmed and in one piece."

Her tears slowed and her tongue darted across her lips. "Okay," she said with a shaky voice.

"There's no easy way to tell you this, so I'm just going to tell you and whatever happens, happens. The reason Charlie asked about your father and your job is that those discrepancies are why you're here. I don't work for your father, but I think you understand that he's not on the level. You wouldn't be so frightened if you didn't know at least that much."

"I'm starting to learn that."

"Good," he said. "It's important you know that so you understand why we took you."

"How did you save my life?"

Her innocent question squeezed his heart. He wished he had told Schaffer to leave it up to the feds to talk to her about Langston and Mathers, but the situation left Logan little choice but to convince her of the truth and do the job the feds couldn't.

"If you had married Mathers today and gone on your honeymoon, you would not have come home alive."

Her expression cleared and her lips parted. "Why not?"

"Because your father hired someone to kill you."

Sara pulled her head back and her eyes widened. "What?"

"Your father hired someone to kill you because of the questions you were asking about the discrepancies in the accounts. We kidnapped you so that wouldn't happen."

Her hands clasped the back of her neck. She rocked back and forth, her face contorting as she digested his words.

"The organization I work for needs you alive," he said. "I need you alive. So does the FBI."

Her eyes turned to him at his last words. "FBI?"

Logan recognized from her change of tone that he went too far. He never should have pursued the direct route and he should have left the conversation in Charlie's capable hands. Instead, he backed himself into a corner with the mention of the FBI. Anything short of a full confession could make the situation worse.

"What does the FBI have to do with this?" she asked.

"They want to put you into WITSEC so you can testify against your father."

"What's WITSEC?"

"The Witness Security Program."

"You mean witness protection?" She dropped her hands and smiled. "Witness protection?"

Her laugh set Logan back on all the progress he thought he had made. "Sara, this isn't a joke. It's very serious and your life is at stake."

"Witness protection," she said again, as if not hearing him. "I guess I should give you credit for coming up with an interesting explanation for kidnapping me."

"It's the truth."

"Yeah, because the FBI goes around kidnapping people to place them in witness protection."

"I'm not with the FBI. I was hired to take you to them."

She threw her arms to the side. "Then where are they? I've not met one FBI agent during the entire time you've held me against my will."

"They couldn't approach you in your daily life without your father knowing about it."

"Why not? What organization are you with that advocates kidnapping?"

Logan held his breath and bit back any words he might regret. Her questions were becoming more sarcastic and thinning his patience. "The organization I work for helps with things that fall outside the parameters of the law."

She watched him for a moment. "So you're a criminal."

"Not exactly—"

"The FBI hired some criminals with a criminal organization to kidnap me and keep me captive so that my father, who they call a criminal, couldn't have me killed on my honeymoon. That's the most ridiculous thing I've ever heard."

Logan pushed his chair back and stood up. He held up his hand, but closed his mouth before he could say anything. Picking up the chair, he left the room and locked it behind him. There was no reasoning with her. The information needed to sit with her for a bit, where it could hopefully penetrate her resistant attitude.

He had told Charlie not to hit her with everything at once and then he did it himself. He should have listened to his instincts instead of taking the direct path. She needed an hour, maybe longer. That was if he decided to go back in there before she fell asleep. He didn't have much tolerance left.

In the living room, he greeted Jack and Charlie. Before they could ask any questions, he made his way down the main hall to the front door. A cool breeze met him, as he stepped off the front porch and into the large yard. He moved to the shady oak tree and leaned against the bark. Looking up into the night sky, he stared at the full moon. He pulled in a deep breath, letting the air open his lungs and calm him.

The moon called to him, hypnotizing him with its memories. Karen always loved full moons, one of the many wonders of nature in which she found delight. Whenever the sky granted them one, she would stay up late just to see it among the stars. He couldn't count the number of times she had dragged him outside to take a look with her. There wasn't a doubt in his mind that she watched it with him now.

His chest swelled with the pain that accompanied thoughts of her and he closed his eyes. He had only spoken with Sara a handful of times and already the job had taken its toll. He wondered if he was being hard on Sara because of the things her father had done, though he couldn't blame her for her lineage.

Schaffer was right to put Logan on the job, but he may have been wrong to put him in charge. Logan wasn't able to protect Sara any more than he could save Karen, not just because of who was after him, but because of how Sara's indirect association with

Karen affected him. He turned to go back inside the house so he could call Schaffer for guidance.

Walking into the living room, he noticed Charlie on the couch. "Where's Jack?" he asked.

"He just went to bed."

"Do you mind going to check on Sara? See if she needs anything, food or water, a breathing treatment, whatever."

Charlie nodded. "I'll make sure she's okay."

"Don't mention anything else to her," Logan said. "She's had enough for one night."

Charlie disappeared down the hallway, leaving Logan alone to use the phone. He spoke briefly to Kyle before Schaffer came on the line.

"I need you to put someone else in charge," Logan told him after they exchanged greetings.

"And why is that?"

"I'm no longer effective."

After a long pause, Schaffer blew out his breath into the phone. "Sorry, Logan. I'm not reassigning the job."

Logan hesitated. Schaffer would never leave someone in a position if they couldn't do the job, but Logan no longer believed he could perform as expected. "I need you to. Jack is just as capable—"

"Jack doesn't have your experience. You're also vested in seeing this job through to the end and making sure it's a success."

"That's precisely why I need you to put Jack in charge. I'm too vested. I made a mistake tonight and I don't want to be in the position to make another one."

"What mistake?"

"I gave Sara too much information at once. She wasn't ready and I tried forcing it. Now she thinks we're all crazy. She won't listen to the truth, especially coming from me."

"Yes, that was a mistake, but you're the one who came to me and hinted that there's a leak. If for no other reason than that, I need you in charge. I wouldn't put you in this position if it wasn't absolutely necessary. There's no one else who can—"

"There has to be."

"There isn't. I know how hard this is, but Sara had nothing to do with Karen's death. She has nothing to do with anything that Langston or Mathers or anyone else has done."

"I know."

"Then quit blaming her. You need to see her as a person, separate from Langston and Mathers. Get to know her. Recognize she's someone who needs our help. Your help."

Logan knew pushing the subject would end with another admonishment. If there was a leak, no one else could ensure Sara's safety. Passing her off to someone else could get her killed.

"Can you handle that?" Schaffer asked.

"Yeah," Logan said. "I thought about taking her out in the morning to run with me and Jack."

"That's a start."

"Any news on the leak?"

"I've been examining your recent jobs to look at your teams. I've also reviewed all of the debriefs."

"And?"

"And nothing. You consistently use the same teams on your jobs. Nothing stood out as being odd in the debriefs."

"Who knew about my jobs?"

"Jack, Les, Charlie, Kyle, Doctor Connors, and myself. Occasionally you use Austin or Phil."

"I trust all of them, which is why I use them all the time. What about the intel from this job? Is there anything unusual about that besides the amount of it?"

"I have a friend at the Bureau looking into that."

"When will they be ready for us to bring her in?"

"Three more days. Can you manage?"

"Yeah, but this is it for me. I'm taking time off after we're done here."

"Take as much time as you need, but when you come back, I'm taking you out of the field except for a job here and there. Time for me to start thinking about retirement and time for you to take over. If you still want to, that is."

"I do," Logan said. "You saved my life and gave me a second chance. We need to continue that work for others like me."

"Good. I don't want anyone other than you in this position. Karen would have wanted that for you, too."

Logan didn't respond directly to the statement, but instead ended the call. He didn't want to think about his future, but Karen did want him to be happy with everything he did. She reminded him every second of the three years he spent rebuilding roads with a construction crew of how much he needed to go back to The Boys Club and do what he loved. The problem with pursuing that path presented itself when Langston had a bomb planted in his car. Now that Logan was alone without his wife, spending his remaining working years heading up The Boys Club wasn't such a bad idea.

He just wished he wasn't alone. As much as he didn't want to admit it, Jack giving him permission to find someone else opened up a new door for his thoughts to explore. Maybe it was okay to find someone else, someone he could love as much as Karen. Someone with whom he could share every bit of his life, even the bad things. Someone kind, understanding, intelligent, soft, and beautiful…

Someone like Sara.

Logan chased away the crazy, stray thought from his mind. He headed back outside to spend more time in the clear air under the full moon, alone with his memories and regrets.

Chapter Twenty-three

As soon as Logan shut and locked the door, Sara turned on the bed. Throwing her back up against the wall, she crossed her arms. Who the hell did Logan think he was? From the way he had spoken to her since the beginning she expected honesty from him, not some half-cocked story about her father and the FBI. He acted as if she were the stupidest person in the world, but expected her to trust him and only him.

She lowered her head and massaged her temples, her growing headache the least of her concerns. Though the whole of Logan's tale made no sense, some of it rang true. Her gut instinct over the past few months told her that her father had mishandled his money and not on accident. The runaround he gave her and the simple explanations Stephen spit out only fueled her suspicions.

She knew how to recognize the signs of money laundering. Though she didn't want to admit it before, she knew that's what he had done. He had quite possibly been doing it all along. Logan telling her that he was up to no good cemented that thought, but the idea of the FBI investigating him seemed far-fetched. Or did it? She only saw the accounts of the one company. His illegal activities could span across everything he did.

What she had problems reconciling was that he wanted her

dead. Sure, they weren't always on the best of terms and the thin ice she skirted across to please him had plenty of cracks, but he wouldn't kill her. He wasn't that kind of criminal.

Sara gasped as the word rolled across her brain. *Criminal.* She had thought it before with regards to her father, but never connected the two into one idea. It was the same thing she accused Logan of being, and yet Logan had treated her far better than her father ever had. Could Logan be one of the good guys despite having kidnapped her?

The lock on her door clicked and the doorknob turned. "I just wanted to check on you," Charlie said, as he stepped through the narrow opening. "Are you doing okay?"

An exasperated laugh left her lips. "I don't know what 'okay' means anymore."

Charlie sat at the end of the bed, unfazed by her comment. He hiked his leg up on the bed and faced her. "What's going on?"

Sara shrugged. "Logan said all kinds of things about my dad. I don't know what's true, what's a lie, and what's skewed."

"I can't talk to you about that without Logan here." Charlie started to move off the bed. "I can get him and we can talk—"

"No!" Sara reached her hand out to stop him. "I don't want to talk to him. I want you to tell me the truth about why you kidnapped me."

"I don't know what Logan told you or didn't tell you and I'm not supposed to talk to you about any of this without him here."

Everything went back to Logan. Her frustration grew, but she didn't want to take it out on Charlie. "Just one question," she said, keeping her voice even-keeled. "Did my father hire someone to kill me on my honeymoon?"

He slid off the bed and studied her for a moment before folding his arms across his chest. "Again, I don't know what Logan told you," he said, "but whatever he said is true. Logan doesn't lie. He doesn't know how. Now, is there anything you need? Food, a breathing treatment?"

Tears welled in her eyes and she shook her head. Charlie slunk out of the room, leaving her alone once again when she wanted nothing more than to talk to someone about everything Logan had said. She had hoped Charlie would give her answers, not more questions. Logan had his thumb on every part of the kidnapping, right down to who could tell her what. Charlie's statement that Logan didn't know how to lie scared her even more. If Logan didn't lie, her father hired someone to kill her. And Stephen might know about it.

She shook the thought from her mind and went into the bathroom to get ready for bed. It was far easier to stay mad at Logan for fabricating her reasons for being there rather than believe her own father and the man she agreed to marry might want her dead.

Chapter Twenty-four

Logan dragged himself out of bed after another restless night of very little sleep. He figured he would be half dead by the time the job ended if he didn't find a way to rest soon. Already asleep when he came back into her room, Sara also seemed to suffer from anxiety during the night. She tossed and turned in her own bed, all while staying in the grip of sleep, adding to his insomnia.

Throughout the night, he wandered between his bed and hers, watching over her while she fidgeted in her sleep. At one point her lips moved and an inaudible utterance emerged, letting him know just how distressed he made her with his narrative. His stomach twisted at the thought of upsetting her. He hadn't intended to be so forward, but once he started speaking, he couldn't stop.

Schaffer's suggestion to get to know her, to see her as a person, also contributed to his unrest. He wanted to do that, to understand her and get her to trust him, but a strange unsettling surfaced in his gut every time he considered knowing her more. In the early morning hours, he finally realized why. He already saw her as more than a person who needed saving. He saw her as a woman, one who had caught his eye when he first saw her, and he couldn't control his attraction to her.

Once he admitted his fascination with her, he understood

why Karen plagued his thoughts. He never thought of Karen while involved with Allie, but only because he knew his relationship with Allie ended with sex. Sara intrigued him on a different level, the same one on which Karen entered his life. The idea of meeting someone else he could see as part of his life frightened him in a way he hadn't experienced since he first lost Karen.

More than that, Sara represented nothing more than a fleeting moment. She would leave his life as quickly as she came into it. In a few days, the FBI would take her away and she could quite possibly spend the rest of her life in hiding. He wouldn't see her again after she disappeared into WITSEC and he couldn't do anything to change that outcome.

Logan left the room when Charlie got him for breakfast. He opted for fruit instead of a large meal, as he had already decided to take Sara out running. For a moment he considered getting Les and Jack to do it for him, but he couldn't take a chance with the leak still uncovered, no matter how much he believed his team wasn't involved. At least having Jack with him would provide a buffer so he could ignore Sara.

After he swallowed half a cup of coffee, he found Jack in the backyard. They planned a route across the four acres of land behind the house. Though Sara ran five miles a day, they decided half the distance would be best at first. If everything went well, they could increase the distance for their next run. They agreed to hang back and let her run in front of them to give her a sense of freedom. Both men could outrun her if she tried to escape and keeping her contained between the house and the trees at the back of the property held little risk.

Back in the house, Jack detoured into his bedroom to change while Logan made his way to Sara's room. He knocked and waited for her permission to enter before unlocking the door. Logan pushed the door open and found Sara sitting up in bed, the comforter pulled to her chest and her childlike eyes fearful. The sight battled for control of Logan's good spirits and he reminded himself that his reason for being there would soon change her demeanor.

"How about a run this morning?" he asked.

Sara eyed him for a long moment before responding. "That would be nice, but I don't have anything to wear."

"You do, in the suitcase. I made sure of it. I'll have Charlie bring it back for you. Do you want to eat before we go?"

"I can eat and shower afterward."

"Just come out when you're ready." He closed the door behind him, but left it unlocked to help her feel more comfortable. He spoke to Charlie about the suitcase, then went into the guest bedroom and changed into a pair of shorts and a T-shirt. He had not gone running in over a week and the idea of the fresh air and exercise made all the negativity from the night before disappear.

When he emerged from the guest room, Sara turned the corner with timid steps. "I wasn't sure where to go," she said.

"You're fine." He motioned for her to walk in front of him and they started down the hall. "Jack is meeting us out back."

As they entered the living room, she twisted her head to look at him. "Jack is one of the others here?"

"Yes, him and Les. We might see Les out on our run, but he usually keeps himself busy in the shed."

Her eyes roamed around the living room, examining every corner. Logan interpreted her actions as looking for weapons or a way to escape, but he had no fear that she would leave. Though he made a mistake in dumping all the information about her father and the hit on her at once, he had also planted enough in her mind to create some doubt about her family.

On the back porch, Logan introduced her to Jack, who gave her a firm handshake and a warm smile. Sara tucked her chin down and shrugged with a shy hello. She seemed to struggle with how to act around them and Logan wanted nothing more than for her to feel comfortable. The more she trusted them, the easier it would be to get her into WITSEC.

As she stretched in preparation for their run, Logan's eyes wandered to the side. Her palm flat against the side of the house, she pulled her foot up, until her heel was flush against the back of her thigh, her clothes hugging every curve. He turned and tried to stretch himself, but looked back at her when movement caught his attention. From the corner of his eye, he watched her bend at the waist and reach for her running shoes.

Logan cleared his throat and walked away from her. When he reached Jack, he started to speak, but noticed Jack looking around him to catch a glimpse of Sara. Logan tightened his mouth to avoid laughing at Jack's obvious behavior.

"How far ahead of us do you think we should let her go?"

Logan asked.

"Ten feet at the most," Jack said. "I think this will go a long way in getting her to warm up to us. We should let her stay out of her room the rest of today, too."

Logan wondered how much of Jack's request was oriented to the job, but he couldn't deny the logic. "Keeping her prisoner all day in that room doesn't seem to be working."

Jack grinned. "Just leave it to me and I'll have her warmed up by the end of the day."

Logan started to reply, but stopped when he heard Sara behind him.

"I'm ready," she said in a quiet voice. She tucked stray strands of dark hair behind her ear.

"You can go ahead of us and we'll stay back a little ways so you can have some privacy," Logan said.

"Like my security detail does."

"Exactly like that," he said. "You're not going to try and give us the slip, are you?"

She flinched and her eyes flew up to his face. "You know about that?"

"We know a lot of things," Jack said, "but taking off on us never crossed your mind, did it?"

"No."

"Whenever you're ready," Logan said.

Sara turned and started with a slow trot. They quickly picked up speed and settled into a comfortable pace. Jack rambled from topic to topic, filler to make the time go by quicker. Logan gave short answers, but focused more on clearing his head so he could start again with Sara. He would keep Charlie with him this time and keep his own feelings about her father at bay. Sara did not know what he had done, and Logan intended to keep it that way.

As they neared the end of the run, Jack nudged Logan and gestured toward Sara. "Check out the view."

Logan glanced at Jack. "As far as you're concerned, there is no view."

"Ah, come on. Tell me you didn't notice."

"I didn't notice."

"Liar."

Logan allowed a small smile. "Alright, she looks... nice."

"What are you, like fifty? She doesn't 'look nice.' She's hot as hell. I can't even look at her without thinking about stripping those sweaty clothes off her body and—"

"You don't want to do anything to her but keep her safe."

"Are you kidding me? Just 'cause you want to walk the straight and narrow doesn't mean we all have to."

"It's not a matter of the straight and narrow. She's the job, not some girl at a bar waiting for someone like you to take her home."

"Why did Doctor Connors have to get her such tight running clothes?"

Logan had wondered the same thing himself, many times during the course of their run. Memories from searching her the day before flashed in his brain. The images reminded him of her timidly standing in front of him with most of her beautiful, fair-toned flesh exposed, enough of it so he could imagine what he couldn't see.

He fixed his gaze on the back of her head, watched her short ponytail bop from side to side, and reminded himself again of his job. He did his best to not let his eyes fall down her body again, but he couldn't help himself.

"Yeah," Jack said. "You noticed."

"Just shut up and run."

Jack laughed and bumped into him, shoving Logan off to the side. Logan grinned and returned the hit. Spending their teen years together had turned them into brothers and allowed them the leeway to still act like it as adults.

Sara's head turned to the side with the commotion, but Logan focused his eyes forward and ran straight ahead, as if being caught goofing off by the teacher. As soon as her head rotated back around, Jack laughed again and jabbed Logan's arm. Logan shook his head and kept running.

Chapter Twenty-five

Sara's lips curled upward into a large smile for the first time since waking up in the strange room yesterday. After having the men steal her away and hold her captive, the sun warming her skin gave her hope that they would soon let her go, even if it was to hand her over to the FBI.

Though her mind seemed to clear with her first breaths of the pure morning air, her confusion built with every fall of her feet. Her anger with Logan had subsided by the time she woke up, and allowing her out of her room to run only made her believe that he told her the truth about her father.

The idea terrified her. Her father had never been happy about taking her in, but hiring someone to kill her took his restrained annoyance with her to a whole new level. But if he had taken out a hit on her, did Stephen know?

The question had plagued her since last night. Stephen worked closely with her father. He seemed to know everything her father did, but she couldn't fathom he knew about the hit. They may not love each other, but they did have some feelings, enough to sustain them spending their lives together.

Stephen didn't know, she decided. He *couldn't* know. Just two days earlier, the same day Logan kidnapped her, they had spent the morning in bed. Nothing in his touch signified that he wanted her dead. If anything, he had been gentler, more attentive. He had told her he loved her, several times, and she almost believed him.

But if he had lied about loving her, the same as she lied to him, everything else in their relationship could also be a lie. Logan said that the hit would have happened on their honeymoon, after he had married into her family, the end game of their forced relationship. Maybe he didn't need her after the wedding.

Sara tightened her jaw and pressed forward, refusing to believe Stephen knew about any of it. She struggled enough with the thought that her father wanted her dead. If Logan told the truth, which she believed more and more, then maybe Stephen could help her. She just needed to get back to him.

She peeked over her shoulder. Jack's lips moved in silent conversation, but Logan held his eyes on her. Guilt overcame her and she whipped her head back around. Her unfair words from last night echoed in her ears. If she had given him half a chance, his explanation would have made sense and she could have questioned him further. He had saved her life by taking her, and she rewarded him by slicing open his arm with glass and going on an angry tirade that downplayed everything he had done for her. Though natural reactions in her situation, his kindness outweighed everything else.

She snuck another glance back at him and saw the men closing in on her. She slowed her pace and waited for them to catch up.

"Ready to go back?" Logan asked.

She nodded and followed his lead to the right. She ran in silence next to him, wishing Jack had stayed behind. She wanted to apologize to Logan and tell him she believed him, but remembered he warned her against trusting anyone but him. Jack seemed nice enough, much like Charlie, but she didn't know how much he knew about her situation. She would have to wait until she caught Logan alone.

Back at the house, she propped her hands on her hips and walked in a circle to wind down. The sight of Logan bent over with his hands on his thighs caught her attention. She detoured toward him, hoping to ask him for a moment alone. As she neared, he straightened up. With his back facing her, he reached over his shoulders and tugged his damp shirt over his head.

Sara's face reddened. Her legs shifted direction and she averted her eyes, as Logan turned around to face her. Having experienced Logan's strength firsthand when he restrained her, she didn't need to also see it. Just the glimpse of his back and shoulders jolted her enough.

Jack walked up to her, saving her from further embarrassment. "Do you like Jim Carrey?" he asked.

Sara's brow furrowed. "Jim… Carrey? The comedian actor guy?"

"Yeah, that's him." A smile accompanied his jovial tone.

"Um… I suppose so."

"There's a marathon of his movies on today. Would you like to join Charlie and me and watch them?"

Excitement coursed through her veins at the thought of being out of her room all day. She didn't care much whose movies played on the television, as long as she didn't have to pass time staring at the wall in a locked room. Logan's warnings about not trusting anyone floated through her mind. Wondering if the question was a trick, she looked at Logan. As the man in charge, she didn't want to do anything without his permission.

Logan gave her a slight nod of approval.

She smiled at Jack. "That sounds great."

"I guess we'll see you after we're all cleaned up." He opened the back door and entered the house.

"Thank you," Logan said, as soon as the door shut.

"For what?"

"For checking with me about what Jack said."

With her eyes lowered, she said, "I'm sorry I was rude to you last night. I thought about it and I think you were telling the truth about my dad."

"I wish it wasn't true," he said, taking a step toward her. "But I'll do what I can to help you until we get you to the FBI."

He reached in front of her to grab the doorknob. She shuffled sideways to move away from him, but stepped on her shoelace as she crossed her foot over the other. Logan reached out to grab her, but she stumbled in the wrong direction and he missed her. Her palms cushioned the painful fall onto the concrete patio.

Crouching in front of her, Logan asked, "Are you okay?"

She lifted her hands and brushed them against each other. "Just clumsy, I guess. I'm sure I'll have plenty of bruises later on."

"Here," Logan said. He stood up and held out his hand. "Let's get you up and make sure you're okay."

His hand swallowed hers and he pulled her to her feet. The momentum brought her closer to him than she liked. The air thickened around her and her heart crashed into her stomach. Her eyes landed on his and her lips parted. She dropped her gaze and took a small step back, hand still in his.

"I, uh…" Although she felt like she needed to say something, her mind blanked.

"You sure you're okay? No twisted ankle or anything?"

Against her wishes, her eyes moved down his contoured body. She gasped at the number of scars spread across his shoulders, chest, and stomach. "Were you in a car accident?"

"No." He let go of her hand. "I guess I'm a little too good at my job sometimes."

"I see."

He opened the door and gestured for her to go in first. She instinctively reached for her ring finger, her fingertips circling the naked skin. Walking past Logan into the house, her forehead wrinkled, she could no longer deny her attraction to him, as much as she wanted to, but the impossible situation confused her. Grateful that she would spend the rest of her day with Jack and Charlie, her feet picked up speed so she could go to her room to shower and get as far away from Logan as she could.

Chapter Twenty-six

"Any news on the leak?"

"Nothing that can tie it to one person," Schaffer said.

Logan slouched over the kitchen counter. "What have you found?"

"Everything seems to be in order. The intel was vetted as much as it could be before it came to us. The feds found nothing out of the ordinary on their second look-through."

Logan narrowed his eyes. "As much as it could be?"

"The job was handed down to us an hour after it was received. They had very little time with it before it came to me."

"Why the shortened timeframe?"

"Because Sara's life was on the line. They didn't have a choice but to rush it through, same as us."

Logan straightened up and ran his hand over the stubble on top of his head. "That's just what they wanted."

"What do you mean?"

Logan lowered his voice to make sure no one else heard. "Whoever is working with Langston didn't want us to have a lot of time to look into the intel. They made it so we focused more on saving Sara's life rather than on where the intel came from."

"The source was anonymous," Schaffer said.

"Wait. Was the source on my last job also anonymous?"

"Yes, but that isn't proof they're related."

"Not definitively," Logan said. "One in five jobs come from anonymous sources."

"Two in a row could be a coincidence. Or maybe it isn't."

"That's what I'm thinking. Have you traced the hit?"

"We don't have enough info to do that."

Logan closed his eyes and shook his head. "What if there is no hit?"

"No hit?"

"What if this isn't about Sara at all?"

"It's possible they used her to get you out in the open. But saying there's a hit on her is pretty severe if there wasn't one out there. They took the chance we would find out the truth."

"But they made sure we didn't have enough time to do that. Now I'm in the open with Langston's daughter."

Schaffer didn't respond.

"We need to find out if this hit is real," Logan said. "Either way, Sara's still in danger as long as she's with me. The men coming after me may not care about collateral damage."

"I'll focus everything on the hit. Do you have a backup plan yet? You need a way to get her out of there if someone comes after you."

"I'll get one ready now."

After they ended the call, Logan walked over to the breakfast bar and peered out into the living room. Sara sat between Jack and Charlie, and occasional laughter tinkled out of her as they watched television. She turned her head to Jack and exchanged inaudible conversation for a moment. Her lips mesmerized him as she spoke and smiled. He hadn't dreamed they would be able to lift her spirits while she stayed with them, but Jack and Charlie had managed to make her happy, if only for this afternoon.

Her head turned and she glanced at Logan, sharing her warm smile with him. Logan tore his eyes away from her and walked back to the refrigerator. He wanted to smile back, to share even one little moment with her, but doing so was counterproductive to his job. The stress of protecting her, the knowledge of a mole working against him, the lack of sleep... all of it had already worn him down. Feeling something for her would make things worse, especially when she had to leave with the FBI.

He fished a bottled water out of the refrigerator and walked out of the kitchen. Sara's eyes bore into him as he walked past the living room, but he did not look over at her. He had a job to do.

Chapter Twenty-seven

As she watched Logan walk toward the front door, Sara frowned at his blank, unreadable stare. She turned back around to face forward on the couch and sighed.

Jack and Charlie had calmed and relaxed her for the past few hours while they watched television. She worried at any time they might lock her back in her room, but the unfounded concern didn't stop her from enjoying herself.

Except for when Logan looked at her.

Ever since they had spoken on the back patio after their run, uneasiness plagued her chest. She didn't think he posed a threat; rather, his presence wrapped a blanket of security around her. Though she didn't feel as safe with the others as she did with Logan, that same comfort also caused her fear and anxiety.

When she tried to smile at him, he dismissed her with an indifferent glance before walking away. She didn't think she had done anything wrong, but she couldn't shake the feeling that he wanted nothing to do with her.

"Does Logan hate me?" She posed the question to no one in particular.

Both men turned to face her. "Hate you?" Charlie asked. "What makes you think that?"

She stumbled on her words. She didn't even know she felt

that way until now. "I don't know exactly. He avoids me and it seems like he's angry with me for some reason."

"Oh, yeah," Jack said. "He doesn't hate you. It's just that whole thing with Karen that bothers him."

Sara flinched at the unfamiliar name. "Who's Karen?"

"His wife—"

"Jack," Charlie said.

The last thing Sara expected to hear, her eyes widened. "Logan's married?"

"We're not supposed to talk about it," Jack said. "Especially in front of you."

Charlie groaned. "Damn it, Jack. Stop."

Sara turned to Jack since Charlie seemed unwilling to answer her questions. "What do you mean?"

"Does anyone want some water?" Charlie asked, standing up. "I think it's time for something to drink." He walked off without waiting for a response to his question.

Sara moved to the edge of the couch and turned to face Jack. "What are you talking about? Why aren't you supposed to talk about Logan's wife in front of me?"

"She died a couple of years ago, but it's still an open wound for Logan. We don't talk about it in front of him."

Logan's behavior finally made sense to her. He went through the motions of his job, of protecting Sara and doing what needed to be done, but did so in a constant state of mourning. If she outlived Stephen it would be hard enough to lose him, but she couldn't imagine how hard it would be to go through life if she lost someone she loved as much as Logan must have loved his wife.

Jack's words about not talking about it in front of her came to mind. "Why aren't you supposed to talk about it in front of me?" she asked.

"Because Langston—"

"Alright, that's enough talk," Charlie said, as he walked back into the room with a glass of ice water. "I'm ready for the next movie and then I'll start working on tonight's dinner feast." He moved to the center of the couch and sat his cup down on the coffee table.

Sara scooted over to the end of the couch so Charlie could sit between her and Jack. She wanted to ask more questions, especially with the mention of her father, but Charlie's deliberate separation of her from Jack warned her against further discussion.

Chapter Twenty-eight

Logan walked into the dining room after spending the afternoon working on his backup plan for Sara. He hoped he wouldn't need it, but his gut told him otherwise. If there was a leak in their organization, which seemed more and more likely, then things had been much too quiet since kidnapping Sara. Someone would eventually come for her, and he needed to be prepared.

Charlie came into the room with a plate full of corn on the cob. "Just in time for dinner," he said.

"I see that," Logan said. "Can I help out with anything?"

"I have plenty of help. Just sit down and enjoy."

"Hot, hot, hot!" Sara ran in behind Charlie, a round casserole dish in her hands. Charlie jumped out of the way and she rushed to get the glass dish onto the table.

"Why didn't you use oven mitts?" Charlie asked.

"I couldn't find any. I searched all the drawers—"

"They're in a cupboard above the coffeemaker," Logan said. "We've never been too organized around here."

Sara glanced up at him and smiled. "Good to know. Um, Charlie said you didn't like corn on the cob, so I heated up some green beans for you. I hope they're okay."

Logan flinched. Sara had come a long way since their

confrontation last night. "I'm sure they're great," he said. "Thanks for thinking of me."

"Couldn't let you go hungry," she said, flashing a grin his way.

Logan looked down at the spread on the table, mainly to stop himself from staring at Sara. "You've made quite a feast tonight, Charlie."

"Steaks, roasted potatoes, corn on the cob, green beans, rolls. All with Sara's help."

"Don't forget the pie," Sara said.

"Did someone say pie?" Jack asked, as he came into the room with Lester in tow.

"I didn't know you baked, Charlie," Lester said.

"I don't," Charlie said, gesturing to Sara.

"You made pie?" Jack asked.

"I hope you don't mind," Sara said. "There were some fresh strawberries in the fridge and you had all the ingredients to make up a crust. It's a pie I used to make with my mom."

"You went to a lot of trouble," Logan said, as he pulled out the chair at the head of the table.

Sara shrugged and sat in the chair adjacent to his. "Charlie said this might be one of our last dinners here and I wanted to do something as a thank you." She glanced around the table at all the men, who were all now sitting and passing around food. "It's just a small thing, but I didn't know how else to say thank you for saving my life. I know I was a bit of a pain in the beginning—"

"You weren't a pain," Charlie said, handing the bowl of potatoes to Lester. "A little spirited, maybe, but definitely not a pain."

Jack, who sat beside her, rested his hand on her forearm. "I think I speak for all of us when I say you've brought a lot of light into our world. Our jobs normally aren't this interesting. It's not every day someone we kidnap makes us a pie."

Sara laughed. "I really hope I'm the only one you've kidnapped."

"The first and last," Lester said.

During the friendly exchange, Logan focused on his plate of food and tuned everyone out. The light banter around him reminded him too much of how well Karen fit in with his team. After dating her for several months, he slowly introduced her to his job and coworkers. All of the men took to her and welcomed her into the fold. They embraced Sara much in the same way, as if they still missed that connection with Karen as much as he did.

"Of course, I did some cage fighting back in the day," Jack said.

A laugh bellowed out of Lester. "You did not."

Logan lifted his head at the new conversation. "I'll vouch for Jack. I saw a few of his matches when we were younger."

"I still don't believe it," Lester said. "No cauliflower ear, no cage fighting."

"I do too have some cauliflower ear!" Jack said.

Sara stared at Jack's left ear. "I don't see any here."

Jack pushed his chair out and turned his head. "It's on the right one."

Logan shook his head and resumed eating his steak.

"Yeah," Sara said. "Still don't see it."

Jack huffed and pulled his chair back up to the table. "It's there."

"Did you win any matches?" Sara asked.

"My record was 8-0."

"8-1," Logan corrected.

"Everyone knows that last fight didn't count," Jack said.

"Not this again," Charlie said, as he munched on a corn cob. "Every time he talks about his cage fighting stint, it's always that the last match doesn't count."

"I'm still trying to come to grips with Jack cage fighting," Lester said.

Jack glared at him. "Let's go out back and I'll show you a takedown or two."

"After which I'll ground and pound you into early retirement," Lester said.

Sara and Charlie joined in with Lester's laughter while Jack muttered under his breath.

"Did you ever cage fight?"

Logan looked up at Sara. Her raised eyebrows and curious smile warmed his heart, but he didn't show any emotion on his face. "I didn't," he said. "That was Jack's thing."

"He knew I could beat him," Jack said. "He was too scared to face me in the cage."

Sara shifted her gaze between the two men. "Sorry, Jack. My

money's on Logan."

Charlie and Lester exclaimed with surprise at the same time, while Logan smiled on the inside.

Jack shook his head. "And just when I was getting to like you," he said, nudging Sara's arm.

"You still like me," she said with a teasing tone.

"Maybe." He winked at her and grinned. "Of course, there's plenty of time for you to win me over."

Sara's cheeks flushed and she looked down at her food.

Though Logan knew Jack's flirting was harmless, he couldn't help a small twinge of jealousy from hitting him. Before Karen died, Logan had no problems with women. Her death had zapped out all need to have fun with chasing a woman he found attractive, not that he bothered to ever initiate that chase with any woman.

Allie had been the only woman in his life in any capacity since Karen, and even then he had fallen into their casual relationship without much thought. She had approached him, hinted at wanting something more, and actively pursued him. The only part he had in it all was kissing her first, and that was only after she told him she wanted him to do it.

Women no longer came naturally to him, not that he needed one in his life anyway, at least not for anything more than what he had with Allie. That was not a path he wanted to go down again and risk hurting someone else if they decided they wanted more. He also didn't want to get involved with someone on a deeper level, especially not a woman who would disappear into WITSEC in a few days. It was far better for Jack to flirt with Sara and for Logan to ignore his own attraction to Sara. It wasn't like anything could come out of it anyway, even if he did decide to pursue her.

Chapter Twenty-nine

Sara swallowed the last bite of strawberry pie and pushed her plate away. "I don't think I've ever eaten that much."

"This is pretty standard for us," Jack said. "Well, maybe not the delicious pie. Charlie will have to learn to bake now."

"I *loathe* baking," Charlie said.

"We could just take Sara with us on all our jobs," Lester said. "Make her our official pie chef."

Sara laughed. "Tell you what. I'll give Charlie the recipe before we leave. Then he can decide if he wants to use it."

"Oh, I'll make him use it," Lester said.

Sara's stomach felt like it would burst open at any moment and all she could think about was walking off the meal. "I'd love to take a walk before bed," she said. When no one responded immediately, she looked at Logan. "If that's okay with you."

He pushed his chair out from the table and stood up. "Of course it's okay. I'll go with you."

"You guys go ahead," Charlie said. "Les and I are on dish duty tonight."

"A walk sounds like a good idea," Jack said.

Logan held up his hand. "Sara and I should be fine by ourselves. Right, Sara?"

She read the meaning of his words in his tone. "Maybe we

can go running again tomorrow morning, Jack."

Jack smiled. "It's a date."

Sara said her goodnights to the other men, thanked Charlie again for dinner, and followed Logan out of the dining room. Stepping onto the back porch, she took a deep breath of the cool night air. Chirping crickets greeted them, and she relaxed with their pleasant song.

"Did you enjoy dinner?"

She looked up at Logan and smiled. "It was wonderful. I liked getting to know everyone. Thank you for letting me spend time out of the room today."

"I had no intention of making you stay in there for long. I just didn't want you trying to leave without knowing your life was in danger."

The mention of the hit brought her back to reality. "I am grateful that you all saved my life, but it's still a bit difficult to grasp that my own father wants me dead."

"If I know one thing about Hugh Langston, he doesn't care who he has to kill to get his way."

"He's done a lot of things wrong, hasn't he? More than just money laundering."

"I'm sorry to say it, but money laundering is just one of the many criminal ventures he's involved in."

Sara didn't want to know any of his other activities, although murder seemed to be one of them. "How do you know so much about him?"

"I used to work for him."

Surprise stopped Sara's feet from moving forward. "You worked for my dad?"

Logan turned to face her. "Unfortunately, for almost a year. My organization needed someone to infiltrate his operations. The government had tried time and again and fell short. Schaffer offered me up as someone who could do it, and I did."

"What kind of work did you do for him?"

"I started out as a grunt, but I worked my way up the ladder. I had to do a lot of illegal things, but Schaffer helped fix them on the back end. I never killed anyone, though. Somehow I always managed to weasel my way out of that."

"Killing people?" Sara's head spun with the words. The real Hugh Langston was nothing like the father she thought she knew.

Logan started walking again, and she fell into step beside him.

"Did you get to know my father well when you worked for him?"

"Too well. About nine months into the assignment, I met him for the first time. He took to me, which was good for our end game, but it also put me in jeopardy of being caught. I had to play it very carefully for a long time."

"Did we ever meet?" Since he confessed to working for her father, Sara had tried to remember if she saw Logan during school breaks or in the summer.

"No, we didn't. I spent a lot of time in his home, but I think you were in school when I came around. I heard your name from time to time, but that was about it. Never even saw a picture of you until this job came around."

"He was never the sentimental type to keep pictures of family in the house. How old were you when you worked for him?"

"Seven years ago… that would have made me 24."

"I would have been 19. My freshman year in college."

"Sounds about right. I remember Langston mentioning something about you being in college."

She shook her head. "That's unbelievable. I had no idea you knew him so well."

"Both him and Mathers."

Sara's heart skipped a beat at his revelation. "You knew Stephen, too?"

"Almost as well as your father."

Logan's words about how she didn't want to marry Stephen came back to her. "I'm guessing you didn't get along."

"No, we didn't. Mathers is a wild card, someone I never knew how to act around. He came up the ranks, much like I did, but he was always suspicious of me. It may have been because your father was looking for a new second-in-command and Langston took a real liking to me, while Mathers would have done anything for that position. He questioned everything I did, had me followed, tapped my phone, bugged the safe house I was living in for the job."

"Stephen did all that?"

"He thought I was working for someone on the outside, which I was. He did his best to convince Langston of that, but until the end, it didn't work. Then I made a mistake and it all went to hell. I got out as fast as I could, but a couple years ago, Langston found me and learned my real name."

Though afraid to hear the answer, she desperately needed to know every ugly truth about her father. "What did he do when he found you?"

"He hired someone to kill me." Logan took a deep breath before continuing. "But they missed."

With his words, a strange bond formed between them. Both targets of her father, both still alive. Yet with her father as the common thread, she had a good guess as to why Logan had been so eager to save her.

"Is that why you're so interested in saving my life?" she asked, looking up at him. "So you can get to him through me?"

"I can't say that has nothing to do with it because it does. I'm vested in seeing Langston pay for what he's done and I will make him pay for it, one way or another." After a moment of hesitation, he said, "But if I had a choice between saving your life and putting Langston behind bars forever, I'd go after him another time. Your life is worth so much more than getting revenge for his past misdeeds."

Her heart skipped a beat, then resumed thumping at record speed. She ripped her gaze away from him and focused on the ground beneath her feet. Something in Logan's voice when he spoke about saving her made her body tremble.

She pushed away her attraction to him once more. Still engaged to Stephen, thoughts about another man had no place in her world. With everything Stephen had done to Logan, after all the revelations about him, one question about her fiancé plagued her, one she hoped Logan could help answer.

Terrified to speak and learn more about her father and fiancé, Sara finished their walk in silence. Before they reached the back porch, she worked up the courage to talk again. She couldn't go another night not knowing the truth about Stephen's involvement in her current situation.

"Does Stephen know about the hit?" she asked.

They stopped a few feet from the back door and Logan turned to her. "I believe he does. The others think maybe he doesn't. As far as I know, Langston doesn't do anything without Mathers. If Langston put a hit on you, he wouldn't hide that from

Mathers, especially since you two were getting married. To do it behind Mathers's back would send the wrong signal to Mathers and the rest of his guys."

Sara's heart sunk. Logan had intimate knowledge of both her father and Stephen. Given everything she had learned about the two just tonight, Logan seemed to know them better than even she did. She didn't want to believe Stephen knew about the hit, that he would marry her knowing she would soon die. That he would spend their last morning in bed together, pretending to love her, using her for his own gratification instead of truly caring for her.

"I'm sorry, Sara. I know it's got to be hard to hear these things and I wish I could tell you it's not true."

She raised her eyes to Logan's face. "Is there a chance he didn't know?"

"There's always a chance."

Her fingers reached for her necklace. She tugged on the locket and moved it up and down the gold chain. "It's all so surreal. Just two days ago I was preparing to marry someone I thought I'd spend my life with. Now I find out my dad was trying to kill me and my fiancé may have known about it. Instead of spending my life with Stephen, I'm going to spend my life in witness protection."

"But you don't love him."

She froze. After a moment, she lowered the locket back down on her skin. "I don't love him," she said. "I never have and marriage wouldn't have changed a thing."

"Then why were you going to marry him?"

Remembering Mary's words at the beach, Sara smirked. "Because Daddy told me to. Ever since my mom died, I've been told what to do. What's best for me, what I need, what I want. Nothing is ever my decision. Everything I do is decided by either my dad or Stephen. It's like I can't take care of myself, or at least no one ever trusts me to.

"And now I have to go with the FBI, where I'm sure someone else is going to tell me what to do and I won't have a choice in any of it. They'll tell me where to live, they'll change my name. So I'm stuck again, not having a voice in my own life."

Logan caught her eyes. "I know you're frustrated. If you weren't, you wouldn't have ditched your security detail. It's like you had something to prove, to do something that was your decision."

"I didn't mean to do that, it just happened. The moment

came and I went for it. Mary is always telling me to do what I want, and I do have some little things that are all mine that Dad and Stephen have nothing to do with."

"Like what?"

"It's stupid, really."

"Tell me."

She shrugged and a smile took over her face. "There's a food truck down at the beach Mary and I always get tacos at. Stephen doesn't know about it, at least I don't think he does."

His eyebrows jetted up. "A food truck, huh?"

"A little weird since we can eat anywhere we want, but we love the food there. The owners are a couple brothers that have had the truck for a little over 10 years. They're both married with young kids and they drum up a living with their truck and the best tacos in the world. And then after we get our food, Mary and I always walk across the street and sit on the short wall at the beach. I love walking barefoot in the sand."

Logan didn't respond, but instead watched her. Uneasiness crawled across her skin at his stare, the same one she could never read.

"I'm sorry," she said, to break the silence. "I didn't mean to ramble on about it."

"You're fine. I was just thinking that in the short time I've known you, I already know you're nothing like Langston or Mathers."

She wrinkled her nose. "Is that a bad thing?"

"Not at all. It surprises me that you spent so much time with them and yet it's like you've never been around them a day in your life. None of their influence rubbed off on you in anything."

"Except for the fact that I let them tell me what to do all the time."

"You are your own person, Sara. You always have been. Them telling you how to live your life is one thing, but you constantly rebelled and remained true to yourself. It shows in the little things, like your personality and the way you carry yourself. They may have told you what to do, but they didn't control who you were or who you became."

"I'm not quite sure who I am anymore. Everything's changed so drastically in such a short time and it's going to change even more, but again, it will be out of my control."

Logan stepped forward. "You are going to have to surrender some control of your life to the feds, but not like you have with Langston and Mathers. Think of this as a chance for you to find yourself. It's not ideal, but it's your second chance at having the life you always wanted."

"I hadn't thought of it like that, but you're right," she said.

"But, Sara, when the air clears and Langston and possibly Mathers are behind bars, and you're out there finding yourself, do one thing."

"What's that?"

"Don't marry someone you don't love because someone tells you to. That's not how it's supposed to be. You deserve someone who loves you more than life itself, who will take care of you and keep you safe. Someone who is willing to give everything he has if that's his only chance of being with you. Don't settle for anything less than that."

His eyes held hers captive and his words opened her heart. She always believed in that kind of love, unconditional and unrelenting, but in committing to marry Stephen, she thought her chance had passed. Though horrified at the thought of her father trying to kill her, with it came the opportunity to start again, to find love, to be happy.

Still mesmerized by his gaze, guilt flooded her again. "I'm so sorry I cut you with the glass," she said. "I shouldn't have done that."

"You didn't know me and you were scared. I don't blame you."

"I hope it doesn't scar."

"I'll just add it to the others."

She chuckled. "I guess it does give you something to remember me by."

"I don't need something to remember you." Though his face remained stoic and largely unreadable, emotion danced in his eyes under the glow of the back porch light. "You are someone I'll never forget."

Sara swallowed hard and her tongue flicked across her lips. Whereas Jack's flirting at dinner had been fleeting and fun, Logan's eyes held something more permanent. Whether real or imagined, her heart crashed into her stomach. The mystery of the man in front of her ran deep and with each layer she peeled back, she only wanted to unravel him more.

She opened her mouth to say something, anything to break the tense, emotionally-charged silence, when the back door opened.

"There you two are," Jack said, stepping onto the back porch. He aimed his large smile in her direction.

Sara blushed and averted her eyes, not so much at Jack's obvious flirting, but at him catching her and Logan in a moment, though she was still unsure what had transpired between them.

"We were just heading inside," Logan said.

"That's why I was coming to get you," Jack said. "The news says there is a hell of a storm heading this way."

Sara looked up at the dark skies, but could only see the clouds around the full moon. A flash of lightning in the distance caught her attention.

"We better get you inside," Jack said, holding his arm out to her.

She glanced at Logan for direction.

"You two go ahead," he said. "I'm going to stay out here for a bit longer."

"Did you want to stay up with us and watch television?" Jack asked.

"I think I'll just head on to bed. I'm pretty tired and I want to be rested for our run in the morning."

"Goodnight, Sara," Logan said.

Sara watched him walk toward the woods until he disappeared into the night shadows. She turned and slid her arm through Jack's.

Smiling, Jack escorted her in the house and back to her bedroom. "Last chance," he said after they reached her room. "In a few days, you'll be with the FBI and they are not nearly as good looking as I am."

Unaccustomed to having a man so straightforward with his flirting, Sara laughed and a deep blush crept into her cheeks. "I'm sorry. I need some good sleep tonight, but tomorrow night I will. I promise."

"I'll hold you to that," he said with a wink.

As soon as he shut the door, Sara's smile fell. As sweet and cute as Jack was, Logan had not left her mind since she came inside. She didn't know what would have happened if Jack hadn't come outside when he did, but she had a strong sense that Logan would have kissed her. Though surprising, that she had wanted him to do it shocked her even more.

She moistened her lips and lowered herself on her bed. "What the hell is happening to me?" she whispered aloud. She had never so much as fantasized about another man since she started dating Stephen and now she couldn't stop thinking about what Logan tasted like. Between that and the revelations about Stephen and her father, it would take a miracle to fall asleep.

Chapter Thirty

After several hours of tossing and turning in bed, sleep finally embraced Sara, but not for long. A strong hand over her mouth dragged her out of her peaceful dream. Her eyes popped open to find a face hovering over hers.

"Don't scream." Logan's whisper cut through the silence and set her on edge. "We have to go."

He removed his hand from her mouth and she drew in a jagged breath. Despite the seriousness of his voice, her body froze with fear.

"Now, Sara."

She didn't hesitate. The desperation in his command told her everything she needed to know. He handed her a pair of jeans and shoes, and she quickly slipped them on while he waited.

When she stood up, he grabbed her arm. "Stay behind me."

Sara's body stiffened against his, her hands on his back for protection. His hand reached behind him and held onto her arm, guiding her to walk with him. With every step she worked to control every frightened breath that left her lips, scared that whoever Logan sheltered her from could hear her.

Logan stopped and told her to step to the side, behind the door. His fingers never left her skin as he poked his head out the door. Faraway voices filtered through the crack between the wood and the wall, and he eased the door closed.

"We have to go through the window," he whispered, as he locked the door from the inside.

"How?" Sara asked.

He knelt down to his mattress, lifted it, and picked something up. He handed her the item.

She ran her fingers over the cylindrical, heavy metal while he dragged the mattress in front of the door. "A crowbar?" In all her time looking for a weapon or means of escape, she never dreamed he kept the one thing she needed so near.

He had her stay behind the door and he took the mattress from her bed and added it to the makeshift barricade. He took the crowbar from her hands, picked his bag up from the floor, and told her to stay in front of him. As they walked to the window, with his body shielding her from the door, adrenaline coursed through her limbs to the point that they ached. He pushed her to the side when they reached the window, and her fear increased tenfold.

The crowbar slipped between the board and the wall and with a strong pull, the board let loose on one side. He had her hold the board while he worked on the other side. Together, they set the board down with care. He gave her the crowbar again, slid the window open, and pushed out the screen.

Encouraging her to go first, he helped her up, and she crawled through the window and into the night rain. After he climbed outside, he took each strap of his bag and brought them over his arms, securing the bag on his back. He turned his head from one side to the other, scanning the terrain ahead. Sara handed the crowbar to him. Her tense neck snapped around when the noise came from her bedroom, the sound of men breaking through the door.

Logan circled his hand around her wrist, and she looked up at his stern face. "Run as fast as you can toward the barn and keep up," he said.

As they raced in the direction of the barn through the pellets of rain, Sara focused on her breathing to avoid thinking of the danger behind them. She didn't know if the men had broken through the door yet, or if they were right on their heels, and she didn't care. She only thought about her breathing and keeping pace with Logan, a much faster runner than she.

Under the full moon, a man emerged from the side of the

barn. Logan skidded to a stop and held out his arms to catch her. He pulled her behind a nearby tree. Trapped between the bark and his body, she leaned her head against his chest and closed her eyes. She wanted to ask about the others, but something told her not to. She held as still as possible, scared to take even a breath.

One of his hands rubbed up and down her chilled, soaked arm. "It's okay, Sara," he whispered, as if he sensed her fear. "I've got you."

A momentary calm rushed over her soul. She knew he would do everything he could to keep her safe, just as he had since he kidnapped her to save her life.

Logan backed away from her and she lifted her eyes to his. "Ready?"

"Yes."

He slid his hand around hers, his other hand grasping the crowbar, and guided her into the thickening trees behind them. She again kept up the best she could, as they dodged trees and ducked under low-hanging branches. Moving deeper into the woods, the darkness camouflaged the oncoming obstacles and they slowed their pace.

Sara gripped Logan's hand tighter. Her lifeline to safety, she stayed right behind him and matched his steps without complaint.

Chapter Thirty-one

Nothing else went through Logan's mind except Sara's safety. He took every step and made every turn knowing he could not fail in his job.

She didn't know yet about the rest of his team and until they stopped in a safe place, he wouldn't tell her. Lying awake with another restless night, he had heard the unusual noise coming from another part of the house and his instincts kicked his gut. After leaving the bedroom, the first body he stumbled over was Charlie at the end of the hall. A glimpse into the living room showed two more shadowed bodies, one on the floor and one on the couch, right where he had left Jack and Lester when he went to bed.

Creaks coming from the loft above him had spurred him into action before he could investigate further. He didn't know why those that killed the others had yet to find him and Sara, but he took advantage of their mistake to get her out of the house.

As he emerged from the woods with Sara, he closed off all thoughts of his team so he could work out their next movements. It wouldn't be long before the men on the property found their way out here, but Logan had led them to a dead end. In front of them, the edge of the small mountain had a long drop to a lower ledge, far enough down for both of them to break some bones if they tried to jump.

He had not been to this safe house in some time and did not have an escape route planned that didn't include the cars in the barn. The rain only compounded the situation. Peering over the edge again, he saw headlights coming from the winding main road that they had driven on their way to the house. He just needed to find a way down there.

He told Sara to stay with him and they ran along the edge until he found a mostly hidden dirt trail that appeared to lead down to the ledge below them. From there they could better figure out how to get to the main road.

"We're going to have to separate," he said, as he stopped walking.

Sara looked at him, her fear apparent. "You can't leave—"

"I'm not leaving you for long. I want you to take this trail down to the next ledge. Then run north for ten minutes and find a place to hide. If the path ends before ten minutes is up, turn east and run in that direction for the rest of the time." He removed his watch, illuminated the face, showed her the compass on it, and handed it to her. "No more and no less than ten minutes. If I'm not there in forty-five minutes, find a way down to the main road and follow it to the next town to get help. Don't let any cars see you, but run along the side and keep hidden behind the trees."

"What are you doing?"

"I need to even out the playing field a bit or we'll never get out of here."

"What do you mean?"

He nodded his head in the direction of the woods. "We have at least two men on our heels. Wherever we go, they'll go. Just do what I tell you. Ten minutes north."

"Logan, I can't—"

"Yes, you can."

"But what are you—"

"I'm going to slow them down." He rested his hand on her shoulder. "Do you trust me?"

"Yes, I—"

"Do you trust me?" he asked again, stressing each word.

She hesitated and her dark eyes found his. "I trust you."

"Good. Now go." He watched her take off down the trail. He hated leaving her on her own, but he couldn't let her see what he needed to do.

As soon as she left his view, Logan removed his bag from his back, retrieved his knife, and secured it on the left side of his belt. He preferred using his gun, but he couldn't draw attention to their location with the noise. He stashed his bag in between the branches of a tree near the edge of the woods and moved toward the sounds of the men searching the trees. He hoped he only had to take care of two of them.

Voices came at him from the right. He ducked behind a large tree and plastered his back against it. Peering over his shoulder and around the tree, two men stood several trees away from his position.

"We've searched the woods already and they aren't here," the first voice said.

"We have to be sure," the second man said. "They could have come back here after we searched."

"They're long gone. We just have to tell him that—"

"I'm not telling anyone anything until we search these woods again. They told us to keep searching until we find them and we haven't found them. Head out that way and I'll take this half. That should make it quicker."

Logan unsnapped the knife holster for easy access if he needed it. Closing his eyes, he focused his attention on the sound of footsteps. Shoes hit the wet leaves on the ground, and he determined the man approached from his left.

Within seconds, the man passed him by, without bothering to look to his sides. When he passed, Logan launched himself at the man. His left hand smothered the man's mouth to silence him and his right arm wrapped around the man's neck. He contracted the muscles in his arm. The man struggled, but not enough to get out of Logan's grasp. Logan held on long after the man passed out to finish the job. He couldn't risk the man coming to and revealing their location.

He lowered the man's lifeless body onto the leaf-covered ground. He took the gun out of the man's hands, turned the safety on, and tucked it into the waistband at his lower back. Now he had to find the other man before he noticed his partner's absence and called in the rest of the troops to the area.

Keeping his footfalls light, he crept through the woods, with long pauses between each footstep. Ears alert for any sound, he heard nothing until he was a good distance away from the first body. He ceased moving at the sound of rustling leaves coming in his direction, and he wrapped his hand around the handle of his knife. A figure emerged from the shadows, and Logan reassessed his plan. The position of the other man eliminated another stealth attack.

Logan dashed to the side, behind another tree before the man could see him. His movements alerted the other man to his presence, but he had little other choice.

As expected, the man stopped walking. "Don?"

Anticipating the man to keep moving past the tree, Logan inched to the left to stay hidden. A branch cracked under his soles and within seconds the man stood at Logan's side, gun aimed and finger on the trigger.

"Let's go," he said, walking backward. "Where's the girl?"

"She's gone," Logan said, as he raised his hands up in front of his shoulders.

"You're lying. Where is she?"

"We moved her this afternoon."

"We know she wasn't moved."

Logan took uneven steps in a diagonal direction, trying to guide the other man's backward steps and get him away from the tree where he could act. He needed a lot more room if he wanted to turn the situation around.

"You obviously have old information," Logan said. "She was across the state line before sunset."

The man followed Logan's lead. "She's here and we'll find her. You were easy enough to get to. I've been looking forward to this. You killed my cousin a few days ago, Logan."

That the man knew his name gave Logan pause, but only for a moment. "Ah, is that who that was? Tell me, was he the dumb one or the stupid one? Whoever he was, you can tell him hi for me in a few minutes."

"That ain't gonna happen. I'm the one with the gun here."

Logan shrugged. "Details. Don also had a gun, but that didn't seem to matter much."

"You killed Don?" He stumbled over a hidden obstacle in his path.

Logan sprang into action. As the man tried to regain his balance, Logan knocked the gun out of his hand and snatched his throat. Pushing him back against a tree, he asked, "Who gave you our location?"

The man laughed, and Logan tightened his grip on his throat until all noise ceased. "You have two choices. Tell me or join your buddy over there." He relaxed his hand to give the man a chance to talk.

With narrowed eyes, he said, "You're getting nothing from me."

Logan pressed his forearm against the man's chest to keep him against the tree and reached for his knife. The blade flew up to the taut flesh around the man's throat. "Who are you working with?"

The man seemed unruffled by the new threat. "What does it matter? Won't be long before Langston has you and the girl."

"Give me a name."

"When he does get you, I'll have my turn with you. Maybe with the girl, too, although for much different reasons."

The knife melted into the man's skin, just enough to demonstrate his intention. "A name. Now."

"Your dead wife."

Logan faltered and the knife almost fell out of his hand.

"Too bad it wasn't you in that car instead of her. Waste of a nice piece of—"

He buried the blade in the man's neck. Warm blood spurted onto his face and clothes, as he sliced through the carotid artery. The man's body tumbled to the ground as soon as he withdrew the embedded knife. With every muscle in his body tensed, he focused his energy into kicking the dead man several times before tiring.

He crouched on the ground and lowered his head with the tip of the knife handle against his forehead. Anger and pain mixed in his veins and shook his arms. He wanted to rush to the safe house and kill every man in it and around it, but he held himself back. Somewhere on that trail, Sara waited for him. He couldn't save Karen, but he could still save Sara. Through her, he could find the vengeance he sought. He could find peace.

Logan swiped the blade of the knife on his shirt and sheathed it. He tugged his shirt over his head, turned it inside out, and cleaned as much blood off his face and neck as he could. He dropped his shirt on the corpse. He didn't want to leave his shirt somewhere that would tip them off to where he and Sara had gone.

He made his way back to his bag at the edge of the woods,

where the rain fell more freely outside the cover of the tall trees. Cupping his hands, he collected as much rainwater as he could and splashed it over his already soaked face to wash the rest of the blood off his skin. He dug around in his bag until he found a clean shirt. After he put it on, he secured his bag on his back and headed for the trail where he last saw Sara.

Skating down the slick, steep mud trail, he caught his balance several times. His mind wandered to Sara and he hoped she had been able to make it to safety without hurting herself. At the bottom of the trail, he turned north and started his run while keeping time. Trees covered most of the part of the path, and Logan found it easier to keep steady and not fall.

Approximately nine minutes, he converted his run into a brisk walk. Sara may have stopped short or run too far, and he did not want to accidentally pass her. He also had to keep his eyes peeled so he could spot her before she did him. He didn't want her thinking one of the men from the safe house had found her.

A noise startled him, and he slowed down and crept along the tree line. Out in the open and at a strong disadvantage, he hoped it was Sara and not another one of the men.

"Logan?" Sara's hushed whisper came from between two trees.

Tension flowed from his shoulders and back, as he moved toward her. "It's me, Sara," he said.

She ran out from behind a tree and dropped a large rock from her hands. Tears streaming down her cheeks, she hopped up on her tiptoes when she reached him. Her arms flew around his neck and her body pressed against him. Face buried in his shoulder, Logan couldn't understand any of her garbled words. Instead of asking her to repeat everything, he tightened his hold on her and let her have a moment to decompress.

When her hold on him loosened, Logan pulled back and took her arms. He locked eyes with her and asked, "Are you okay?"

She pressed her quivering lips together and nodded. "I'm sorry."

"Don't be," he said. "I wish I didn't have to leave you alone like that." He looked over her head and scanned the landscape. "We need to find a place to sleep tonight."

"What about going down to the main road?"

"We can't chance that they would drive by. They might

expect us to take that route."

He took her hand and coaxed her to follow him into the trees. Not far in, he found a fallen tree with enough brush over it to act as a shelter. Leaning against the rock, the nature-made cave provided the perfect amount of cover from the elements and their enemies so they could rest.

"This will work," he said. When she hesitated, he gently rubbed her back. "You're freezing and we have little choice. They won't find us in here, but if they do, we'll hear them coming."

Sara ducked under the branches and nestled herself inside the shelter. Logan took his bag off his shoulders and followed. He noticed her arms wrapped around her legs, as she rocked back and forth to try and get warm. He leaned his back against the rock and opened his bag.

"Take off your shoes and socks," he told her. "They're soaked."

He waited until she complied, and then did the same. He pulled out two fresh pairs of socks from his bag and handed her one. "I know they're not your size, but we have to make do."

"I'm not complaining," she said. Once they were on her feet, she tucked her legs back up against her body.

He took the confiscated gun out from his waistband and put it into his bag, then removed his own gun and the blanket. After loading his gun, he set it on the ground, then grabbed the blanket and fanned it out. "Come here," he said, gesturing for her to move closer to him. "It will be easier to stay warm together.

She looked at him for a moment before scooting a little closer to him.

"I'm not going to bite," he said.

She smiled and moved under his arm. With her body close to his, he covered them with the blanket. She snuggled up against him, pressing her cheek into his shoulder and gripping his shirt. Her chest heaved with every breath, and desire for her stirred in the pit of his stomach.

He reminded himself that he was there to protect her, nothing more. He pulled his hand out of the blanket and grabbed the gun off the ground next to him. He held the gun over the blanket in front of him, his finger twitching under the trigger, ready to act if anyone dared to disturb them.

But he couldn't ignore the way her body felt against him and how she clung to him for protection. For a moment he wondered if she wanted him as much as he did her. He hoped she didn't, but given a choice to think about her or about the three friends he lost tonight, he preferred to keep her in the front of his mind.

"Did you kill any of them?"

Sara's quiet question dragged him back into reality. Logan didn't want her knowing the dirty side of things, but he also didn't want to lie. "Yes."

"How many?"

"Two."

A long moment passed, and Logan worried he had upset her by being honest.

Sara gripped his shirt tighter and moved even closer to him. "Good."

Her matter-of-fact answer did little to still his growing need for her. Logan closed his eyes and prayed sleep would soon find him to destroy all of his indecent thoughts about Sara.

Chapter Thirty-two

Sara stirred to life, but kept her eyes shut. Her stomach growled a bit. Though eager to get up and find some breakfast, if she was lucky, Stephen would keep her in bed for a bit longer. Smiling, she stretched her hands around his torso, slid her fingers down to his hips, and nuzzled her cheek into his chest, hoping he would take the hint.

The corners of her mouth fell and she realized she wasn't cozied up with Stephen in her bed. His body never felt as good as the one she woke up against. Memories of Logan getting her up in the middle of the night and whisking her to safety colored her face and neck with a deep blush. She sealed her eyelids closed. Her embarrassment kept her frozen in place. Maybe she could pretend to still be asleep.

"Sara? Are you awake?" Logan's soft voice told her he either didn't know she was awake or he knew and was offering her an out from the awkward situation.

She wished herself to disappear, but there she remained, her head against his warm body and her fingertips still grazing his lower back. She opted to play dumb and she popped off of him, her hands pushing him away.

"Good morning," Logan said, with the same expression he always wore, the one that gave her no indication as to his thoughts.

"Morning." Sara lowered her head so as not to look directly at him. She had to be a mess, having slept in the wilderness after a long race to safety.

"I have some water and granola bars for breakfast, if that's okay."

"That sounds great," she said, as if he had offered up a large feast. "I, uh…" She looked around at their camp and saw she still wore his oversized socks on her feet.

"Our shoes should be dry by now if you need them."

"I need to, um…" She chewed on her bottom lip and blushed again.

Logan reached for his bag and opened it up. He pulled out a roll of toilet paper and handed it to her. He dug around in his bag again and handed her a shirt and a pair of jeans. "I managed to grab a couple items out of your suitcase for you in advance, just in case we had to leave without your clothes. It's not much, but—"

"It's perfect. Thank you for doing that." The words gushed out with a breath of relief. She reached for her shoes to put them on. "You're very prepared."

"I've never needed the go-bag before last night, but it's definitely coming in handy."

"I'm grateful for it. I'm going to… I'll just be back in a minute."

"Take your time. Head away from the trail and watch out for any wildlife, especially snakes."

"Snakes. Of course." Anxiety filled her chest at the mention of creatures. She hadn't given them a thought last night when they camped out and she was now glad she hadn't. She had never been a woodsy person and she didn't intend on becoming one anytime soon.

"Do you want me to come with you? I can make sure it's safe for you first."

"No, I think I'm okay." She started out of the structure, but paused and looked over her shoulder. "Thank you."

He nodded and resumed rummaging through his bag.

Sara took a moment to stretch out when she exited their sleeping quarters. A crick had worked its way into her neck while she slept and she hoped it wouldn't bother her all day. She stepped carefully through the trees, picking out landmarks to remember her location.

Morning birds chirped overhead and she paused to enjoy the sound. A small rustle in a nearby bush startled her. She held still, wondering if she should call for Logan. He had offered to help and he wouldn't think twice about coming to her aid.

A rabbit jumped out of the bush and Sara sighed with relief. She continued on her way, determined to take care of this one thing herself. Ever since her mother passed away, men had told her what to do. They had carved out her life for her, always making sure she did the "right thing." Much like with ditching her security detail, she had something to prove, a small demonstration that she could take care of herself without the help of a man.

Logan's question if she wanted him with her struck her as being different than her father or Stephen. He had asked, whereas they always stated their intentions. Where to go to school, which friends she could have, what occupation to choose, who to marry, where to live. Even small things like when she should do a breathing treatment seemed to be planned.

But Logan asked. He gave her a choice. He had given her choices for most of the time he'd had her under his watch, except when he had to search her. It seemed such a small gesture, asking if she needed help versus telling her she did, but one that she appreciated more than he could possibly know.

On her way back to their camp, she prided herself on her ability to take care of herself. Almost like a new step in life, she wondered what else she could do with her newfound freedom. She could change careers, maybe even go back to school to try something new. She could buy a house on the beach. She could go on a vacation where she wanted. She didn't have to marry Stephen.

She stopped walking with the thought. She didn't have to marry Stephen. She didn't need to be tied to someone she didn't love for the rest of her life. She could be free to find someone else, to date for the first time. She had been bound by her father's rules for so long that she wasn't even sure what kind of man she was attracted to. Though Mary always talked about the men she found attractive, Sara paid only a little attention to it. She was never free to do much more than listen to the dreams of others. Did she even like men who looked like Stephen? Or would she go for someone different?

Taller, she decided. She knew for a fact she liked tall men and Stephen was an average height. Maybe a lighter hair color than

Stephen. The hands were very important, too. She wanted strong hands, a bit calloused even. Hands that could make her feel safe, but desired at the same time. And blue eyes. Definitely blue eyes.

She giggled at herself. Stranded in the middle of the woods with her father sending men to kill her, and she was thinking about men. Mary had finally rubbed off on her. When she saw her again, she'd have to share it all with her. Mary wouldn't hesitate to rush her off to the bars to find her blue-eyed, strong-handed man.

Sara ducked under the top of their camp and Logan looked up as she entered. He held out his hand to help her inside, and she hesitated. She had described Logan in her mind, down to the strong hands and light blue eyes.

She took his hand and crawled under the makeshift roof. She sat as far away from him as possible before handing him the toilet paper roll and her dirty clothes to put back in his bag.

"You okay?" he asked.

She shrugged, hoping he wouldn't notice her ever-evolving attraction to him. "Everything was fine. No snakes. I can take care of myself."

He frowned at her last statement. "Of course you can. I'm sorry if I implied earlier that you couldn't."

Sara wanted to strangle herself. She hadn't meant any disrespect or to diminish his concern for her wellbeing. "I didn't mean that. I'm sorry, I'm not sure where it came from."

His expression cleared. "Don't worry about it. I know how stressful this situation is for you and I'm going to do everything to get your life back to normal. Well, as normal as it can be with the FBI poking their heads in it."

"Thank you," she said.

"For what?"

"You've done a lot for me and I'm sure you've sacrificed a lot. You've saved my life more than once now and I know I'd be dead if it wasn't for you—"

"You don't have to thank me. It's my job to make sure you're safe."

"Right, your job." Sara lowered her eyes and wondered if everything he did for her was only because of the job. "Still, thank you."

"Are you hungry?" He held out a bottled water to her.

"Famished. You mentioned granola bars?"

He grimaced and dug around in his bag. "It's not much. You have the choice of peanut butter or chocolate chip. I recommend the peanut butter ones so you get some extra protein."

"I can't," she said. "I'm allergic to it."

"That's right, I forgot." He handed her two packaged granola bars. "Chocolate chip it is then."

"Can we go back to the house after we eat?" she asked, as she opened the plastic wrapping. "I need my inhalers."

He reached into his bag and tossed her a small plastic bag. "You should have everything you need there. I also have a nebulizer in here and some EpiPens in case you accidentally eat the peanut butter granola bars."

Sara smiled at his subtle joke. "How did you manage to get everything before we left the house?"

"I didn't. I had Allie give me duplicates of everything just in case something like this happened."

She took a small sip of her water. A pang of unfounded jealousy touched her at his mention of another woman's name. "Who's Allie?"

"Doctor Connors," he said. "She's a doctor at the Church. You'll probably meet her when we take you in. She'll want to look you over before you go with the feds."

His words relieved the ridiculous envy that she had no reason to feel. "What's the Church?"

"Our headquarters. You'll see. For now, we need to get to a phone and talk to Schaffer, my boss. I need to tell him what happened and find out what he wants us to do next."

"When are we meeting up with Jack, Charlie, and Les?"

Logan looked away and bit off part of his granola bar.

"We are meeting them, aren't we?" she asked.

"No, we're not."

Her stomach dropped with his response. She didn't want to ask any more questions, but she couldn't stop them from flowing out of her mouth. "They're dead?"

"Yes."

Sara set her water down on the uneven ground and closed her slack jaw. She had held up so well under the stress, but knowing that the other three members of Logan's team had been killed brought reality front and center in her mind. Her father was trying to kill her and he sent men to do just that. Instead of her, they killed three very capable men. She and Logan were beyond lucky to be alive.

"I'm so sorry, Logan." She knew the words would do nothing to take away the rawness of his pain at losing his friends, but she had to say something. Then another thought entered her mind and she raised her fingers to cover her mouth. "This is all my fault," she said, looking away from him.

"It's not your fault."

"Yes, it is. None of you would be here if it wasn't for me and it's my dad who sent people to kill us. It's entirely my fault."

Logan stared at her during an uneasy, tension-filled minute. Sara could not interpret his expression and tears flooded her eyes. She had gotten three men killed, three men that she had come to like, all of whom had saved her life. And still Logan was willing to put his life on the line for her. She couldn't handle being responsible for his death, too.

He moved closer to her and gently took both her arms. "I want you to listen to me. This is not your fault. Nothing that your father did last night, nothing he's ever done, and nothing he does in the future is your fault. I don't want you to think that for a second. As for the others, every time we leave the Church, we know there's a possibility we won't come back. All of us had the opportunity to reject this job and none of us did. We knew who we were up against and we all believed it was far more important to save your life than to walk away and knowingly let you die. This is not your fault."

Sara's chin quivered and tears jumped from her eyes. Logan climbed on his knees and gathered her to him. Meant as comfort, the gesture only succeeded in making her cry harder. She gushed out a series of muddy apologies against his shoulder. He didn't speak, but held her tighter, his hand caressing her back and stirring up more guilt in her soul. It wasn't her friends and colleagues who had died, but his. She shouldn't be the one that needed comforting, yet she couldn't help falling apart in his arms while he remained stoic and strong.

After she cried herself out, she pulled back from him and kept her reddened face hidden in her hands. Logan handed her a wad of toilet paper and she turned to the side to erase the evidence of the breakdown from her face.

"I'm sorry," she said, as she wiped the remaining dampness

off her cheeks. "I don't know what's wrong with me."

"Nothing's wrong with you," Logan said. "You've been under an incredible amount of stress and emotional trauma. This just pushed you over the edge."

"I still feel bad. I never wanted anyone to get hurt and now all these people are dead." A thought entered her mind and she caught her breath. "Is Mary—"

"As far as I know, she's fine. Her team moved her to a new safe house yesterday afternoon, where she was reunited with her parents. If Langston sent out a team to the safe house she was originally at, then the attack most likely would have been coordinated with the attack on our house. That way no one from either house could warn the others. Mary would have been long gone."

"How do you know that's what he would have done?"

"If I had planned it out, that's what *I* would have done. It's the smart way to hit your enemies in two locations without one having time to warn the other. Your father is incredibly smart and methodical in everything he does."

Sara took slow, deep breaths and tried to calm herself. Logan's words made sense and she had no reason to believe anything had happened to Mary. "So what are our next steps?"

"We'll head down to the main road and follow it east, in the direction of the Church. We need to stay hidden in the trees on the side of the road. We can't take a chance that they are still out here looking for us. We'll find a phone and call Schaffer to get direction from there. No matter what, we have to get out of the open by tonight."

"I know I don't have my driver's license, but I could stop by a branch of my bank and try to get money for a hotel for us—"

Logan held up his hand. "That's a generous offer, but you can't have any communication with anyone. Your picture is all over the place and the minute you try to take money from your account with a teller, the police and the feds will swoop in. We should also stay out of public places, like hotels."

"I thought the FBI knew about this."

"They know we're bringing you in and they know we had to bend the law to do it, but it's a very small handful of people who know we're involved. The agents searching for you don't know anything about this. Neither do the police. If they find you, they'll take you back home and I'd spend some time in jail waiting for Schaffer to bail me out. Once I got out, I don't know if I could get to you again or how long it would be before they attempt another hit. It could be hours, it could be days, weeks, or months. I refuse to take a chance with your life."

Sara offered a strained smile. "I don't know how to thank you. I know you don't have to stay with me, especially after what happened to your friends, but—"

"I won't leave you, I promise. Not until you're safe with the feds and on your way to a new life." He picked up his water bottle and motioned toward her. "It's going to be a rough day, so you should finish your breakfast."

She had lost her appetite as soon as she heard about Logan's team, but she nibbled her granola bar. As they ate in silence, she noticed dried blood on his jawline, a reminder of what he had done a few hours earlier to keep them safe. If they were out in the open today, blood on his face would draw attention.

"You have some blood on you still," she said, gesturing to the right side of her jaw to mirror the location of the blood.

He took out some toilet paper and wet it with a bit of water. He wiped at it blindly, missing it entirely.

Sara held her hand out. "Here, let me get it for you."

He placed the damp paper in her palm, and she rose up on her knees. She wrapped her hand around his jaw and turned his head so she could see the blood better in the light. Being so close to him again kick-started her nerves. Her fingers trembled as she touched the makeshift cloth to his cheek. The stubble on his cheek ripped through the paper, but she managed to get him cleaned up. She rotated his face in the other direction and held up his chin to check for other blood, but found none.

"I think you're good now," she said, grateful that she found no other blood so she didn't have to keep touching him. Every time her fingers grazed the rough growth on his face, her heart dropped a little more. She wanted to run her hand over his skin and couldn't stop imagining what it would feel like against her own cheek, neck, and the rest of her.

Her face heated up as she sat back down and sipped on her water. She had to stop thinking about Logan in terms other than a protector. Even though she knew she didn't want to marry Stephen, she was engaged to him and shared a home with him. Her inability to love him didn't matter. She still wanted to be faithful to him. While letting her lustful thoughts wander about another man took her mind off all the bad that had happened in the past few days, it also set her on a dangerous path.

Besides, Logan didn't want her. He barely looked at her and held her at arm's length at all times. Sure, he had comforted her and let her sleep next to him, but it was only because the circumstances called for it, not because he wanted to be that close to her. Now that her father had his friends killed, she doubted he would ever want anything to do with her. She was nothing more than a bad reminder of the horrible things her father had done.

Afraid to let her thoughts continue to fill the silence, she said, "I haven't had granola bars since I was a kid. I didn't remember how good—"

Logan held up his hand to silence her. Eyes narrowed, he leaned forward, his ear pointed to the opening of their camp.

Sara jumped at the snap of a tree branch not far away from their location. She looked at Logan for guidance. He opened his bag and motioned for her to put everything in there. He lifted his gun and crawled to the entrance. After a moment, he turned to Sara and waved at her to follow him. She picked up his bag and handed it to him once they were out of the shelter.

He secured it on his back and turned to her. "We have to move slow," he whispered. "Just follow me."

She nodded and started behind him. Ten steps into their escape, a large man emerged from behind a tree and punched Logan in the jaw. Sara stifled a scream and watched Logan hit the man several times.

With his arm around the man's neck, Logan yelled at Sara. "Run!"

Sara didn't hesitate. Unsure of which way to go, she took off toward the path they traveled the night before. As she crossed over to the other side of the path, she glanced over her shoulder to see if Logan followed. Not seeing him, she turned her head in time to see another man jump out at her. His arms encircled her and Sara screamed.

"There you are," he said. "Just come with me, sweetheart, and all will be good."

He took hold of her arm and Sara backed up half a step. Her knee flew up into his crotch and he doubled over with a loud cry.

She balled up her hands and brought them down on his back twice, but it didn't seem to hurt him. She ran a few steps before he caught up with her again.

His strong hand pushed her and she smashed into a tree. Sara fell to the ground and scurried away, but he caught up to her before she got too far. He grabbed her arms, pulled her to her feet, and pushed her against a nearby tree.

Sara lashed out at him with her fists. He grabbed at her hands and, one at a time, he wrestled her arms away from him and stopped her attack.

"No, no, no!" She struggled against him, but his tight grip kept her from hitting him again.

He pinned both of her hands over her head with one hand and raised his other hand to strike her. "You stupid—"

A gunshot rang out and she screamed again. The man fell at her feet and she jumped to the side.

A hand grabbed her arm and she whirled around. She threw out her fist again, but the new man caught her wrist before it connected with his body. Only then did she see Logan's face. Her shoulders dropped and she took a jagged breath.

Logan cupped her face in his hands and looked her over. "Did he hurt you?"

"No, I'm fine. I'm sorry that I—"

"Don't worry about it." He released her. "There are going to be more of them and they would have heard the shot. Can you run again?"

"Yeah."

Though sore and tired, adrenaline coursed through her veins. Her legs moved without thought and she followed Logan's lead. They raced down the path, hugging the left side where the trees acted as cover from anyone on the ledge above them. Despite the burning in her lungs, Sara kept her pace up to match Logan.

Thoughts swirled through her mind and she tried to process everything that happened. The man falling down dead in front of her and the assumption that Logan killed the other man, too. No matter how gruesome the thoughts, she kept coming back to the idea that Logan would go to any lengths to keep her safe. She wanted him to kill every last one of them.

Chapter Thirty-three

I need to stop."

Logan stopped walking and glanced at Sara. One hand rested on her chest, which heaved with shallow breaths, and the other one on her hip. They had walked for a little over three hours without finding anywhere they could safely stop for a phone. The temperature rose substantially during their journey, slowing Sara down the hotter it became. He had encouraged her to keep going all morning and they were close to a rest stop, but the fatigue on her face told him she couldn't make it much further, not in her present condition.

"Let's rest for a bit," he said.

He led the way to a nearby tree and dropped his bag to the ground. Sara placed both palms on the tree and rested her head down on the backs of her hands, but made no move to sit.

"Do you need your inhaler?"

She nodded, but didn't look at him.

Logan helped her sit and crouched down beside her. Handing her the inhaler, he grew concerned at her pale color. She had finished her water bottle off a couple of hours into their trek, so he gave her his water to drink.

"It's only going to get hotter," Logan said, once her breathing seemed to get back under control. "We need a car."

"Wishful thinking."

"No, we're going to get one."

"If we're trying not to reveal ourselves to anyone, how are we getting a car?" She paused for a moment and her eyebrows shot up. "We're going to steal one?"

"I'm going to steal one from the rest stop. You're going to hide."

"Logan, we can't steal someone's car. That's not right."

"No, it's not right, but what choice do we have?" He recognized the conflict on her face. "Listen, whatever we do wrong will be made right. We'll find a phone, I'll give Schaffer the details. Someone will pull up the police report, contact the owners, tell them they're with some governmental agency, and spin a tale as to why their car was stolen. If we can't return their car in the same condition we took it, they'll get a new car, fully loaded and fully paid. No matter what, they'll receive a large amount of hush money. It may not seem like it at first, but whoever's car I steal is about to have one of the best days of their life."

"Since you put it that way," Sara said, standing up.

"Where are you going?"

She pointed in the direction they were heading. "To the rest stop so you can steal a car. The quicker we get there, the quicker we get to enjoy the air conditioning."

Logan got to his feet and put her inhaler back in the bag. They continued walking for another twenty minutes, stopping in a good location near the rest stop. With the trees in front of them, they could hide in plain sight while still scoping out the parking lot for the perfect car.

"Which one are we going to take?" Sara asked, as she sat next to the tree.

"One that's as close to us as possible, but far enough away from any of the other cars. It might take some time to find the right one."

She shrugged and pulled her knees up to her chest. "I guess I have nowhere else to be right now."

Logan settled onto the ground and stared at the parking lot. Though he saw several cars he'd like to take, the bustling rest stop didn't provide the opportunity to do so without getting caught.

"How did you get started doing this?" Sara asked.

"Stealing cars? Schaffer taught me."

"No, how did you get started doing whatever it is that you do?"

"That's a long, tedious story."

"It's not like we don't have time. You don't have to tell me if you don't want to. I'm just curious."

He didn't have anything to hide, but very few people knew about his past. He glanced at Sara, who waited anxiously. He figured it wouldn't hurt to tell her a bit about his life, and it could go a long way in getting her to trust him and feel more comfortable around him. Waiting in silence would leave his thoughts to wander to his team and the great loss he had suffered. With that came the blame game, the same one he played every time he thought about Karen. He preferred conversation over tormenting himself.

Logan sighed. "I guess the quick version is my mom was a prostitute who dropped me off in front of a hospital when I was 4-years old with a backpack and a note saying she didn't want me anymore. I have no idea who my dad is, but I assume he was one of her johns.

"I was shifted around from foster home to foster home, and finally ran away when I turned nine because I was tired of one of the older boys there beating me up all the time. I ended up across state lines and in another foster home. Every time I ran away, I'd get caught, stuck in a juvenile hall for some petty crime, then I'd go back into foster care.

"The last foster home I was in, I took off when I was 13 and got pretty far away. I found some other kids on the streets and they taught me the ropes. I survived out there for two years until I was caught burglarizing a home. That's when Schaffer found me and recruited me for his program, and here I am."

"That's awful," Sara said, her hand half covering her mouth.

"You didn't ask for a happy story."

"I'll remember that next time. What was it like living on the streets?"

"There was a whole different set of rules out there. People stuck to their own kind. The drug dealers all hung together, the prostitutes, the gang bangers. I didn't belong to any of the groups, so even though I knew some of them, I stayed with the other kids that didn't fit in anywhere. One of the older kids taught me how to pickpocket and shoplift, so that's what I did."

"Were they all kids?"

"All of them. The adults stayed in different areas than we did and they also went to shelters, which we didn't do. None of us wanted to end back up in the system, so we stayed away from places like that."

"What about that car?"

Logan followed her extended finger to a white Prius that pulled into a parking spot closer to them and far away from some of the others. He considered it for a moment, but then a black Escalade pulled up next to them.

"Damn it," Sara said.

"And that's why we wait. One will come along soon."

"Why do you do it?"

"Do what?"

"Your job. You had a horrible start to life. No one seemed to show you kindness until Schaffer came to you, so why do you go and help others out? Why are you risking your life to help me?"

Logan kept his mouth shut and scanned the parking lot. He had never been so honest with someone outside of Schaffer and Karen. The idea of opening up to someone new terrified him. If he revealed his weaknesses to others, they could exploit them.

Yet, telling Sara about his childhood happened without concern, as if he already trusted her completely. The woman had been in his life for a few days and already she had broken through his cement walls. Then, in a few days or less, it would end and Sara would be nothing more than a wisp of beauty who floated into his life on a summer breeze, only to vanish into a faded memory.

None of his thoughts stopped him from answering her question. "There was a girl on the streets with us. She was only 14 and a prostitute, but we got along well. We'd hang out from time to time and since I was 15 at the time, I thought maybe there was something to it. But she had a mean pimp—he called himself her 'manager'—who ruled his lot of kids with an iron fist. If any of them stepped out of line, he beat the crap out of them.

"I went off with Schaffer to pursue my new life and all these kids I knew were left behind. I suddenly had a purpose for being alive, where they didn't. I wasn't complaining, but I'd often think about them and wonder what happened after I left."

"Did you ever find out what happened to the girl?"

"A couple years later, I talked to Schaffer about her. I wanted to find out where she was so we could somehow set her life straight. He warned me against it, but I was on a mission to save her. I found out that just a few months earlier, she'd been knocked up by someone. Her pimp forced her to have a back alley abortion, after which he put her right back to work. Didn't take but a day for her to die from internal bleeding."

Sara wiped at the dampness in her eyes, but didn't speak.

He took a deep breath and smothered the anger that always came when he thought about his past. "I spent the next month thinking if I had just gone looking for her sooner, I could have saved her. I could have pulled her out of that life and shown her a better way. Who the hell knows if I could have done all that, but you asked why I do this. I do it for the ones out there who can't save themselves, exactly as Schaffer did for me."

Sara lowered her eyes and her voice. "You saved me. I couldn't save myself, but you did, even if I didn't want you to at first."

"And that's why I do it." He jetted his head forward a bit to catch her attention. She looked up at him, a pained look on her face. "I'm going to keep you safe, Sara. I promise no one will hurt you."

Her forehead creased. "But what if they hurt you first?"

He laid his hand on her forearm. "No one is going to hurt you."

She gave him a quick smile and nod, but then turned her head to look at the rest stop.

Logan took his hand off her skin and let his eyes drift back to the parking lot. The Prius and Escalade had both left. After a moment, an older model Escort pulled into the spot closest to them. A young couple climbed out of the car and ambled toward the scenic trees behind the restrooms, hand-in-hand. The man swung a camera by its strap in his free hand.

"That's our car," Logan said, pointing at the Escort.

Sara took a deep breath and blew it out. "So what's the game plan?"

"I'm going to go hotwire the car. Get a good look at the couple. I want you to walk around the back of the restrooms and toward the rest stop exit. Keep your eye on them for me. If they start heading back before you're past the restrooms, find a way to stall them, but only if you have to. Don't let anyone see you unless absolutely necessary."

"Where do I find you?"

"At the exit. I'll pick you up there. Be ready to jump in and go."

She nodded, but still stared wide-eyed at the car.

"Can you do this?"

Glancing at him, she said, "Absolutely."

The strength in her voice convinced him she would do fine. "Give me a quick head start before you leave." He got up and hurried toward the car, keeping an eye out for the couple and anyone else that might take notice of him.

Chapter Thirty-four

Sara watched Logan walk in the direction of the car for a moment before she gathered the courage to move. Her heart slammed against her ribcage with each beat and she wondered if others could hear her fear.

As Logan had instructed, she moved around the back of the restrooms, keeping her pace even and steady. She tried not to think about Logan and if he would be successful in hot-wiring the car. If someone caught him and he didn't get away, he could end up in jail, leaving her all alone. It had been hard enough with just the two of them. If Logan disappeared, she would never survive.

She smiled at a woman and child passing by, then returned her eyes to the couple Logan told her to watch. The woman was sitting down under a tree while the man snapped pictures of her. Sara wasn't sure how much time Logan had, but it didn't appear the couple would leave soon.

Picking up her pace, Sara shifted her direction when she passed the restrooms and headed toward a tree near the rest stop exit. She turned her head to look for Logan and the Escort, but the many cars and trucks in the parking lot blocked her view.

When she reached the pavement, she shoved her hands into her jean's pockets and sauntered alongside the on-ramp. A diesel truck whooshed by her, making her heart jump into her throat.

Only then did she worry about how long Logan was taking to hotwire the car. She didn't know the timeframes involved with something like that, but she had assumed it would be quicker than this.

The Escort pulled up next to her. Logan shouted to her through the open window and she raced to the door. She had barely pulled her feet inside when he took off again. She slammed the door shut and turned to look out the back window. The couple ran into the parking lot, screaming and waving their hands, but they quickly disappeared into the horizon.

Sara put her seatbelt on and laid her head back on the headrest. "They're probably calling the cops right now."

Logan held up a black cell phone. "They probably are, but only if one of them still has their cell phone with them." He chucked the phone out the window and rolled it up.

"Couldn't you have used that to call Schaffer?"

"Can't risk it. We need a good old-fashioned payphone."

"What happens if the police catch up with us?"

"They won't," he said, his voice much calmer than Sara could ever be in the situation. "There are a few highway interchanges ahead, which we'll use to put some distance between us. Then we'll move onto some back roads. The highway patrol will probably stick to the interstates and highways to search for us, but they'll give up soon enough."

"I feel so bad for them."

"Don't," Logan said. "They'll be well taken care of."

"I know that, and I believe you, but I don't know how you do this." She shook her head. "Too much excitement for me."

"Trust me. I prefer my jobs much quieter than this one's been."

Sara twisted her neck and stared out the window, as Logan took an on-ramp onto another highway. No cars followed them onto the new stretch of road. "Do you know where we're going?" she asked, turning back around.

"I have an idea of where Schaffer might send us, but first we need to find a phone. He may have already sent a team out to the safe house to find out what's going on since we've been out of communication for about 12 hours now."

"How often do you normally talk to him?"

"Protocol is to check in every two hours. That's why we have to get to a phone. He needs to know I'm alive and you're safe."

The thought of another team going out to the house to find the bodies of Logan's friends saddened her again. Though Logan told her she wasn't to blame, she still felt responsible for their deaths. She had just started to get to know the others, and then they died, all because her father wanted to kill her.

Sara leaned her head back against the headrest and watched the mountains fly by outside her window. Life had changed so drastically in the past few days, leaving her feeling out of sorts and scattered. She wanted to talk to Logan to pass the time, to take her mind off everything, but making small talk seemed a ridiculous idea.

"What are you thinking about?"

She raised her head at Logan's question. Shrugging her shoulders, she said, "Nothing, really." She paused for a moment, then turned to look at him. "I guess I'm not sure what I'm thinking about. I just feel so lost right now."

Logan kept his eyes on the road in front of them. "I can't imagine. Honestly, I'm not sure how you've kept it together, not with the bombshell we dropped on you about your father and with everything that's happened since."

"How have you kept it together? Your entire team is gone."

"We've lost people before. It doesn't happen very often, but it does happen."

"But you seemed so close to them," Sara said. "Especially Jack."

Pain flashed in his eyes and he grimaced. "Jack and I practically grew up together."

A hint of melancholy mixed with sadness laced his voice, and Sara wanted nothing more than to comfort him. "I am so sorry," she said.

He shot her a sideways glance. "You have nothing to be sorry for," he said, ending the discussion.

She frowned and focused on her hands in her lap, trying to think of something more to say.

"What was it like growing up with Langston?" Logan asked after a few moments of silence.

"Our relationship was disconnected. I never knew him. I guess I still don't." She sighed and turned her eyes back to Logan. "I was always gone from the house and when I was there, he wasn't too interested in me. I think he was happy when he passed me off to Stephen. It was like the best thing about me graduating from college and being an adult was that he no longer had to take care of me. I became someone else's problem."

"When did he introduce you to Mathers?"

"A little over a year ago. I tried to break it off a few times, but Dad kept pushing me to stick it out." She shook her head. "All because Stephen is his number one."

Logan remained silent while Sara mulled over her last words. An unbidden thought entered her head, one she hadn't considered before. Realization dawned on her, and her eyes glazed over.

"His number one," she said under her breath.

"What's that?" Logan asked.

"Didn't you say that Dad was grooming you to be his right-hand man? But Stephen wanted the job, so he did all those things to try to prove you weren't legitimate?"

"Yes."

"If you were legitimate and not working at The Boys Club, would you have gotten the job?"

"I think so," he said. "I worked very hard to get to the top in a short amount of time."

"That's so weird." An incredulous smile crossed her face and she shook her head. "If you had been legitimately working for my dad and moved into Stephen's position instead of him, then my dad would have pushed me to marry you, not Stephen."

Logan's eyes widened, but only for a moment. "I suppose you're right."

"Strange how that worked out," Sara said, shaking her head. "Now you're protecting me from him."

"I guess I never thought about that before. I'm glad that's not the way it was."

Sara's eyes flew to his face. "Thanks a lot," she said, overplaying her sarcasm.

"That's not what I meant. You shouldn't have let him push you to be with Mathers to begin with, so I'm glad it wasn't me that he tried to force on you."

"Something tells me if you had worked for him legitimately, you never would have gone for it. You're a much different person than Stephen. And, though the circumstances could have been better, I'm glad it happened this way."

His eyes connected with hers for a moment. "Me, too."

"You know, I never dated anyone before Stephen." The words tumbled out of her mouth and she instantly regretted sharing something so personal.

"Never?"

Sara shook her head. "Dad didn't like the idea of me dating anyone. Sometimes I wonder if he always had this plan to marry me off to someone high up in his organization."

"He may have," Logan said. "He always thinks about the long-term when he makes a decision. But how did he stop you from dating if you were never around him?"

"My security detail did his dirty work for him. I guess I did go on one date before I met Stephen. I was 16 and this guy took me to a movie. We were sitting in the back of the theater, and I was so nervous since it was my first date. After the movie started, we held hands, and then about halfway through the movie, he kissed me." Sara smiled at the memory. "My first kiss."

"So what happened that you stopped seeing him?"

"My dad happened. He had told my security detail that I wasn't allowed to have any physical contact with the guy, so in the middle of a crowded theater, they yanked us up and dragged us out of there. They pushed the guy around, made sure he understood he couldn't come near me again, and then drove me back to the dorms."

"That's pretty extreme."

"I was so embarrassed. The theater was filled with kids from our school, so word spread pretty quickly. No guy even would talk to me after that, let alone ask me out on a date. Then, somehow, the story followed me to college. It was my curse. That's what it was like growing up with Dad. If I should even call him that anymore."

"It's hard, growing up with the feeling that no one cares about you. I know you had your mom, but after she passed away and you were left with Langston, it was probably a lot like what I went through on the streets. No one seemed to care."

"We do have that in common, I suppose. Although I wasn't homeless."

"I wasn't for too long. Schaffer took me in after a few years."

Sara studied Logan's face for a moment and thought she caught a hint of a smile. "He sounds like a wonderful man. I can't wait to meet him."

"You'll get along with him very well."

She leaned her head back again and turned to the window.

"Why don't you try to get some sleep?" Logan asked. "I'll wake you when we get near a stopping point."

Until he suggested it, Sara had not noticed her exhaustion from their adventurous morning. Her eyes grew heavy and she yawned. With Logan next to her, she could rest comfortably again, knowing he would do everything he could to keep her safe.

Chapter Thirty-five

When Logan pulled the car into a truck stop two hours later, Sara was still in a deep sleep. She had barely moved since drifting off, and Logan did not want to wake her. Though he had chosen a parking space at the far end of the lot, closest to the pay phone, he could not go inside and leave her in the car for a nosy patron to find her and possibly recognize her.

Logan touched her shoulder. "Sara?"

She stirred a bit, but didn't wake.

"Hey, Sara," he said again, his tone light. "Time to wake up."

Her eyelids snapped open and she jumped forward in the seat. Frantic, her eyes darted about the car before landing on Logan.

"You okay?" he asked.

She lifted her hand to her chest. Taking deep breaths, she said, "I thought something was wrong and they had found us again."

"It's okay," he said. "We're not going to let that happen."

She looked out the windshield, toward the truck stop. "Can I go inside with you?"

He grabbed his bag from the backseat. Digging through it, he found his stash of money and handed her six twenties. Gesturing to the pay phone near the car, he said, "I'm going to use the phone to call Schaffer. Go on into the store, use the restroom or whatever, and get some food and water. The safe house won't have anything for women, so get what you need for two or three nights. Keep your head down and don't linger. Don't look anyone in the eye if you don't have to. I'll meet you in there."

"I'll be as quick as I can," she said.

Her confident tone erased any doubts he had about leaving her alone for a few minutes. "I won't be long," he said, opening the car door.

Logan watched her walk to the gas station, her head bowed as he had asked. When she disappeared behind the door, he made his way to the pay phone, nervously jingling change in his hand. He deposited the coins, waited for the dial tone, and punched in the numbers for Schaffer's emergency cell phone. He didn't want to risk the leak answering the phone at the Church.

The phone clicked, but no one spoke on the other end. Logan recognized it as Schaffer being cautious. "It's me," he said.

A sigh of relief came from the other end. "Logan," Schaffer said. "Where the hell are you?"

"Just across the Arizona border at a truck stop."

"I sent a team to the safe house when I hadn't heard from you. What happened?"

"We were ambushed. Jack, Charlie, Les…"

"Damn," Schaffer said. "We didn't know who the bodies were."

"What do you mean?" When Logan saw the lifeless bodies of his friends, he knew immediately who they were, even in the darkened room.

"The safe house was burned down. There were just three bodies, but we had no way to identify them. I'm glad you're safe. Is Sara with you?"

"She is. What about the team that has Mary?"

"They're fine," Schaffer said. "They relocated Mary two days ago. She reunited with her parents and now they're all in a safe house up in Oregon. As soon as Sara is with the FBI, we'll look at getting Mary back to her normal life."

"Sara will be glad to hear that, but I need to get her to a safe place. What's our next move? I thought maybe you'd send us to Flagstaff."

"That's the best place to be right now, so head to the safe

house there. But I want you to get to the Church tomorrow."

Logan hesitated. Though he wanted to get back more than anything, he still had no idea who was working with Langston from the inside. "I can't bring her there, Schaffer. Not until I know who the leak is." He tightened his hand around the receiver. "They've killed three of us now. Jack... Jack's gone—"

"I know this isn't easy for you, but I need you to stay focused on keeping Sara safe. I'm still working on the leak from this end, but we have to get you both out of the open. Call me when you get to the safe house. Tomorrow, we'll figure out where to go from here."

Logan ended the call and leaned against the top of the pay phone with his eyes squeezed shut. He had been so focused on his job until now that he hadn't thought about his friends being killed. He knew he had to get Sara to safety, but he didn't know how much more he could handle before he broke.

He took several deep breaths to decompress and align his thoughts with Schaffer's instructions. Sara's life now rested entirely on his shoulders and he could not fail, not after three men gave their lives for her. As he walked toward the truck stop to find her, he resolved to stop at nothing to bring Langston down.

Chapter Thirty-six

Sara accepted the change from the cashier without looking directly at him and turned around to head to the bathroom. She tried to stay conservative while shopping, settling on a couple T-shirts, a few personal items, some water, and food. The truck stop had no jeans or other clothes for her, but she figured she could make do with whatever they had at the next safe house. It would only be for a few more days at the most, she hoped.

In the restroom, she stood over the sink and used paper towels to soap off her face, neck, and arms. After drying her skin, she went into the handicap stall and changed into a clean shirt. She wanted nothing more than to climb into a hot shower and change into fresh clothes, but she reminded herself it wouldn't be too much longer before she could do that.

Back at the sink, she took the toothbrush and toothpaste out of the bag and worked on getting her teeth cleaned. Between that and the sponge bath, she already felt much better, but was a long way off from being back to normal.

"Screw you, too, Vern," a female voice came from just outside the bathroom.

The door swung open and Sara froze at the sink as a stout woman wearing a flannel shirt walked in.

"Men," the woman said. She stepped up to the basin next to

where Sara stood and looked at Sara in the mirror, as if they shared some common bond. "You can't live with 'em, but you can sure as hell live without 'em." Her laugh echoed through the small bathroom.

Sara gave her a brief smile, but returned her attention to brushing her teeth. She spit out the last of the toothpaste. Leaning over the sink, she cupped water in the palm of her hand and brought it up to her mouth.

"I've had to do more than one of these truck stop clean ups," the woman said, washing her hands. "Not the best in the world, but it works. Where you heading?"

Sara hesitated, unsure of what to say. "Um, just taking a road trip, that's all."

"I see, I see," the woman said, eyeing Sara in the mirror. "Me and Vern are heading over to Nebraska. Have a load to drop off there by tomorrow. Looks like you've been on the road quite a bit already."

"Not for too long," Sara said. She worked on packing her things back in her bag to leave.

"Yeah, you're a bit worse for the wear. Still adorable as a baby chick, though." She moved to the paper towel dispenser and yanked out several sheets of rough, brown towels. "You driving with your man or with a friend?"

Sara grabbed her bag and headed for the door. "A man... I mean, a friend. He's a man, but he's a friend." She pulled open the door as a flush crept into her cheeks.

The woman laughed again and followed Sara out of the restroom. "I know that type of man friend," she said.

Sara stopped to look around for Logan and considered her exit strategy. She didn't want to be rude to the woman, who was friendly enough, but she also couldn't keep talking to her in case someone noticed them or the woman happened to recognize her from the news.

"Over there," the woman said, her short arm extended and pointing to the hot dog warmers. "That's my Vern right there."

Sara smiled at the sight of Vern, who scratched the top of his head and messed up his comb over.

"I sure do love him, but sometimes spending all day together in that truck of ours gets the better of us. You'll find out at the end of your trip with your man, I'm sure. Which one is yours, now?"

Sara's stomach knotted as she looked around for Logan. She wanted to hurry and get back to him, away from the prying conversation.

"That's him coming in now," the woman said. "I know it sure as I know my name. He seems like your man, at least."

Sara swallowed hard at the sight of Logan walking into the truck stop. She latched onto her locket and swung it back and forth on the chain.

"Yeah, that's him," the woman said. "Man alive, he sure is something."

Logan stopped when he saw Sara and stared at her with his trademark, unreadable expression.

Sara kept her eyes on him, immobilized by her thoughts. She didn't know what he was to her, other than her protector, even though she felt something more when he looked at her. Any day now, he would walk out of her life, and though she could not fathom why, that was not an acceptable outcome for her. He seemed to be the only thing she had left to hold onto before the FBI took her away and she did not want to lose the one person who tethered her new life to her old one.

"It was nice talking with you," she told the woman.

Logan's eyes shifted to the cash register. He looked back at Sara with a frown before walking toward her.

Sara wondered what he saw that changed his demeanor so suddenly. She turned her attention to the cash register.

"Oh my goodness," the woman said from beside her.

Sara's jaw dropped and her heart jumped when she saw the television behind the counter. There, for the whole store to see, was her picture. Information scrolled across the bottom of the screen beneath the word "MISSING" in large, block letters, just above a phone number.

"That's you," the woman said. "You're that girl they're looking for in California."

"Time to go," Logan said when he reached her. He grabbed her arm and guided her lead-filled legs to the exit nearest them.

"Wait!" the woman called out.

Logan picked up the pace. As soon as they went through the door, he coaxed her to run. She barely heard the commotion of people behind them over her heart thudding in her ears. They both jumped into the car and Logan fumbled for a second with the keys.

Her eyes landed on the woman running out with Vern and a few other patrons right behind her. She noticed a man on his cell phone gesturing wildly, occasionally pointing in her direction.

The engine revved up and Logan tore out of the parking lot. She watched the side mirror for the first few miles, but didn't notice anyone following them.

"We have to get on some back roads for a while," Logan said.

"I'm so sorry," Sara said. "That woman wouldn't stop talking to me and—"

"It's okay, Sara. There's nothing you could have done once it was on the TV. If she didn't recognize you, someone else would have. We're just lucky there were no cops there at the truck stop."

"It was my fault," she said. "I should have walked away from her as soon as she started talking to me and came out to find you. I just didn't want to be rude to her."

"Stop worrying." Logan touched her arm and glanced at her. "You did nothing wrong. We were in the wrong place at the wrong time. It's as simple as that."

"Are you just saying that to make me feel better?"

"Of course not."

Sara crossed her right arm over her chest and placed her hand on top of his. "I don't want to screw up again," she said. "I don't want anything I do to end up with you getting hurt."

"Don't worry about me."

She squeezed his hand and placed her hands in her lap. Turning to look out the window, she realized with horror that she had just touched his hand. She had done so without thinking, as if it were a natural exchange between them, and embarrassment flooded her mind. The more time she spent with him, the more comfortable she allowed herself to become. She needed to remember he was just a man assigned to protect her. He wasn't Stephen, and they weren't even friends, but two people thrown together in a strange situation, one that would soon end.

"By the way," Logan said, breaking into her thoughts. "Schaffer says Mary is fine."

Sara let out her breath and relief overcame her. "Where is she? Is she safe?"

"She's with her family in Oregon, at one of our safe houses there. They'll keep her there until it's safe for her to go back home."

"I hate that she's involved in this," Sara said.

"We didn't want to take her when we picked you up, but we had no choice. That was our only window of opportunity to get to you."

"I'm just glad you're making sure both she and her family are safe." Sara glanced at him, pushing the awkwardness of grabbing his hand aside. "Can you get me in touch with her? I want to explain this all to her."

"She's been told everything already, but I might be able to get a call in between you two once we get to the Church."

"When are we going there?"

"I'm not sure. Could be tomorrow, could be in a few days. Right now we're heading to a safe house a couple hours away from here. You can get a good night's sleep and tomorrow morning, we'll figure out our next move."

Sara nodded and rested her head against the seat. She looked out the window and tried to enjoy the scenery to pass the time.

Chapter Thirty-seven

For two hours, they shared off-and-on light conversation about the less important things in life. It helped pass the time and Sara was grateful for no more emotional discussions about their situation or about his history with her father and Stephen. For their lunch, they ate the beef jerky and sipped on the bottled water she purchased at the truck stop.

At one point, Logan turned on the radio and surprised Sara by tuning it to a country station. She thought he would have gone more for some brand of rock. She had never been one for country music, but she let him keep the radio on the station without speaking up and soon found the twang in the songs oddly soothing.

A few miles after the "Welcome to Flagstaff" sign, Logan took several side streets into an upscale subdivision. Though Sara did not care for beige, gray, and tan cookie cutter homes, she could find nothing to complain about with these homes. The sight of them signified she would soon get a hot shower and a warm bed.

Logan pulled the car off to the side of the curb near a home and turned off the engine.

"Is this it?" Sara asked, as she unlatched her seatbelt.

"It's a few blocks over." Logan turned around in the seat and grabbed his bag from the back. "We're going to walk over to it and scout it out first. I don't want the stolen car anywhere near us.

When we get to the house, I'll call Schaffer with its location and he'll send someone to get it."

Sara watched as he took out a T-shirt and wiped down the steering wheel. He then used the shirt on the dashboard and any instruments he had touched. He put the car keys under the floor mat and used the shirt to open the door. She took the shirt from him and followed his lead, wiping down her side of the car before opening her door. Once out of the car, Logan had her watch for nosy neighbors while he wiped their prints off of the outside handles.

Stuffing his shirt back in the bag, he motioned for her to walk with him. They moved down the sidewalk and turned right at a cul-de-sac. At the arch of the circle, they walked on the side of a home without a fence and went through the backyard.

"Have you been to this safe house a lot?" Sara asked, impressed with his ability to navigate the subdivision.

"A few times," Logan said. "It's been maybe a year since the last time I was here."

They trudged up a small, grassy hill. At the top, Logan held out his hand to stop her from going further. "That's the house," he said, pointing to a gray, two-story house at the bottom.

Sara knelt down to catch her breath. The other side of the hill was much steeper than the side they just climbed, and her asthma already had her wheezing a bit. "Can I get my inhaler?" she asked.

"Sure," Logan said. He sat down next to her and retrieved it from the bag.

She took two puffs and handed it back to him. Closing her eyes, she rested her hand on her chest and steadied her breathing.

"We can stay here until you're ready. If we need to go back to the car, we can drive there. Then I'll bring it back here and walk to the safe house."

"It's okay. I don't want you going to all that trouble. I'll just do a treatment when we get there."

He studied her face for a moment. "If you change your mind—"

"I'll be okay. Why are you so worried about them finding us at this safe house?"

"There's a leak in our organization," Logan said, still staring at the house. "I kept hoping that maybe I was still wrong, but them finding us at the last one proves it."

"What does that mean, a leak?"

"Someone in my group is working for Langston."

His words clicked in her mind. "That's why you told me not to trust anyone at the safe house."

"I hate that you're exposed to this because a leak makes your already bad situation even more dangerous, but I'm not going to let them find you. Schaffer is working on it to see if we can find out who it is."

"Is that why you don't want to go to the Church today?"

"Exactly," Logan said. "If someone on the inside is working against us, I don't want you to be in even closer proximity to that person."

Sara settled down on the lush grass, pulled her knees up to her chest, and wrapped her arms around her legs. "I can't wait to get into a hot shower," she said. "I feel like we've been on the road for weeks."

"I think that's the first thing we'll both do."

"How many bathrooms in the house?"

"Three and a half, if I remember right."

"Thank God. I thought I was going to have to arm wrestle you to see who showered first."

"I'd have let you win."

Sara flinched and looked up at him. His tone held a hint of humor, but no smile graced his face. She realized for the first time that not once since he entered her life had she seen him smile or heard him laugh. She wondered if losing his wife had created the sadness that ruled him or if his demeanor had always been more on the serious side.

After several minutes passed in silence, Logan said, "I think it's safe to go down there now. We've scoped it out long enough to make sure no one is inside. Are you sure you can make it down the hill?"

She nodded and pushed herself up from the ground. Peering down the steep descent, she said, "Just don't let me fall."

He caught her eyes. "I won't let you fall."

Her heart skipped a beat and her breath hitched. He didn't seem to notice, as he started down the hill. She composed herself and he encouraged her to follow his slow, deliberate steps, and Sara made sure each step she took landed exactly where he had stepped.

He kept his hand out toward her, and after a couple steps she held onto his arm to help her balance. Though she had moments where she thought she would stumble and roll down the hill, Logan kept his word and got her down the hill in one piece.

At the house, he led her into the backyard. Under the wood deck, Logan pressed several numbered buttons on a small, wooden box camouflaged within the beams and retrieved a key. They went up the stairs of the deck, and Logan used the key to open the back door. They entered through the kitchen, and Logan set the bag down on the granite countertop.

Sara took a deep, cleansing breath, and let it out in a loud sigh. "Feels good to finally be in a safe house again."

"I couldn't agree more," Logan said. He walked to the phone on the breakfast bar and picked up the receiver. "I'm going to call Schaffer real quick. Then we'll go get cleaned up and figure out sleeping arrangements."

Sara pulled out a chair at the kitchen table and watched him as he turned to the side and spoke in a low tone to Schaffer. Every so often she understood a word or two, but didn't bother trying to strain so she could eavesdrop. If he wanted her to know what they spoke about, he would tell her.

Instead, she occupied her time by studying his face. From his tightened jaw, his creased brow, and narrowed eyes, she could tell whatever he and Schaffer discussed was quite serious, even heated at times. Her eyes traveled from the rough growth along his cheek and jawline, to lips that moved with intent.

He turned his head, and his ice-blue eyes caught her staring at him. Her cheeks flushed and she jerked her head away to look at something else in the kitchen. Not the first time she had been caught watching him, she reprimanded herself for being so obvious.

Pushing back her chair, she decided to explore the rest of the house while he finished the phone call. Anything to get her out of the uncomfortable situation. She ambled toward what appeared to be the living room, but stopped when Logan called her name.

"Don't wander too far," he said. "I still need to check out the rest of the house."

She nodded and went into the living room. The décor mirrored that of the last safe house they were in, and immediately brought the rest of Logan's team to mind. She ran her hand along the top of the forest green couch, thinking about sitting between Jack and Charlie, watching Jim Carrey movies. They all had laughed so hard, not just at the movies, but at their light conversation that day.

Dinner that night had been a wonderful time, as she got to know all the men better, with the exception of Logan. If only she had known that was truly their last dinner together, if there had been something she could have done differently that would have resulted in their lives being spared, she would have. Even if she had to surrender herself to the men searching for her, the choice would have been easy for her. She would have done anything to keep them alive.

"We're all set," Logan said from behind her.

Sara whirled around and smiled. "Did he say anything about the leak?"

"Nothing yet, but he thinks he found a thread he can follow."

"Hopefully that will lead to something."

"Are you ready to tour the house?"

She followed him up the carpeted stairs at the other end of the living room. At the top of the stairs, Sara noticed a closed door on her right. Logan led her left, passing another closed door. They continued down the hall to a dead end with three rooms, all with the doors shut. Logan picked the room on the left and set his bag down on a queen bed.

"I think I'll have you stay here in this guest room," he said. "I'll stay awake for most of the time you're asleep, but when I do sleep for a few hours, I'll be in the master bedroom near the stairs. That way I can hear anyone coming in the house and get to them before they get to you."

"Do you think they'll come here?"

"I don't know, but I want to be prepared for anything. There's something I need to show you. All of our safe houses have a secret room somewhere in them."

"Like the room I was in at the last safe house?"

"Exactly. If someone does come here, I want you to hide right away and don't come out until I get you."

"Where is the secret room?"

"It's been a while, but it's somewhere in here." His eyes traveled over the walls of the room until they landed on the closet.

"Right there." He examined the seams in the drywall, pushed on the upper corner of the wall next to the closet, and a hidden door swung open.

Sara jumped back. "That's amazing!"

"There's a handle on the inside for you to pull it shut once you're in there. You can also use that to push the door back open, but like I said, don't come out until I get you."

As he closed the door, she memorized the release latch's location in case she needed to use it. "Where can I take a shower?"

"The bathroom is down the hall, on your left, just before you reach the stairs. I'm going to head down to the master bathroom and shower as well after I check out the rest of the house."

"I need to do a breathing treatment first," she said, "so you'll probably be done before me."

"I'll leave my bag with you since the master bedroom should have clean clothes that fit me. You're welcome to go through the dresser in here and use whatever you need. There should also be some things in the bathroom that you can use if you need to."

"Thank you, Logan."

"I'll see you in just a few minutes."

She waited until he left before opening his bag and pulling out the nebulizer, once again amazed he had thought so far ahead to get duplicates of all her medications. She found an outlet near the bed, plugged in the machine, and prepared her treatment.

Sitting on the bed next to the bag, she clamped her lips around the mouthpiece and breathed in the familiar medicated steam. She coughed a couple times, but settled down almost immediately.

Boredom struck a couple minutes later, as it usually did during a treatment. She fumbled with the handle of the bag for a moment before unzipping it just a bit, then all the way. Not wanting to be caught snooping, she looked at the door and wondered if Logan would come back in. She shrugged and decided she could make up a story if he did.

She pulled out the T-shirts she bought at the truck stop, followed by some dirty clothes. She rummaged through the rest of the bag, only stopping when her hand came across one of the two guns in the bag. She yanked back her hand and decided going through the rest of it wasn't worth it, especially if she accidentally discharged one of the weapons.

Putting everything back in its place, she zipped the bag back up and resumed her treatment. When the medication in the nebulizer ran out, she disconnected the tubes and cleaned the parts out in the bathroom down the hall. Back in the bedroom, she put the machine into the bag and sat on the edge of the bed to allow time for the shakiness from the treatment to wear off.

She glanced back down at the bag and noticed a small bulge in the pocket on the side. She unzipped the pocket and reached inside. Two items came out with her hand, both surprising her. The men's wedding band broke her heart, as she realized it was Logan's. She rotated it around and tilted it to read the engraving on the inside of the band. The words, "My forever," brought tears to her eyes.

No wonder he had been so passionate when he spoke to her about not marrying a man she didn't love. The love between his wife and he still resonated today, from the words on the inside of the ring to the fact that he still carried it with him. His morose demeanor, a constant reminder of his loss, paid tribute to the pieces of his soul ripped out of him the day she died.

The ring stirred up envy inside of Sara. She and Stephen never had that kind of love, or any love at all. They never would. She doubted she would ever experience something as wonderful as what Logan and his wife must have had, before the cruelty of this world stole her away from him.

She focused her attention on the second item, a worn photograph, the creases in the corners and the upward curvature in the middle letting her know it had been handled far more than any random picture. A beautiful brunette stood in front of a house with a wide smile, her hand resting on her pregnant belly. Sara lifted her hand to her mouth as she studied the woman. From Jack's story, she knew Logan's wife had died, but Jack failed to mention she had been pregnant at the time. She couldn't imagine Logan could do the work he did while raising a child alone, so she could only assume his wife died while pregnant.

With the wedding ring and the photograph still two items Logan kept with him, Sara knew it had to be recently that she died. Not so recent that he no longer wore his ring, but close enough that he still carried the ring and her picture with him. Sometime in the last few years.

He hired someone to kill me. But they missed.

Sara's eyes grew wide as Logan's words from their last night at the safe house raced through her mind. He said her father placed the hit on him a couple years earlier, and thinking about it now, she remembered that Jack told her that his wife died around that same time.

Her father had killed Logan's pregnant wife.

Logan walked into the bedroom, dressed in fresh clothes. Sara rose to meet him, the picture and wedding band still in her hands. He stopped when he saw them. After a moment, his eyes drifted from them to her face.

She could not contain her tears when pain flashed across his face after seeing the wedding band and photograph. "My father did this," she said.

Logan tilted his head. "Sara—"

"He did, didn't he? He killed your wife and baby."

"How, uh... how do you know about Karen?"

Karen. Though she had heard the name of his wife from Jack, hearing it tumble from Logan's lips kicked Sara in the gut. His wife had a name, a husband who loved her more than anything else, and a child on the way. The happiest time of her life, destroyed by Sara's father in an attempt to settle his vendetta against Logan.

"Jack told me," Sara said. "He didn't tell me she was pregnant, but he told me she died a couple years ago." She looked down at the picture and ring in her hands. "I'm sorry, Logan. I didn't mean to upset you or go through your things. I saw something in the side of the bag and I opened it and—"

"It's okay." Logan walked over to her and plucked the mementos from her hands.

"He did this, didn't he?" she asked again.

"He did," Logan whispered.

Sara's eyelids fell and her face scrunched up. She covered her mouth and nose with her hands and leaned forward.

Logan's hand landed on her shoulder. "Sara—"

"How did I not know?"

"Know what?"

She strode away from him and gestured wildly. "He killed your wife and baby, he hired someone to kill me." She turned around to face him. "How did I not know that he was so... evil? What did I miss seeing all those years? I should have known. I should have seen something, *anything* that would have clued me in to who he really is. Maybe if I had paid more attention, maybe if I had listened to my instincts, I could have discovered what he was doing and stopped him somehow."

"Sara, it's not your—"

"You keep saying that it's not my fault, but it sure as hell feels like it is."

Logan remained quiet.

"I'm going to take a shower." She brushed past Logan, raced out the door, and went into the bathroom across the hall. She turned on the hot water and tugged up the diverter. As the water streamed through the shower head, she sat on the edge of the tub and buried her face in her hands.

Chapter Thirty-eight

Logan lifted his balled-up fist to knock on the door, but lowered it before his knuckles connected with the wood. He frowned and stared at the white in front of him, wondering what Sara was doing behind the door. She had shut herself in her room after her shower and spent the last two hours in a self-imposed quarantine. The faster the clock ticked down the minutes, the more Logan wanted to help ease her pain. He understood more than anyone the harm Langston brought into the lives of those around him, and seeing Sara tormented by that monster was too much for him.

The door swung open and Logan stepped back.

Sara jumped. "I was just coming out to talk to you."

"And I was just coming up to talk to you."

She pulled the door back and gestured for him to come in the room. "I wanted to apologize… again."

"There's no need to apologize."

"But there is. I guess a lot of what I'm learning is catching me off-guard and I don't know what to do or how I should feel."

"I've lived with what he can do for years now. You've had an atomic bomb dropped on your life and you're dealing with the fallout."

"I never knew how horrible of a person he was until now," she said, lowering herself onto the edge of the bed. "What he did to you was just awful."

Logan sat next to her on the bed and turned to the side. "I put myself in a position where I could get hurt. I know I was just doing my job, but I also knew that by going undercover and working for him I could lose my life. At the time, I didn't know Karen and I didn't think about what the future would hold. I certainly didn't plan on getting married and starting a family."

"You have told me over and over that it's not my fault. You should listen to yourself a little more. It's not your fault, either."

"But my story's different than yours. My job endangers me and anyone around me. I should have known better than to let someone into my life."

Sara sat sideways on the bed and crossed her legs. "You just said you didn't know her and you didn't plan on meeting her. So it's not your fault. Are you supposed to deny yourself any kind of happiness because you're helping out others?"

"Maybe."

"Well, then by your reasoning, I also shouldn't look to ever be happy because he just so happens to be my father."

Logan opened his mouth to argue, but stopped. Sara's logic could not be denied. He couldn't keep telling her that she wasn't responsible for her father's actions and then hold himself responsible for those same misdeeds. For the first time, he considered the strong possibility that the blame for Karen's death rested elsewhere.

"I've spent the last couple hours wondering about my role in this whole mess," Sara continued. "When it comes down to it, I can't blame myself. I was never around him and I had no idea what he was doing. The thing that gets me, though, is all the damage he has done. He has hurt so many people, destroyed lives, and that's just what I know about. What else has he done that I don't know? How many other people are suffering or have suffered because of him?"

"You can't torture yourself thinking about that. The only thing you can do, now that you know who he is, is stop him somehow. That's why the FBI wants to get you on their team. You have knowledge about him that no one else does. They can use what you know in conjunction with evidence they've collected to put him away for the rest of his life."

"And then we both get some closure and peace."

"That's the plan," Logan said.

Sara sighed. "Then I guess it's in my best interest to cooperate with the feds. So, tell me. What happens when I go into witness protection?"

"The FBI will provide you with a new identity, take you to a secret location, and you'll stay there for the duration of your time in the program. If your identity is compromised in any way, they will move you."

"How long will I be there?"

"Until it's safe for you to come out again. That might be the rest of your life."

"I won't be able to talk to Mary anymore, or any of my friends, will I?"

"I'm sorry."

"Do I at least get to pick out my new name?"

Her sad eyes and downturned mouth made Logan want to give her some hope. "I can't promise anything, but Schaffer might be able to get that worked out for you."

Sara's expression dropped and her eyes lowered to her hands in her lap. "Will you come see me?"

Logan hesitated, wanting to give her any answer but the truth. Settling on being honest, he said, "I can't, Sara. They won't let anyone know where you are, especially not me, not with Langston still coming after me. They can't—*I* can't risk your life like that."

She took a deep breath. "I was hoping Schaffer would have you come with me. You know, so I would know someone."

Logan had hoped that himself. He considered asking Schaffer to assign him to her security, but reminded himself that he couldn't put his own selfish desires over Sara's safety. "That's not the way it works," he told her. "Once this job is over, my part will be done."

"I keep forgetting this is just another job for you."

His fingertips grazed her shoulder. "If I go with you, I would put you in danger. That's the only reason I'm not going with you to watch over you." His fingers trailed down her arm and covered her hand. "But you're not just another—"

A noise from downstairs stopped his words. He whipped his head to the side, eyes narrowed. Voices drifted up the steps and into the room.

He looked back at Sara's frightened face. "The cubby."

They climbed off the bed, and Logan grabbed his bag. He guided her to the wall and he pushed open the door. He wrapped his arm around Sara and forced her into the cubby with him. He shut the door behind them and set his bag down beside them on the floor, careful not to make a sound. His hand cradled her back and she pressed into him.

Squeezed together in the tight, dark space, Logan couldn't ignore her trembling body touching his. Her cheek rested against his chest, with her arms pinned between their bodies and her fingers curling into his shirt. He stared at the top of her head for a moment before raising his eyes to look into the darkness. He focused instead on the noises coming from down the hall and prayed the men didn't know about their hiding place.

Sara moved her head. He glanced down to see her looking up at him.

"Logan—"

He touched her mouth to silence her whisper. As soon as his fingers caressed her soft lips, a dam broke inside of him. He drew back his hand as if bitten, but he couldn't tear his eyes away from hers. They remained still, as voices came from the other side of the door, accompanying the sound of the men ransacking the room.

Logan tried to listen to the voices, but Sara held him captive. She extended her arm upward, touching her shaking fingertips to his cheek. He took her hand and he lowered his head, as she rose on her toes to meet him. Their lips met in a soft, tentative kiss. Her mouth lingered next to his, their eyes studying each other, as if neither were sure of the next move.

He let go of her hand, which reconnected with his face. His palm slid around to the back of her head, tangling his fingers in her hair. Her chin lowered just a bit, enough to force Logan to take action before he lost the moment. His mouth crushed hers in a fierce kiss, one that she reciprocated. Sara freed her other arm from between them and threw it around his waist. Her fingers tugged at his shirt while her other hand latched onto the back of his neck.

Another voice came from the room, reminding Logan of their company. Every sane part of him screamed that continuing to kiss Sara would lead down a dangerous path for them both, but he couldn't help himself. While Allie only succeeded in awakening his physical needs, Sara aroused every part of him, waking him up for the first time since Karen died, something he never thought he would experience again. Now that he tasted her, fueling a new addiction, he wasn't about to stop.

Logan ignored the warnings and lost himself in his almost frantic desire. No sound came from either of them, their forced restraint building his need for her to uncontrollable heights. His mouth never strayed from hers and they could barely move in the cubby, but the tight quarters didn't stop him from exploring the sensual curves of her body through her clothing.

He didn't know how much time passed before he realized the men had long since disappeared. He did not want to let go of her, but they also could not stay in the closet. Breaking away from her, he ran his thumb over her cheek.

"Stay here," he whispered.

She moistened her lips and nodded.

Pushing the door open, he squeezed past her, into the room. The harsh daylight seeping through the curtains seared his eyes, reminding him of his priority to keep her safe. Without looking at her, he closed the door behind him. He crept into the main hallway and waited, but heard nothing. He opened a small slit in the blinds covering the window at the end of the hall. Looking down, he saw no cars in the driveway or on the street near the house.

Once he searched the house and confirmed the men had left, he went back upstairs to get Sara. His heart grew heavier with each step. He had crossed the line with her, a line he had managed to stay clear of since the first time he saw her. He couldn't take back what happened, but he also couldn't ignore it.

He opened the door to the cubby. "It's safe."

She stepped out, but avoided his gaze. After putting several steps between them, she asked, "Do we need to leave?"

He had wondered that himself, but the lateness of the hour made him reconsider getting back on the road to move her again. "We'll be fine for tonight. There's no need for them to return again tonight since they already ruled out this house for our location. In the morning, I'll contact Schaffer. He will let us know if we're staying here or moving somewhere else."

"Would he have us go to the Church tomorrow?" Her innocent sounding question held hidden meaning, one he recognized. As soon as they were back at the Church, they would be separated and she would be whisked away by the FBI.

Everything that just happened would soon be a memory, an unfulfilled desire.

"I don't know yet," he said. "He wants us to come in, but I'm not so sure it's a good idea."

"Oh."

Her eyes shifted around the room, and Logan tried to find something to look at other than her. Reminders of the closet filled every second of silence, and he regretted his actions. He knew better and could have displayed more self-control, if only he had tried.

"We should—"

"What if—"

Their words came at the same time and they chuckled. He turned his head and seeing her in his peripheral vision caught his attention. Though her eyes pointed at the floor, her flushed cheeks and timid fidgeting hypnotized him. His job no longer mattered. He took a step in her direction. She blinked and looked up. Their eyes locked and everything he felt in the closet rushed back into him at once.

Sara moved toward him, but stopped just before she reached him. She crossed her arms at the wrist, grabbed the hem of her T-shirt, and pulled it over her head. As she dropped the shirt to the ground, his eyes roamed over her skin and heat filled every inch of his body. She reached behind her back and unhooked her bra. It fell loose at the sides, but stayed in place.

He closed the gap between them and lifted his palm to her cheek. "I don't want to take advantage of you."

"You're not."

His thumb traveled over her parted lips, and she closed her eyes. His hand moved down her neck to her shoulder. He slipped his fingers between her bra strap and shoulder.

"I also don't want to stop kissing you."

"Then don't," she whispered. "Don't ever stop."

Chapter Thirty-nine

Lying on the soft carpet, Sara rolled toward Logan and slid her hand across his contoured torso. The scars scattered across his skin mesmerized her. Though she had seen them before, in the aftermath of being with him, they had a much different impact on her. He accumulated each one of them doing his job, protecting someone, saving someone from evils of which she knew nothing. Now she was his job, the one he protected, the one he saved time and again, in more ways than one.

Her stomach bottomed out with the rush of memories of him kissing her, of clothes flying off, of him picking her up. Her face flushed with thoughts of her legs wrapped around his hips and her back slamming into the wall, both engrossed in a never-ending kiss while her fingernails dug through the layers of skin on his back. Sex had never been so intense with Stephen. She wondered if it was always like that with Logan or if it was only because of the circumstances. She really wanted to find out.

Logan raised his head. Wrapping his arm around her, he brought her body in close to him. With her cheek resting on his warm shoulder, he kissed the top of her head. She closed her eyes and enjoyed the feeling of his fingers combing through her hair.

"I'm sorry, Sara."

She angled her head so she could see his face. "Why are you

sorry?"

"I never meant to…" His gaze wandered away from her face. "I tried hard not to—"

"Don't be sorry. I'm not."

"You're not?"

Emboldened by their encounter, she inched up his body until her face floated above his. "Not at all."

"Then I'm not either." His hand pressed down on the back of her head, bringing her lips to him.

Sara lost herself in his kiss again, as if something possessed her body and mind. Having only been with one man before now, she didn't know how to distinguish normal from extraordinary. Stephen and Logan were day and night in every comparison, and she very much preferred the night.

Desire stirred in her and she lifted her head away from him. He took her face in his hands, his thumbs moving over her skin. Her eyelids dropped at his stimulating touch.

"Don't close your eyes," he said, as he brushed the backs of his fingers against her cheek.

She opened them again and smiled. "Why not?"

"You have the most beautiful eyes."

She laughed and shook her head. "I have dull, brown eyes, the same as millions of other people."

"No, you don't. I love your eyes. I've always thought that, since the first time I saw you."

"Are you kidding? Your eyes are the ones that are worth mentioning. They were the first thing I noticed." Even now, she slipped away into a hypnotic state as she stared into them. "I don't know what to call them. Ice blue, translucent, incredible." She folded her arms on his chest and rested her chin on her hands, still captivated by him.

The corners of Logan's mouth twitched and turned upward. In the few days she had known him, he had only given a couple hints that his lips could move in that direction. As his smile grew, it lit up his eyes and warmed Sara's heart.

"You're smiling," she said, her own mouth evolving into a large smile. "I didn't know you could do that."

He laughed and his lips parted, his smile now fully formed. "I know how to smile," he said.

"You should do it a lot more often."

Something in his eyes flickered and his smile died down. The sudden change in his expression reminded her of reality. They were still in danger and would be until he got her into the hands of the FBI, who would make her disappear for however long it took to put her father in prison for life. Tomorrow could be the last day she ever saw Logan, something that passionate sex and sweet exchanges would not change.

Logan gently rolled her over onto her back and hovered several inches over her. "Sara, nothing about our situation is good," he said, as if reading her mind. "Even if it was, I don't…" His words drifted off and he tucked strands of her hair behind her ear.

Pain clenched her heart. She had become attached to a man she barely knew in a complicated scenario. More than that, she was still engaged to another man. By sleeping with Logan, she cheated on Stephen. Lying with Logan now, his naked body covering hers like a blanket, the desire to be with him again surged through her veins, refusing to be ignored. All of it, cheating. There was no taking back what happened between them, though she wouldn't change it if she could.

Logan ran his tongue over his bottom lip and he took a deep breath. "If our situation was different, I wouldn't waste any time. Right now, though, where I am, even if we could do all that, I'm not…" He looked down and his mouth tightened as pain flashed in his eyes. "I'm not free to—"

Sara touched her fingers to his mouth. She lifted her head and brushed her lips against his. "I'm not either, Logan. I wish I were and I wish you were, but that's not the way it is for us." She lowered her head back to the carpet and laced her fingers behind his neck. "But as much as it will rain all over us tomorrow, for tonight, can't we just… pretend?"

He nodded and a small smile contorted his mouth. "Until this ends."

Chapter Forty

Sara stretched awake on the floor of the guest bedroom. Her eyes fluttered open and she smiled to see Logan next to her. As she studied him, she sucked in her bottom lip. He seemed so peaceful in sleep, unlike during waking hours, when he carried more than his fair share of burdens.

She got to her feet and crept through the room to the hallway. She made her way down to the restroom, grateful Logan suggested they get dressed before falling asleep. Though he wanted to be dressed in case they needed a quick getaway, her own insecurities made her happy to not have to walk down the hallway naked in the middle of the night.

After using the bathroom, Sara decided to wash up before going to bed. Excitement coursed through her body and she knew sleep would not come easy. With every kiss, every moment spent with him, she grew a little more addicted to Logan.

She couldn't take back what she had done, yet she felt no hint of guilt she would have expected from cheating on her fiancé. In the past two days, having distanced herself from Stephen, she realized marrying him would have been the worst mistake of her life. She never wanted to spend her life with him, but had only agreed to the relationship because of her father. Now that they were apart, she recognized the ridiculousness of the arrangement.

Stephen never made her feel as important, protected, and loved as Logan did when he made love to her... whether frantic and greedy as he was the first time or tender and gentle as he had been the second time. Her bond with Logan ran deep, encased in unbreakable cement, yet pulled them together with its strong, magnetic force. She had never once experienced those emotions with Stephen, and no matter how many years they would have spent together married, she never would have.

More than that, she had experienced how incredible it was to be with someone who shared a mutual attraction with her. To look into the eyes of someone and see the reflection of her own wild, reckless desire. To soak up the touch of a man who cared about her, and not because of her father. Logan represented everything that was missing in her dead-end relationship with Stephen. The passion, desire, need, urgency, respect, and care. And one day, maybe even the love.

Sara leaned against the bathroom counter, rested her palms on the edge, and closed her eyes. A large smile overcame her face and she bounced up and down with her thoughts about Logan, as if a giddy teenager took over her mind and body. She wished she could share her experiences with Mary right now. They were too amazing to keep locked away for long.

Footsteps coming down the hall interrupted her thoughts. She stared at the door, knowing she should go out and meet Logan, but terrified to move. Seeing him outside the bedroom would be strange the first time it happened, yet she desperately wanted to be close to him again.

She grabbed the doorknob and pulled the door open. A man she didn't recognize grabbed her arm and yanked her to him. She yelped as she collided with him. He slapped his hand over her mouth and lifted a gun to her head. "Quiet, darlin'. No one's gonna hear you anyway."

Her eyes widened and flicked to the left, toward the bedroom where she left Logan.

"He can't help you now," the man said. "Let's go."

He dragged her down the hall to the bedroom. When her eyes adjusted to the dark, she saw Logan on the floor with a shotgun to his temple. She lurched forward, but the man tightened his grip on her and put the barrel of his gun to her head.

"Let's get them wrapped up and out of here," the man with

the shotgun said. He grabbed Logan's arm and lifted him to his feet.

Logan locked eyes with her. "Just do what they say," he whispered, "and you'll be just fine."

"What about you?" The words gurgled out as a whisper.

"He'll be dead," said the man who held her. His cruel laugh bounced around the room and brought tears to Sara's eyes.

"Don't hurt him," she said. "I'm the one you want, not him. He was just doing his job."

"You don't know what the hell you're talking about," the man with the shotgun said.

Sara heard footsteps behind her, but the gun against her head scared her into not turning around.

In front of her, Logan's eyes narrowed as he looked past her. "What the—"

The man with the shotgun smashed it into Logan's head, knocking him to the ground. Despite Sara's cries for the man to stop, he hit Logan again, and Logan stopped moving.

"Blindfold her," a man's voice said behind her.

Sara only had a second to think about the somewhat familiar voice before a blindfold wrapped around her head, covering her eyes. The man next to her took her arm again, escorted her out of the room, and helped her down the stairs. Toward the bottom of the stairs, the clunk of Logan's body being dragged down the steps tore into her heart.

After going outside into the cold night air, a car door opened from somewhere in front of her. The man pushed her into the seat and she slid over until she ran into someone else on the other side of her. The man climbed in next to her, and the feeling of two large bodies on either side of her made her claustrophobic.

"Put your wrists together on your lap," the man said.

She obeyed, and someone wrapped a tight binding around her wrists.

"Now, just sit there and be a good girl," he said. "We have a bit of a drive ahead of us."

"Where are we going?"

"No talking," the man told her. "I wouldn't want to have to knock you out like we did Logan."

Sara lifted her bound hands and lowered her head, touching her forehead to her fingers. Silently, she prayed like never before.

Chapter Forty-one

I've been in far worse spots than this.

Logan chanted his mantra over and over until he gathered enough strength to open his eyes. He lifted his aching head and took inventory of his surroundings. The gray concrete beneath his boots and the concrete walls stained from water damage told him it was an unfinished basement, but he didn't know where. His location wouldn't matter until he freed himself from the metal chair to which he was bound.

The handcuffs that restrained him to the chair bit into his wrists, but he could freely move his head to look around. He leaned forward and made note of the several knots in the rope that secured his ankles to the legs of the chair. He reclined back in the chair, tensed all his muscles, and tried to rock the chair out of position. The chair didn't budge. He alternately moved each of his legs up and down, but the rope was too tight to work his way out of it. He'd have to find another way to free himself.

Looking to his left, he saw a rusty, metal tray with tools on it. It sat too far away for him to reach it, but not so far that he couldn't identify each tool. Pliers, knives, cutters, a drill, a hammer, and a saw. All useful in the art of torture. Langston would never allow him to leave this world without experiencing a bit of pain first.

To take his mind off his immediate future, Logan searched the depths of his memory for anything that could help him figure out his location and who had him. He thought about his night with Sara and how amazing it felt to hold her, touch her, and kiss her. After wanting her for so long, the release of being with her was incomparable. He had not wanted to take advantage of her vulnerability, but she had assured him that wasn't the case.

He had opened up to her and allowed her inside his world. In turn, he let his guard down and they were both taken by the very men from which he swore he would protect her. He had failed again, in so many ways, and while he would probably not get out of the situation alive, Sara's future was uncertain. He hoped Mathers and Langston would grant her life, but what kind of life would that be, married to a man who used her for his own gain and could turn on her at any time when he decided he had no more use for her? How would she ever feel safe again? How could she ever trust anyone? Sara deserved so much more.

A memory sparked in the back of his mind, of lying on the carpet with the shotgun barrel flush against his temple. Sara had come in with the other man holding a gun on her, a terrified expression on her face. Then, another man walked in. Someone familiar. Someone he knew.

No.

"Good to see you're awake," a man's voice came from behind him.

Logan squeezed his eyes shut, not wanting to believe his ears. He knew to whom that voice belonged, knew it almost as well as he knew his own voice. But surely his eyes and ears had deceived him. It wasn't possible.

It couldn't be.

The man walked around to the front of him and Logan opened his eyes, bracing himself to finally face the mole, the leak in The Boys Club. The man who had betrayed him, betrayed Karen. The last person on earth he expected to see standing in front of him.

"You don't look very happy to see me," Jack said. "I thought at the very least you'd be surprised."

"I am surprised," Logan said with a strangled voice. "I saw your body—"

"But you didn't stop to check, did you? That's 101 stuff,

Logan. Always check the bodies. Make sure someone is dead."

"I shouldn't have had to check to make sure my best friend—my brother—was dead. I never thought he would do something like this."

"Then maybe you didn't know me as well as you thought."

"What did you... I mean, why? How?"

Jack let out an incredulous laugh. "Well, I wasn't dead."

"Clearly."

He pulled a chair up in front of Logan and sat down. Resting his elbows on his knees, he said, "After you left your undercover job working with Langston, he spent a lot of time searching for you. Once he learned your identity, he also found out I worked with you. That's when he approached me."

"You've been working for him all this time?"

"Not at first, of course. A lot of threats were made, but I eventually came around to his way of doing things. Plus he pays a hell of a lot more."

Logan forced his next question out. "You knew about Karen?"

"No," Jack said, remorse crossing his face. "Karen was never a target. She wasn't supposed to be there—"

"You *knew* he was coming after me?" Logan's stomach churned. "That he would do it at my house?"

"She wasn't supposed to be there!" Jack walked around behind his chair and rested his palms on the back. "You talked so much about how she was going to her parents' house for the week. You said she was leaving the day before—"

"But she didn't leave!"

"That's not my fault!" Jack stared at Logan, his anger and hatred emanating from his eyes. "That wasn't the plan."

"Your plan backfired." From the angry expression contorting Jack's face, it was as if Jack blamed Logan for Karen's death just as much as Logan blamed himself. "You were never one to complain about the pay, so why the hell would you work with Langston?"

"You are always the hero," Jack said. "Everyone always looks to you to solve a problem, to take on the tough jobs. I grew up in the shadow of the great Gabe Logan, knowing I'd never be good enough to be at the top. Didn't matter how hard I worked or how many times you messed up. Schaffer always elevated you and left the rest of us scrounging for scraps."

"So you wanted me dead over what amounts to little more than a jealous temper tantrum? Daddy loved me more than you or something immature like that?"

"You can joke all you want, but you're the one tied up right now, not me. You always were on top. Work, Karen, everything. You had your perfect life, married with a kid on the way. The rest of us had to pick up the slack when you left, and all Schaffer could talk about was how he wanted to get you back so that you could take over one day. You didn't even work there anymore! And then Karen was in the car instead of you." Jack stormed over to him and pushed his finger in Logan's face. "You were supposed to die that day, not her!"

Something in the way Jack responded twisted Logan's gut. A strange, jealous rage punctuated his words and consumed his face.

As much as he didn't want to, Logan kept his eyes locked onto Jack's. "So, kill me and leave her alone, pregnant? Or what *was* the plan there, Jack? Were you trying to eliminate me so you could take my place with Schaffer and with Karen?"

"You were never good enough for her," he said.

"You're right. I wasn't. But you sure as hell weren't, either."

Jack's fist connected with Logan's cheek. Logan straightened out his neck from the blow and ignored the pain. He had to somehow get through to Jack, to make him realize he could still turn around and make the right decision.

"Whose body was in the safe house in your stead?"

"One of our guys you killed in the woods."

"Yeah, sorry about that."

"He was a nobody. Expendable."

"Except everybody that works for Langston eventually becomes expendable."

Jack chuckled and shook his head. "I see what you're doing. Trying to make me think that one day, Langston will get rid of me. That's not going to work, Logan. Langston needs me too much."

The black hole of his situation swirled around Logan, swallowing him up the more Jack spoke. "What does he need you for?"

"What do you think?" Jack asked, throwing his hands out to the side. "To take down Schaffer. Take down The Boys Club."

Logan closed his eyes and gave up on Jack. He was lost to

Langston's cause, brainwashed by the scent of money and the promise of revenge against Logan for whatever perceived wrongdoing. He had to find a way to get out of his restraints and get to Sara, but that wouldn't come through Jack.

"You see, Logan, with you gone, there's nothing stopping me from rising to the top and giving Langton the information he needs to get rid of Schaffer and his band of vigilantes."

"And just how do you explain that you're not dead?"

"I miraculously escaped the safe house, but you were captured with Sara. Schaffer needs someone new to take your place, and I'm next in line." He walked around behind Logan, leaned over, and spoke in Logan's ear. "Of course, Doctor Connors has an opening for someone new, too, doesn't she?"

Logan clenched his teeth and jerked on his bindings, but the cuffs only dug further into his skin.

"You broke her heart and then ran off and died on her. She'll need someone to console her through the late nights, to let her know that there are much better things on her horizon."

"Leave her out of this," Logan said.

Jack rose back to his full height and sat back down in his chair. "I don't think you have a say in it any longer." He leered and his eyes widened in an innocent manner. "I promise to treat her right."

"You son of a—"

"Speaking of which," Jack said, "I see you treated someone right just as soon as you were alone with her."

Logan froze. How could Jack possibly know about his night with Sara? "I don't know what you're talking about."

"Ah, come on, now. When we were tying you up, the back of your shirt slipped down a bit and I noticed what I thought was a cut. Turned out, they were fingernails, running straight down your back. Only one way that happens."

Logan's heart stopped. If Jack told Mathers or Langston about his time with Sara, it would not end well for either of them.

Jack propped his elbows up on his knees. "You thought your team was dead and you just broke Doctor Connors's heart. You couldn't even wait until we were in the ground and the good doctor wallowed in her pound of consolation ice cream before jumping in bed with Sara? She was the *job*, Logan. Guess you decided not to follow that straight and narrow, after all."

Logan tightened his lips and remained silent, while staring Jack down. Yes, he had screwed up, and he was a bastard for it. He had toyed with Allie's heart and then slept with Sara. No matter how he justified his actions, he was wrong. But Jack's statements also made him realize how hard he had fallen for Sara to do those things.

"Don't worry," Jack said. "I won't tell Mathers about any of this. If he knew, he just might shoot you and take away all my fun."

"I don't know what it is that I did to you," Logan said, "but whatever it is, I'm sorry. I always regarded you as my closest friend, as family. I would never intentionally hurt you, Jack. Not now, not ever."

Jack's expression turned serious. "It's a little late for that now, don't you think?"

The door behind Logan opened again, and Jack rose to his feet. A hefty man of about 250 pounds of muscle spread out over six feet of height walked up to the tray with the tools. Logan made note of the key ring on his belt, which held the key that appeared to belong to his handcuffs cuffs.

"Logan," Jack said, "I'd like you to meet my friend Xander." He turned to the goliath. "Xander, this is Logan, my former friend." Jack grinned at Logan. "You two will be spending some time together. In fact, Xander is going to get to know you very intimately over the next several hours."

Watching Xander fumble with the tools on the tray, Logan tried to remain stoic, but failed in that task. Unless a miracle happened, the only thing he could hope for was a quick death.

Chapter Forty-two

Sara rocked back and forth on the edge of the bed and stared at the door in front of her, waiting for someone to come through it. The more time that passed, the more her body trembled at the unknown. But as much as she worried about her own fate, Logan remained a constant in her mind. The men that took them had no regard for him, not with the way they knocked him out and let his body flop down the stairs.

When the men had brought her into the room what seemed like forever ago, they removed her blindfold and restraints. After shutting her in the bedroom, Sara explored the room, much as she had when she first woke up after Logan kidnapped her. The bedroom contained the standard, expected bedroom furniture: bed with an intricate, iron frame, large oak dresser with an attached mirror, matching bedside table, and an armchair in the far corner.

She checked the drawers of the dresser and bedside table, but found them empty. The closet also had nothing she could use as a weapon, and trying the mirror trick again without a towel to hold between her and the glass could prove painful. With nothing left to lose, she twisted the doorknob back and forth, but a lock prevented the door from opening.

Sitting on the bed, Sara's anxious thoughts kept her company until a key entered the lock on the door. Sara jumped off the bed, ready to face her kidnapper.

Stephen walked into the room and stormed toward her. Before she could get a word out, he grabbed her arms. Shaking her, he asked, "What the hell are you doing with Gabriel Logan?"

"He kidnapped me, him and some other men."

"That was two days ago! His team is dead, and my understanding is he was very lax on your security. You could have easily gotten away from him."

"I was scared, Stephen! I didn't know what to do. He said..." Sara shuddered with her tears. "He said Dad was going to have me killed on our honeymoon and that you knew about it. Maybe you were even involved in it."

Stephen let her go and walked around her.

"I didn't believe him about you, but it still frightened me. I'm still not sure what—"

Her words faded at his laugh. "Son of a..." His laughter grew.

Sara's brow creased and her stomach dropped at the rising pitch of his laugh. "You did know, didn't you?"

He looked in her direction and smiled. "You are in way over your head here."

Sara shook her head. Somewhere deep inside, she had held out hope that even if her father did put a hit on her, at least Stephen wouldn't have been involved. But Logan had been right. Stephen knew all along. He knew while they wrapped up their wedding plans, while he made love to her the morning of her kidnapping, and while he lied to her about loving her.

"How much?" she asked.

"What?"

"How much did you and Dad pay someone to kill me?"

His tongue jetted across his lips as he stared at her. "$50,000."

Sara's jaw dropped at his admission.

"If it's any consolation, that's a large amount to pay for a hit."

"Consolation? That you could even put a price on my life at all is..." Numbness crawled over her brain and she wandered away from him. Leaning against the wall, she said, "I can't believe you were in on it. I thought you loved me, at least I wanted to think that. I was willing to spend my life with you, to try and love you.

And you were going to kill me."

"You weren't going to die. Yes, Hugh took out the hit and wanted it to happen during the honeymoon, but I told him I could contain you."

"Contain me?"

"The kidnapping was orchestrated to get to Logan. I told Hugh that we could use the hit to draw Logan out into the open and get him to kidnap you. Then, when he had you at the safe house, we would come in and get you. We didn't anticipate a few mistakes that the team made or that Logan would get you out. You were never in danger there, though. I wouldn't have let you die."

Sara could only focus on Stephen's earlier words. "Contain me? What does that mean?"

"It means that I could get you to take the teaching job or stay at home as a wife and mother and we wouldn't have to worry about the accounts you worked on."

"You paid someone to kill me on our honeymoon."

"Yes, but I also talked Hugh out of killing you."

"So, instead you used me as bait to get to Logan."

Stephen moved over to her and caressed her cheek. "I know it's hard for you to comprehend, but I never would have let someone kill you. You're too important to me."

"I'm only important to you so you can marry into my family."

"That's true, but my reasoning doesn't make you any less important. Now that this is all done, we're going to forget all of this and go on with our lives."

"Go on with our lives? You mean get married and start a family, as if nothing has happened? After Dad tried to have me killed, which you knew about, and then you used me as a pawn in your sick little game?"

Anger flashed across his face and he tightened his hand around her arm. "I'm willing to admit I was wrong in helping your dad out with this and I'm talking him into keeping you alive, but you need to watch yourself. After things settle down from your reappearance, we will get married. If you want to live, you have no choice."

Sara squirmed under his hold, the evil in his eyes terrifying her. She had never experienced that side of him and she didn't want to keep provoking him.

"I want to live," she said.

He loosened his grip. "That's the right answer."

She lifted her hand to rub her sore arm, and he snatched her wrist.

"Where the hell is your ring?"

"They... they forced me to give it them. I didn't want to, but they made me. It must have burned up in the fire at the safe house."

"This just keeps getting better and better." Stephen huffed. "I guess we'll have to get you a new one."

Sara let out a shaky breath, grateful that he didn't press the issue. "What are you going to do with Logan?" As soon as the question left her lips, she knew she had made a mistake.

The back of Stephen's hand crashed into her cheek. "Logan is none of your concern. I never want to hear that name come from your mouth again."

Salty tears crossed over her stinging skin and invaded her mouth. "I'm sorry," she said, reaching for her cheek.

He stared at her for a moment. "Maybe you should see what we're going to do with Logan. It will do you some good to understand just how lucky it is that you're more use to me alive than dead."

Stephen grabbed her wrist, dragged her out of the room, and forced her down the steps to the basement. At the end of the dimly lit hallway, he opened a door. Bound to a chair, Logan sat in the middle of the concrete room. His hands were cuffed to the arms of the chair while rope secured his legs to the chair.

Sara's heart broke at the sight of his bloodied face and the swelling over his left eye. It appeared the men had continued their beating once he woke up here. She wanted to run to him and free him from the restraints, but Stephen's arm circled her waist and held her to him.

"You see, babe," he said into her ear, "your little friend here and I have a long history together. He's been quite the detriment to your dad's dealings over the past several years. He betrayed us in the worst possible way. These two men are going to make him suffer a lot before they let him die."

Sara raised her eyes to the two other men, shocked to recognize one of them. "Jack!"

"Hey there, Sara," Jack said. "Sorry about all the deception."

Sara flinched at Jack's matter-of-fact statement. He didn't seem to care about the gravity of his involvement. Logan believed he had lost his friend, yet he was alive and working for both Stephen and her dad. Logan had told her he thought there was a leak in his organization, but she couldn't imagine what Logan was going through knowing his closest friend had betrayed him.

Her eyes fell on the metal tray next to Logan and the instruments sitting on them. "You don't have to hurt him," she told Stephen.

"But we do," Stephen said. "He's hurt us all and he deserves it. Jack, why don't you and Xander give Sara a little taste of what he will experience before he dies?"

Sara shook her head as hard as she could. "Don't do this."

The large man she didn't recognize, Xander, walked over to Logan's left side and lifted his index finger. He wrapped his fingers around it and snapped it upward.

Logan gritted his teeth and let out a loud groan. Xander then gripped Logan's thumb and broke it as well.

The sound of cracking bone and Logan's outcry resonated in Sara's ears. "Stop it! Please don't hurt him anymore."

"There are so many body parts that can be removed from a person," Stephen said, as Xander picked up a large pair of cutters. "If done right, one can practically dismember a man before killing them. Fingers, ears, tongue, teeth, nose, eyes." He pressed his mouth to her ear. "And then there's everything below the belt."

Sara's stomach revolted and she doubled over, but Stephen straightened her up. He wrapped his hand around her face and forced her head up.

"No, no," he said. "You're going to watch this. I want you to see exactly what's going to happen to him."

Xander moved back to Logan's left hand and placed the cutters around the bottom of his little finger. Logan tightened his jaw and kept his eyes on hers.

"Don't hurt him," she said. "Stephen, please don't—"

"Hearing you beg for mercy makes me want to hurt him all the more." Stephen gripped her tighter. "Why don't you move that up a knuckle?" he asked the man. "Gives us more to work with later when we're running out of parts to take from him."

As Stephen directed, Xander adjusted the cutters until they rested between the first and second knuckles. Logan's chest heaved up and down with rapid, audible breathing.

"No!" Sara cried out. "Don't!"

Xander squeezed the cutters, severing the finger. Logan cried out, but then clamped his mouth shut and lifted his eyes to the ceiling.

Sara could barely see him through the mess of tears coating her eyes. "No," she whispered, suddenly drained of all energy. Her weak limbs collapsed into a mass of jelly beneath her, but Stephen kept her standing up.

"I trust you two can handle this," he said. "I know you're eager to get to it, but spread it out so that it takes all night. When he arrives in the morning, Hugh will want to see Logan alive, but that doesn't mean we can't have a little fun until then." He planted a kiss on Sara's cheek, lingering for a moment.

"No." The word gurgled out of her without any forcefulness. She wanted to save him, but even if Stephen wasn't restraining her, there was nothing she could do with the others in the room.

"I'm going to spare Sara the rest of this," Stephen said. "I'll be back to check on your progress in a few hours."

Sara watched Logan for as long as she could before Stephen turned her around and led her out of the room. When they reached her room, he said, "You wanted to know the truth about what we did. That's what happens to people when they cross either me or Hugh."

She had no strength left in her body, and it took every ounce of it she could find to remain standing. She leaned against the wall with her hand pressed against her nauseous stomach. "You're a monster," she whispered.

"That's no way to talk to your future husband, is it?" Stephen wiped her tears from her face. "What's happening to him is a long time coming. Once he's in pieces and dead, Hugh will be happy and won't mind that I'm letting you live. Logan thought he'd play the hero and save you, so think of it as him trading his life for yours."

Sara couldn't think at all, let alone follow his rationale. Fresh tears replaced the ones Stephen brushed off her cheeks. When he pressed his mouth to hers, she didn't try to fight against the soul-sucking kiss, not after seeing what he had done to Logan. In her mind, she couldn't stop seeing Xander cutting off his finger, and Stephen's promise to do much worse to him rang in her ears. The first moment Stephen left her alone, she had to find a way to get to him. Every second she was away from him was one more opportunity for them to kill him a little more. She had to get to him fast before there was nothing left of him to save.

Chapter Forty-three

Logan lifted his sweaty head, his eyes following Jack as he walked over to Xander and spoke in a low tone. The pain from his left hand radiated up his arm and into his core. It was nothing compared to what they had in store for him, but he tried to focus instead on his escape route.

Sara now knew without a doubt the evils that lay behind Mathers's shiny exterior. That she had witnessed them torturing Logan hurt him more than Xander ever could. Her life didn't cross over into this nasty world of evil and criminals, of pain and greed. Logan wished he could take that image away from her so she wouldn't be scarred with the sight forever, but the only thing he could do was to get her out of this no-win situation and over to the FBI where she could start anew.

Before he could do that, he had to escape.

The tray Xander left next to him had enough tools on it that he could easily kill both Xander and, if it came down to it, Jack, but first he had to take advantage of the one mistake Xander had made during his short torture session. The only way to do that was to keep Jack talking long enough to give him the opening he needed.

"Tell me something, Jack," Logan said.

Jack whirled around and fixed a curious stare on Logan. "What's that?"

Behind Jack, Xander walked away, and Logan smiled inwardly at the sound of the door opening and closing. As soon as Jack let down his guard, Logan could act.

"Why didn't you kill me in the barn last week?" Logan asked. "You had the perfect opportunity to kill me or take me."

"When I went to the barn, you were already supposed to be on your way to Mathers. I didn't expect you to get out and kill my men. I had orders to bring you in alive, and if I took you in, my cover would have been blown."

"No," Logan said. "You wouldn't want anyone knowing who you are. Then how was it that you didn't find us in the Flagstaff safe house the first time you came?" Logan asked. "We were hiding in the cubby Schaffer had built, which you knew about."

"I wasn't there that time," Jack said. "I was a few hours away in the wrong direction. Otherwise, you would have been found."

"Guess you didn't communicate too well with your boys there," Logan said. "Same way as they didn't know to find us in the secret bedroom at the first safe house."

Jack huffed and sat in the chair in front of Logan. "I wouldn't be talking like that if I were in your shoes."

Glancing down at his left hand, the pain stabbing through his arm, Logan shrugged. "What more do I have to lose at this point? Mathers was pretty clear that I'm not getting out of this thing alive and I won't die before Hugh comes in the morning."

"But we still have the okay to deliver a lot more pain to you before the sun rises."

"You've already done your worst. Being in on Karen's death, working for Langston. The rest is just some body parts that I won't miss too much when I'm dead."

"We all do what we have to do," Jack said, with the swipe of his hand and a snide smile.

"Yes, we do. So, at what point did you decide to jump over to this side? Was there an event, something that made you think it was better over here?"

Jack's smile faded and his gaze fell down to the floor. "Nothing clear cut, if that's what you're searching for. It wasn't an easy decision for me. It definitely made it much harder for me to stay after Karen died."

Logan held onto Jack's words and demeanor as hope he could still be reached. "You can come back, you know. You can always come back."

"You and I both know that's not true." He lifted his eyes. "Who says I even want to?"

Silence filled the room, pushing the men further away from each other. Logan couldn't find a way to combat Jack's correct assumption. He could never come back, even if he wanted to, not after everything he had done. He would have to face due punishment, and that alone would be reason for him to stay on Langston's team.

The door creaked open behind Logan, and Jack lifted his head.

"Mathers wants to see you," Xander said, as he walked back to his tray of torture.

Jack rose to his feet and went over to Xander. Looking down at Logan, he said, "We'll begin again when I get back. I'm starting to get bored with the conversation."

Logan squeezed his eyes shut and pulled in as much oxygen as his lungs would allow. He let out the breath when the door shut. He didn't have long to act. After Jack returned, he might not have another chance.

"I'm feeling dizzy," Logan said. "Blood loss, maybe."

"You're not in a hospital," Xander said, "and I'm not your nurse."

"I realize that, but I'm sure Jack doesn't want me passing out for round two. How about some water?"

Xander tugged on each of the handcuffs and ensured his leg restraints were tight before leaving the room.

Logan went straight to work. With both his thumb and index finger broken, his hand was a lot more compact. Since Xander cut off half his pinky as well, it made it much easier to wriggle that finger out of the cuff, although much more painful.

With his entire body tensed and lips mashed together to limit the sound of his groaning, Logan jerked his hand back and forth while pulling out of the cuff. The metal clanked against the chair when his hand came out. Pain zapped his body and threatened to shut him down, but he couldn't give up. Using his middle and ring finger, he picked up a knife from the tray and tucked it into his palm, so the blade rested against his wrist and lower arm. He laid his hand back down onto the arm of the chair, hoping Xander would not notice the missing cuff right away.

Seconds later, the door opened behind him. Hearing only one set of footsteps enter, Logan braced himself to act. Xander moved in front of him and lifted a small cup to Logan's lips. Logan tilted his head back with the cup, as if drinking, and used every bit of strength he could find to bring the knife around into Xander's neck.

The cup bounced off the ground, as Xander reached for his neck. He pulled out the knife, and blood spurted with every beat of his heart. Xander fell to the floor.

Logan angled his body down and reached for the retractable key holder on Xander's belt loop. He pulled it up and unlocked his other cuff. With a functioning hand, he snagged the saw off the tray and worked on the rope restraint around his ankles. Jack wouldn't be gone for much longer, and while Logan had hoped he wouldn't have to deal with him, there didn't seem to be a way around it.

Freed from the last of his restraints, Logan retrieved the knife he used on Xander and wiped it free of blood. He stood on the side of the door, waiting for the doorknob to turn. His mind flashed to his childhood with Jack, their later teenage years playing baseball together with some of the other kids from the Church. He shook the memory away, knowing it wouldn't help him do the inevitable. The man that helped torture him was not the same kid he grew up with. He wasn't even the same man that stood next to Logan at his wedding as his best man. Now, he was the enemy, and he stood in the way of saving Sara.

The knob rotated and the door flung open. Jack stopped after taking only a few steps. Logan held the knife at the perfect angle to strike, and brought it down without hesitation.

Jack whirled around, and the knife scraped across his arm instead of burying itself in his body. He knocked the knife out of Logan's hand and stunned Logan with a quick punch. Jack reached for his gun, but Logan rushed him, knocking him into the metal chair. Logan ignored the pain in his left hand, as he held Jack down and pummeled him with his right.

An arm wrapped around Logan's neck from behind and dragged him away from Jack. The arm tightened against his throat. Logan used his good hand to pull down on the arm, and cracked the man's ribs with his other elbow. As Logan's vision blurred, the man gave into the assault on his side. His hold on Logan lessened.

Logan turned around and threw a knee into the man's stomach. The man doubled over, and Logan brought his head down into his knee. He threw the man back against the wall, just as Jack knocked Logan off his feet.

Logan scrambled back up, jumping to the side as Jack fired his gun at him. He tackled Jack, and the gun clanked against the floor. Logan grabbed the gun and shot Jack in the chest. He turned at the sound of footsteps running toward him and shot the other man in the head. The man fell, and Logan looked back at Jack, who coughed up blood.

Throwing the gun to the side, Logan instinctively pressed down with his palms on the bullet hole, which gushed blood like an erupting volcano. Despite knowing the wound was fatal, Logan still held out hope he could stop the bleeding. That he could somehow save his friend. Jack tried to say something to Logan, but his head fell limp and his body stilled.

Logan kept his hands on Jack's chest for a moment, then sat down on the cold concrete beside his friend. He pushed back his emotion and reminded himself that Sara was still somewhere in the house.

He wiped streaks of blood from his hands across his jeans and grabbed the gun. He found a rag on a workbench in the back of the room and secured it around his throbbing hand as a makeshift bandage. Checking the clip in the gun, he found it full, minus the two bullets he had expended. He made sure a bullet was in the chamber and left the room in search of Sara.

Chapter Forty-four

Logan crept up the stairs to the main floor of the house with the gun leading the way. He remained alert for any sound that would pinpoint Sara's location, but none came. Mathers most likely heard the sounds of the gunshots in the basement, but Logan hoped it hadn't caused him to run off with Sara in tow. If they had left, Logan's chances of ever finding her were slim.

Logan took the last stair through a door and into a hallway. His feet silently crossed over one another, only stopping to check out the rooms he passed. Just as he started upstairs, a noise on the main floor toward the back of the house caught his attention. He changed direction and moved toward the voices, one of which was Sara's.

He stepped into the kitchen, where Mathers had his hand on Sara's back, pushing her toward the back door. "Running away?" Logan asked. "I knew you were afraid of me."

Mathers wrapped his arm around Sara's neck and whipped around. Sara yelped when he thrust a gun against the side of her head. "You don't want to test me, not with her life on the line."

"Stephen—"

He slapped his hand over Sara's mouth before she could say anything else.

Logan took another step toward them, his gun steady in

front of him. "Oh, I don't have a problem testing you. You always were a bit of a pansy when it came to confrontation. Always had to do things behind the scenes so you didn't have to face the consequences."

Mathers narrowed his eyes. "I'm not screwing around with you today."

"Sure seems like it."

"Your problem is that you can't take any situation involving death seriously. Never could. You always had some smart remark for the person on the other end of the gun."

"Maybe that's because their incompetence level was just that ridiculous."

"Put the gun down, Logan," he said. "I know you don't want to see her pretty little brains all over the wall."

Logan held up his hand, but kept the gun pointed at Mathers. "Are you really going to shoot her?" he asked.

"If you force me to, yes."

Sara squealed under his palm.

"Won't that screw up all your plans?" Logan asked. "You need her alive so you can marry into the family and become an heir to Langston's empire. If you don't have her, you're not legitimate in his eyes."

"I'll take over whether or not I have the little whore to help me."

Anger swelled in Logan's chest, but he didn't let it distract him.

"Now, put down the gun," Mathers said.

Logan crouched, as if complying. "We both know you're not going to shoot her," he said. "But I will."

He quickly aimed and fired off a round into Sara's shin. She screamed and slumped down. As soon as her head fell away from the gun, Logan raised his gun and shot Mathers in the forehead. He raced over to pull Sara away so Mathers wouldn't land on top of her.

Gathering her into his arms, he said, "I'm so sorry, Sara." He brushed back her hair from her pained face.

"You shot me," she whispered.

"I know, and I wouldn't have if there was another way."

"Is he dead?"

Logan nodded.

She exhaled and closed her eyes. "This really hurts."

"I know it does, but you have to hang in there for me. You're losing blood, but I can't tie it off without knowing if anyone else is here." He glanced around the floor, but did not see the bullet that he shot into her.

"Your finger… we have to get it."

"It's too late," he said, moving to her side. "Put your arm around me. This is going to hurt a lot, but we need to get out of here."

Sara wrapped her arm around his neck and he held up as much of her weight as he could. He kept the gun raised at his side in case they ran into anyone else. She moaned every time she put a bit of weight on her leg.

Logan stopped walking, bent at the knees, and lifted her up, with his left arm propping her back up and his right hand holding the gun underneath her knees. "Hold onto my neck," he said.

She wrapped her arms around him and rested her head on his shoulder.

He stumbled a few times, but made it to the front door. A man stood next to an SUV, and Logan pulled the trigger beneath Sara's body before the man could get to his own gun. Sara jumped, but Logan held onto her.

"Just a few more feet," he said.

He set her down at the passenger side door of the SUV. She held onto the door while he went over to the man and fished the keys and a cell phone out of his pocket. Logan helped her settle into the front seat and walked back over to the man's body. Ignoring the pain in his hand, he worked quickly to remove the man's T-shirt. His teeth tore through the material so he could rip the shirt down the middle.

Back at the SUV, he used the shirt as a tourniquet around Sara's leg. She cried out a couple times, but he made sure to tie it tightly around her leg. Once the blood slowed its leaking, he moved over to the driver's side. After climbing in, he helped Sara with her seatbelt.

Sara leaned her head back and groaned.

"We'll get you some help," Logan told her. "Just try to sleep."

She turned to him, tears running down her cheeks. "It hurts."

Taking her hand, he said, "Hang in there, okay? It won't be too long."

Her eyes closed. She released his hand and folded her arms over her stomach.

Logan started the vehicle and called up their location on the GPS built into the dashboard. He sighed with relief when he saw they were less than two hours away from the Church.

After maneuvering onto the main highway, he checked Sara. She had fallen asleep, but her breathing seemed a bit shallow. Logan knew the pain could cause that, but it still worried him. He grabbed the cell phone and punched in Schaffer's emergency number. Schaffer answered on the second ring.

"It's Logan."

"Where the hell are you? I sent some men to the safe house in—"

"Mathers found us at the safe house. He had some help, but we managed to get away."

"Did you find out who the leak is?"

"Jack."

Silence came from the other end of the line.

"Are you there?" Logan asked, thinking he had dropped the call.

"How did he… how is that possible?" Schaffer asked.

"He wasn't dead. They put another guy in his place, someone I had taken out, and burned the house down so we'd think he was dead. I never got close enough to his body to know he was still alive."

"Where is he now?"

Logan hesitated, not wanting to rehash everything that took place.

"It's okay, Logan. We'll talk about it when you get here. How far away are you?"

"About two hours. I'm coming in hot, though. Sara's been shot and I've been injured. I need a surgeon for her to remove the bullet from her leg."

"I'll have Doctor Connors get a team in now. What are your injuries?"

"I have two broken fingers and another one missing. All on the same hand."

"I'll let her know that as well so she can determine the

treatment. Do you have the finger?"

"No. It had to be left behind."

"Okay," Schaffer said. "Damn it about Jack."

"We'll talk about it when I get there. Please make sure that a medical team is there when we arrive. I'm very worried about Sara."

"It will be done."

He disconnected the call and looked at Sara. She seemed to be in the same state, still shallow breathing, but sleeping. His own pain flared up and his eyes threatened to close, but he forced himself to stay awake and keep focused on staying in between the lines on the blacktop.

When he pulled into the Church's parking lot a couple hours later, his vision blackened, and he had to hold still for a moment so he wouldn't lose consciousness. He kept himself together long enough to pull the SUV up to the front doors. He jumped out of the vehicle and raced around to the passenger side.

Sara stirred awake when he opened the door. "Are we at the hospital?" she asked, her voice quiet and eyes distant.

"We're at the Church. They have a surgical team waiting for you."

"I don't want surgery," she said.

"They have to get the bullet out of your leg."

She leaned over to try to get out of the car. Logan almost collapsed under her weight, but managed to hold her up. He carried her to the front door, just as Schaffer ran outside. Allie followed with a couple nurses, who guided a gurney through the door.

Schaffer helped Logan get Sara onto the gurney, and the nurses strapped her down.

Logan turned to Allie. "You have a good surgeon?"

"The best. Same with the anesthesiologist. We made up a makeshift operating room, everything is sterilized, and they are all ready for her."

He watched the gurney disappear into the church and started to follow before tripping.

Schaffer and Allie caught his arms and kept him standing. They helped him into the church and in the elevator.

Allie examined his hand as the cab moved down to the basement. "I need to debride this wound. Schaffer tells me you don't have the finger."

All of his energy suddenly zapped, Logan shook his head

instead of responding verbally.

"I'm going to have the anesthesiologist put you out for this. It needs too much work to keep you awake."

"I'll be fine," Logan said. "Just go take care of Sara."

The elevator doors opened, and Logan tried to shrug Allie away as he walked through the doors. He made it halfway down the hall before he fell down and passed out.

Chapter Forty-five

Logan startled awake and sat straight up in bed. He looked around the room and recognized it as being in the Church. He let out a long breath and tried to calm his racing heart.

His left hand throbbed with pain, and he examined the bandage over it. He held it up to his chest and stroked his other hand over his wrist and the bandage. He always gave Allie a hard time about trying to give him pain medication, but for the first time he needed them.

Climbing out of bed, he walked over to the dresser, where his go-bag sat. The dust and grime covering the black reminded him of his journey with Sara. He frowned, realizing he had never been woken up to find out how she did in surgery.

He wandered into the empty hallway outside his room and made his way down to Allie's office. She looked up from her desk as he entered.

"Aren't you a sight?" she asked, with a lopsided smile. "How are you feeling?"

He glanced around the room, feeling a bit disoriented. "How long have I been out?"

"All night." She consulted her watch. "About 15 hours now."

"I guess I needed to sleep."

"When you woke up from your surgery, you were incoherent, confused, dizzy. You were suffering from extreme exhaustion, so I gave you something to encourage your body to do what it needed to do: sleep and rejuvenate. Kept you hooked up to your IV for a bit and let you rehydrate as well. I took that out this morning while you were still sleeping."

Logan touched the back of his right hand, noticing the bandage strip on it for the first time.

"You didn't get a lot of sleep on the job, did you?"

He shook his head. "How's Sara?"

"She's great. She's been up for hours now, has some pain, but nothing that we can't manage."

"When, uh… when are we releasing her to the feds?"

"Tomorrow morning." Allie shuffled some papers on her desk. "She's been asking about you. How you're doing, if she can see you. She's very concerned. I told her that once you woke up, you would check in on her."

"Where is she?"

"In the room next to yours. You should probably get cleaned up and see how you're feeling after that before you start making journeys around the Church." She leaned back in her chair and lowered her eyes back down to her desk. "She's a very pretty girl."

Logan read the meaning in her tone. "Allie—"

She held up her hand. "I can tell she cares about you, with as much as she's asked about you and your injuries. I'm sure when you spend time together in the field under difficult circumstances, you can grow attached to the person you're with."

Logan looked away from her, unsure of what to say.

"I'm not upset," she said. "You don't have to worry about me."

He met her eyes and nodded. They stared at each other for a tense moment, and then he pushed his chair back. Holding up his bandaged hand, he said, "Thanks for fixing me up." He walked toward the door.

"Hey, Logan."

He turned around, eyebrows raised.

"I'm sorry about Jack."

"Yeah," he said. "Me, too."

Back in his room, he took Allie's advice and hopped in the shower. After dressing, he walked to the room next door and knocked.

"Come in!" Sara's voice called through the door.

He eased the door open and went inside. Sara sat up in bed, propped up on pillows, her injured leg bandaged and on top of a wedge to keep it elevated. She threw the book in her hands down beside her.

"You're awake!"

He smiled at her enthusiasm. Allie hadn't lied when she said Sara was doing great. "I'm awake."

He sat on the edge of her bed, and she leaned over. Clamping her arms around him in a warm embrace, she whispered, "I was so worried about you."

They parted, and he said, "You're worse off than I am."

"Yeah, but you slept for so long. I was worried something was wrong."

"I didn't get much sleep on this job. It was time to catch up."

Her wide brown eyes searched his and he couldn't help himself. He leaned over and pressed his lips to hers, engaging her in a passionate kiss. He had not realized until now how much he missed kissing her.

Her cheeks turned pink as they parted. "I'm glad you're okay," she said.

"How's your leg?"

"It's healing okay. Doctor Connors gave me some pain medication, but I'm managing okay without having to take too many of them."

"I'm so sorry I had to shoot you."

She grabbed his hand and squeezed. "You saved my life. You have nothing to apologize for." She moved over in the bed and patted the empty space next to her.

Logan scooted up on the bed and stretched out beside her. "I hear you're leaving us tomorrow."

She sighed. "That's what Schaffer says. I asked him if you could come with me."

His heart skipped a beat, hoping that Schaffer may have granted her request, though he knew better. "What did he say?"

"Same thing you told me. It's too dangerous to have you with me."

"I wish it wasn't like that, but now you've seen what

Langston's men are capable of. I don't want to put you in any more danger. It's best that I don't know where you are."

"I understand," she said, picking up the paperback book beside her.

Logan frowned, as she closed the book. "We have books here?"

She laughed. "Of course you do! Schaffer brought in quite a few for me to choose from. I figure I'll be doing a lot of reading when I'm with the feds, so I wanted to get started."

He took the book from her hands. "*To Kill a Mockingbird*," he said and groaned. "Schaffer had me read this one when I was 16."

Sara tilted her head and grinned. "Oh, really? What do you remember about it?"

"Absolutely nothing," he said. At her laugh, he added, "I hate reading."

"Well, I love reading. I'm not so sure about country music, though."

His eyebrows shot up. "You don't like country music? You never said anything when we were listening to it in the car."

"I didn't want to offend you."

"You're offending me now."

"I guess we'll just have to stop talking then, won't we?" She smiled and gave him a quick kiss. "Do you realize this is the first semi-normal conversation we've ever had?"

"And I'd love to keep having it. I hate that you're leaving tomorrow."

"Me, too. But tonight, can't we just—"

"Pretend?" He rested the palm of his good hand against her cheek. "Until this ends."

Epilogue

Twenty-one months later...

Logan pulled the door open and rushed inside to escape the chilled air. He scraped his snow-covered boots against the black, rubber mat at the front door before continuing down the quiet hall. His shoes squeaked against the waxed floor and bounced off the bad acoustics, as he counted the passing halls until he reached D hall. He had checked out the layout of the building prior to coming here to make sure he took the most direct route. Pulling up the sleeve of his leather jacket, he hoped he wasn't too late. The full parking lot told him he still had some time.

He shoved his gloved hands into his pockets, still trying to warm up from the below zero temperatures. His blood had thinned after years of living and working primarily in warm weather climates. He couldn't understand how anyone would want to live in a place as cold as Kansas. It could be worse, he thought. He could be in Alaska.

Halfway down D hall, he slowed his pace and read the numbers on his left until he found D18. He stopped just before he reached the wooden door with one window. A knot formed in his stomach and he reconsidered his actions. He didn't belong here, so far away from home, not knowing the result of his intrusion.

But his heart overrode his brain, reminding him that after

everything he'd been through in the past four years, he could force his legs to move forward. Just three more feet.

He took the steps, his heart starting its pounding in his throat and head, canceling out everything else around him. Peeking in the window, he caught his breath.

Sara wrote out an unseen phrase on the chalkboard and turned to face her classroom. He heard her voice, but could not interpret any words. He was content just to watch her, with her hair pulled up into a ponytail, much longer than he remembered, and her light makeup accentuating her large, brown eyes. Every movement held an air of confidence and authority, one he had seen hints of during the time they spent together.

She rotated back to the chalkboard, this time in the direction of where he stood. She stopped herself halfway through the turn and the chalk tumbled out of her fingers, as her eyes fixed on his. Her lips parted, and Logan wondered if her surprise was positive.

Her mouth moved a little, as if trying to talk, and then she looked back at her class. He read her rapidly moving lips. "I'll be right back, class."

The closer she got to the door, the more nervous Logan became. She closed behind her, as she stepped out into the hall.

"Logan," she said, with a breathy voice. She covered her lips with her fingertips.

"Hi, Sara."

"How did you... I mean, when did you get here?"

"My plane landed a bit ago at Mid-Continent Airport. I drove straight here."

Her hands dropped to her side, but she remained speechless.

He realized the folly of showing up unannounced and wondered if he had made a mistake. "I probably shouldn't have come without letting you know first."

"No, it's fine. I'm just... I just—"

"It's okay. I should have called before just dropping by." He smiled at her hesitation. "You look great, Sara."

"I could say the same thing. I'm glad to see that smiling thing stuck with you."

Her words made his smile grow. "Maybe just a little. You changed your last name. Sara Bennett."

"I thought it was only fitting to officially change it to my mom's maiden name after everything that happened."

"I'm sure she'd approve of that."

"Schaffer came to the trial. He was there every day. I... I asked about you."

"He told me," Logan said.

Pain crossed her face and creased her brow. "I thought maybe you'd come at least one time with him—"

"I couldn't. I wanted to, but I couldn't."

"That's what he said. But I still kept hoping."

Logan took a step forward. "He told me you were incredible on the stand. That your testimony is what put Langston away."

"That's what they say," Sarah said. "I'd like to think it helped, but it was still scary. As powerful as he always looked in daily life, he looked so old and frail in that orange jumpsuit. It's strange how that one thing changed his whole appearance, but it didn't change my memory of what he'd done to me. To you."

Her gaze dropped to his gloved left hand, and he held it up. "I'm all healed now," he said. "It doesn't bother me at all anymore."

"I had nightmares about it," she said. "I couldn't get it out of my mind."

"I'm so sorry you had to witness all that. I wish I could take that away from you."

"Just knowing you're okay is more than enough for me." She shifted her weight and crossed her arms. "So, what are you doing in town? Do you have a job here?"

"In Wichita? No job. I'm just here to check on an old friend."

Sara smiled and looked down.

"Why move here?" he asked.

"After Langston was killed in prison, I couldn't stay in witness protection. His organization was pretty much dismantled already. I wanted to find a new place to start over. I thought this city sounded as good as any."

When Logan had heard about Langston's untimely end in the prison cafeteria—stabbed with a shank by someone he had crossed years earlier—he wasn't sure how his death would affect Sara. He now saw she hadn't missed a beat, and it probably served to strengthen her even more.

"Do you like it here?" he asked.

"Absolutely. Maybe a little cold for my taste and I haven't

found the ocean quite yet."

Logan laughed. "I only ask because while I'm not here for a job, it is still official business. I heard your teaching contract ends in a few months and you haven't yet signed a new one."

She rolled her eyes. "If I even get offered a new one. There are so many teacher layoffs throughout the country that I was lucky to get this job."

"What if you didn't have to worry about layoffs anymore? Steady, permanent job, great pay, and still doing what you love."

She arched an eyebrow. "And where exactly can I find a job like that?"

"Schaffer is finally retiring at the end of the year, and I'll be in charge of The Boys Club. We thought it would be a great idea to have a full-time teacher on staff. Someone who could help the new recruits with studying for their GED and other teaching duties as needed."

Her lips curled upward into a mischievous smile. "That sounds pretty cushy. Are benefits included in that package?"

"Oh, I don't know." Logan moved to her and lowered his head. "I'm sure we can come up with something."

She lifted up on her tiptoes and met his lips. Logan forgot all about being in the middle of a school hallway, until the sounds of "oohs" from behind her closed door started up. They broke away from each other and chuckled. Peeking over her head, he saw a few of her students with faces pressed against the glass. With a flushed face, Sara waved them away from the door.

When they disappeared, Logan said, "Go finish your class. I have to check into the hotel still. Then I'll pick you up for dinner and we can discuss the details. How's six o'clock?"

"That works." She thumped her forefinger against his chest. "I suppose you already know where I live."

He grinned. "Of course."

"I should have known." She stepped back and smiled. "I'll see you at six, Logan."

"Perfect. Just one last thing, Ms. Bennett."

She tilted her head. "What's that?"

"Call me Gabe."

###

More by Angie Martin

Conduit

Bestseller on Amazon US and Amazon UK for Psychic Suspense
Winner ~ Gold Medal for Paranormal Fiction in the 2014 Reader's Favorite International Book Awards

How do you hide from a killer when he's in your mind?

Emily Monroe conceals her psychic gift from the world, but her abilities are much too strong to keep hidden from an equally gifted killer. A savvy private investigator, she discreetly uses her psychic prowess to solve cases. When the police ask her to assist on a new case, she soon learns the killer they seek is not only psychic, but is targeting her.

The killer wants more than to invade her mind; he wants her. Believing they are destined for each other, he uses his victims as conduits to communicate with her, and she hears their screams while they are tortured. She opens her mind to help the victims, but it gives him a portal that he uses to lure her to him. With the killer taking over her mind, she must somehow stop him before she becomes his next victim.

READER REVIEWS FOR CONDUIT

"Conduit is a unique masterpiece…The amount of details given by the author and the wonderful way it was written causes heart pounding moments, fear of the dark and the need to check behind every closed door." ~ 5-star review from Amazon

"To say CONDUIT is a thriller is an understatement. From the first page to the harrowing conclusion, this is an absolute page-turner." ~ 5-star review from Amazon

"'Conduit' is an absorbing psychological thriller…which blends in more than a little splash of the paranormal as it gets underway with a suitably creepy and curious prologue setting the tone of the book and sinking claws of intrigue in from the word go." ~ 5-star review from Amazon

False Security

Rachel Thomas longs for normalcy, but if she stops running, she could die…or worse. Chased by a past that wishes to imprison her, haunted by dreams that seek to destroy her, Rachel finds solace in a love she could not predict. A love she cannot deter.

Mark Jacobson is the man who never needed love. He has his bookstore, his bachelorhood, and his freedom. In the moment he meets Rachel, he is swept into a world he didn't know existed. One filled with the purest of love. One filled with betrayal, lies, and murder.

Now Rachel and Mark are forced to face her past. The truth may kill them both.

Reader Reviews for False Security

"I HIGHLY recommend this book if you like suspense and surprises. Martin is a master at her craft and I cannot WAIT to read her next novel!" ~ 5-star review from Goodreads

"Ms. Martin had me rooting for Rachel and Mark… As danger escalated, I found it impossible to stop reading. A riveting story: if you enjoy romantic thrillers, you're in for a treat with 'False Security'." ~ 5-star review from Amazon

"False Security by Angie Martin is the kind of book I just couldn't stop reading. It's a new haunting love story…and this author knows how to get me hooked into a tale from the first page. There are…moments of beauty, quiet moments of love, and seething times of terror…False Security is a beautiful love story that you will not want to miss." ~5-star review from Amazon

"Excellent read for lovers of suspense thrillers." ~ 5-star review from Amazon

"…an emotionally gripping thriller." ~ The Wichita Eagle (review of 2004 release)

About Angie Martin

Angie Martin lives with her husband and pets in a Overland Park, KS. She grew up in Wichita, Kansas and has lived all over the United States. Her work reflects her background and schooling in criminal justice. Angie is hard at work on her next projects.

Website: www.angiemartinbooks.com

Fan group: www.facebook.com/groups/angiesconduits

Facebook: www.facebook.com/authorangiemartin

Twitter: www.twitter.com/zmbchica

One Last Thing...

Thanks for reading! If you enjoyed this book, I'd be very grateful if you would post a short review on Amazon and/or Goodreads. Your support really does make a difference and I read all the reviews personally so I can get your feedback. Thank you again for your support!

Made in the USA
Columbia, SC
09 February 2022